BALANCING ACTS

By the same author:

ROUGH STRIFE

BALANCING ACTS

LYNNE SHARON SCHWARTZ

Consume my heart away; sick with desire
And fastened to a dying animal...
W. B. Yeats

LONDON
VICTOR GOLLANCZ LTD
1982

British Library Cataloguing in Publication Data
Schwartz, Lynne Sharon
   Balancing acts.
   I. Title
   813'.54[F]   PS3569.C567
   ISBN 0-575-03086-0

In memory of my father, Jack Sharon,
and his way with words

Printed in Great Britain by
St Edmundsbury Press, Bury St Edmunds, Suffolk

CHAPTER 1

MAX FRIED stepped over the threshold. He set down his navy-blue beret on a gleaming Formica surface and surveyed his new residence. His last, was it not? Its kitchen glistened whitely; every fixture ready and waiting, deceptively virginal. Neatness he liked, but this was antiseptic, reeking already of the purity of the beyond.

All along the counters at arm level he found chrome rails that recalled the hospital from which he had been ejected less than an hour ago. Stuffed in a taxi by his delectable Puerto Rican nurse, Carmela Velasquez, after a month of wry verbal dalliance, and carried to this four-story beige brick building of recent and styleless design— Pleasure Knolls Semi-Service Apartments for Senior Citizens. The knoll was a mild, well-groomed slope on which the building sat in a posture of apathy, uncheered by a warm late-October sun. Max's predilections were urban; driving up the Sawmill River Parkway, he had observed with loathing the wide swatches of Westchester green, buffer zones between clutches of low-roofed commerce. But aesthetics were a luxury at his age. He had no choice, they told him: his heart would not survive another city mugging. Dr. Small had arranged everything. Too kind.

"I can assure you, Mr. Fried, it's no nursing home. It's a health-related facility. You'll have your own apartment and all the privacy you want. But there's a trained professional staff, and you can get meals prepared if you like. It's more comfort than you've had, and not expensive either. You're lucky they had an opening."

"Yes, I suppose some poor fool dropped dead."

Dr. Small cracked his knuckles loudly. "Our social worker, Miss Tilley, went out of her way to find this for you."

Thank you too, Miss Tilley. He opened a canary-yellow cabinet. Smooth white plates, cups, soup bowls—service for four. No wild parties expected, obviously. He advanced to the living room: all

1

suitably autumnal, brown and orange, squarish chaste sofa, wing chair and ottoman with matching rug. Landscape with grazing cattle hanging on the wall. As he stood up on the ottoman to take it down, he could almost touch the low ceiling. Big windows overlooked the back lawn, west, giving good afternoon light—the plants, at least, would thrive. Traffic curled on skeins of road in the middle distance, too far off to be noisy. He drew the curtains and moved along through a doorway. A broad double bed! What did they expect? The decorator, with a burst of unprecedented abandon, had chosen a crazy-quilt spread in hues of bright red and blue and purple. A setting for merriment. Well, it was a comfortable bedroom, unobjectionable, and better than he had had most of his life. He tossed his jacket onto the bed before proceeding to the bathroom, which, offering a medley of orthopedic devices, reminded him of the physical therapy room he used to pass, strolling through the hospital corridors. Hollowed-out people in faded bathrobes doing peculiar exercises; gleaming chrome and wincing faces. He would look away, remembering other antics— ropes and bars and wires, nimble bodies defying the rigidities of bone. He might be shuffling through a corridor in bedroom slippers, but once, oh once, he wanted to shout in protest, he had cavorted on a tightrope in trim silver shoes and been mad for a woman. He did tell Carmela, about the tightrope, not the woman, and she said coolly that she was not surprised; she could see it in the muscles. And for all his joking innuendos, she had managed to embarrass him.

Now he shoved aside a few movable bars near the toilet. Thank God he could still piss without this contraption. Welcome, the inaugural piss.

In the living room armchair, he nudged off his shoes and put his feet up on the ottoman. At eye level, six feet off, waited an empty TV screen. Was this his future, then—night after night falling asleep in the chair, burning cigar holes in the rug, stumbling at last, sleepily, onto the therapeutic mattress? Man acclimates. Not to raging hunger, though. Where was his future grocery store? The smiling information lady downstairs, peppy as a wind-up toy, had promised to tell him everything he needed to know. A large order, he had retorted. Very well; soon he would give her an opportunity to be useful. Meanwhile, he closed his eyes.

He was wakened by a knock on the door. He knew no one, wanted no one, yet there stood a woman built on the grand scale, draped into bright-yellow print, with curly gray-blond hair circling a capable face.

2

A prettiness mellowed by experience. She looked him over; he made a slight bow.

"I'm your next-door neighbor. My name is Lettie Blumenthal and I came to say you can always come in for a cup of tea. I like to be on good terms with my neighbors. Provided, of course, you're a decent sort of person."

"Come in, come in, Lettie Blumenthal." Max shook her hand, large but oddly delicate. "Thank you for your invitation, which I accept immediately, as soon as I put my shoes back on. I assure you I am a decent sort of person."

She stepped inside and gazed around his living room. "Why is the painting on the floor?"

"Have a seat, please." His breath faltered when he bent over to tie the laces. Always, so he couldn't for a minute forget. "My painting is down because its theme did not suit my sensibilities. I prefer a human scene. Cows, I've never felt any rapport with. Do you know what I mean?"

Her knees moved apart; as she smiled, her face broke into furrows, miraculously becoming a face he could talk to. "I know exactly what you mean. I was a city person too. In fact, I'll tell you right off—I was a chorus girl, way back when. Can you believe it?" She was laughing heartily now. "But in the year I've lived here it never occurred to me to take the cows off the wall."

He laughed in return and studied her more closely. Under the mass were good bones. Her features were fine also, shrewd and firm, with light, clever eyes. He walked over to where she sat solidly on the sofa like a flowering plant, and extended his hand once again: "Max Fried, trapeze artist and all-round stunt man, decent and ravenous. Would you have, in addition to the tea, a sandwich?"

"My kitchen is overflowing."

Hunger appeased, Max spent a good quarter of an hour in the late afternoon reading the orderly bulletin board opposite the welcomer's desk. From time to time he glanced surreptitiously at Mrs. Cameron to see if she was observing him. She was, equally surreptitious, but less hostile.

"We have a men's group, Mr. Fried," she ventured at last, "that meets twice a week for a Great Ideas of Western Man discussion."

"Thank you," said Max. "I am not in quest of great ideas."

"Perhaps if you could tell me whether you're interested in something specific . . ."

3

"If I knew what I was looking for, Mrs. Cameron, I would be out finding it. I know better what I do not want. I am reading for enlightenment, to get an impression of the texture of life in this community, henceforth my own, for better or worse, till death do us part." That did the trick. Mrs. Cameron bent her head quickly back over her *Newsweek*.

The prospects were staggering: a Dramatics Group, currently doing a Jerome Kern retrospective, pinochle and poker games, jewelry-making, needlepoint, Chinese cooking, Introductory Spanish (no need; he had had that in the hospital), watercolor painting, woodworking. A man could waste months in self-improvement. He jotted down the hours and locations of the poker games and was about to give up, when a three-by-five card in a low corner caught his eye. "SENIOR CITIZENS," in easy-to-read block letters. "Volunteer positions open in Roosevelt Junior High. Share your skills with children." He copied the address. Skills he had in abundance, but he wanted them to pay.

As he tucked the slip of paper into his breast pocket a siren whined just outside, rising to a horrendous pitch before it trailed off. He turned back to the desk—this time she was frankly scrutinizing him. "Ambulance?"

"Police," she said, and smiled. "They're just a block away. You'll get used to it."

"I suppose I have no choice. Now, Mrs. Cameron, there is something you can help me with."

She rose, levitated by eagerness. "Yes, Mr. Fried?"

"I require a grocery store."

"Oh, yes. Just around the corner on the right, across the street and down half a block, is the supermarket. It's open till seven. We've also got a bus every morning at ten that goes to the main shopping center. You can have a nice leisurely lunch there—a lot of people do that. But for now, we have several shopping carts available, if you'd like one."

Her lust to assist charged the quiet air, depressing Max. "Isn't there a plain dingy grocery, the kind with old cornflakes and a numbers game in the back, where I can get canned enchiladas and brush away a couple of roaches?

"Mr. Fried, the supermarket has everything you could possibly want."

"Not everything, Mrs. Cameron. But no doubt an elegant sufficiency. All right, lead me to a shopping cart."

She opened a closet. "You sound like a highly educated man, Mr. Fried."

"Hardly. I am an autodidact."

She hesitated, as though it might be an arcane perversion. "A what?"

"Self-taught. Little formal schooling. I left home at a tender age—an old, old story."

"That sounds interesting. Perhaps you could give a talk one Friday night to the Fruits of Life Experience Group." Behind the thick glasses her lashes fluttered like moths in their final agonies.

Max spun the cart around on one wheel with the tip of his right forefinger. He twirled his cane in a series of elaborate flourishes and bowed. As he opened the front door he flicked his head back over his shoulder. Her face was glassy, open-mouthed. "Who wants to lecture to a bunch of fruits?" he called, and fled.

On his return he stopped to knock at the door next to his own. When Lettie opened, he thrust at her an enormous bunch of green grapes. "Seedless."

Her surprise lasted only an instant; she took them and tilted her head to bite off two. "They're delicious." She gave him a curious glance. "Thank you. But you really didn't have to."

"My pleasure. Well." Max tipped the cart into motion, then turned back. "Look, I bought a bottle of Scotch—come on and have some with me. I've just got these few things to put away first." He could hardly believe himself; that hadn't been the plan at all. The plan had been merely the grapes, so he wouldn't need to feel indebted.

She came along readily. She was an excellent woman—helped him shelve his groceries and drank her Scotch like a pro. It was he who couldn't meet the demands of the occasion. Halfway through the second bag he faltered.

"You know something?" he said to her. "Why don't we stop and sit down for a while? To tell the truth, I'm a little tired. I must have walked too fast."

"You sit down," said Lettie. She waved him to the living room, brandishing a head of lettuce. "Go ahead, I'll finish. Next time why don't you have them deliver?"

He sat obediently and put his feet up. Listening to her snapping cabinet doors and crumpling bags, he was mortified. He felt as if he were made of paper, not flesh. Parchment—if he moved, if she so much as touched him, he might crackle and turn to dust.

5

"I'm leaving the door open on purpose," she said on her way out. "I'll be back with something."

In less than ten minutes she reappeared bearing a tray. "It's nearly seven-thirty, Max. You're not going to start cooking."

Watching her, lush in her bright yellow and setting down her thick aromatic soup with a steady grace of motion, he had to acknowledge that, even in decline, there were some sights worth hanging around for. "Maybe you'd like the TV, Max? *Good Times* is on tonight. A very nice Negro family. You'll enjoy it."

He gave in.

"You don't need me to stay, do you? I guess you'd rather be alone now."

He nodded; the amenities were too much effort. No way to treat a lady, but he would make up for it later. After the soup he turned off the TV. A nice family indeed, though far too good to be true, with all that tender love, that fine consideration, amid poverty—not at all what he remembered of poverty. He undressed: a disgrace for a grown man to go to bed at eight-thirty. Sitting on the bed, he looked at his pale legs, luckily still strong enough to have gotten him back here. Flying and balancing had kept his flesh hard and compact, if not his heart. In the tumbling acts and the pyramids he used to stand in the second tier. He was not heavy enough to be on the bottom—the support down there was Henry Cook, who resembled a large ape. Max would leap from the highest seesaw and do a double somersault in the air, hugging his knees tight and concentrating on the center inside him, where Susie taught him to imagine a core of white light. He would compress all his energy around this light, which flashed a sustaining beam as he soared through the air, then land on the hairy shoulders of Henry Cook and uncurl his spine to the sound of applause. Four more drumrolls, four bars of ascending music, and Freddie Case came dropping on him like a bag of cement. Freddie never fully mastered his balance. After the thud he would teeter, and Max had to grip his ankles with reassuring fingers till Freddie stopped wobbling. One terrible day Freddie Case fractured his hip falling off Max. They gave him a paperwork job, keeping track of bookings. Max had to force himself to look Freddie in the eye, though Susie and everyone said it wasn't his fault.

He had done it all in his time, walked the wire, tumbled, juggled. Brandon Brothers was too small a circus to afford specialists; they changed costumes hastily in a screened-off corner of the tent, giving

6

the illusion of a host of performers. Except he had never fooled with the animals, never developed any feeling for them. And he didn't clown, only that one time when they put him in to replace John Todd, groaning in his trailer with a wretched case of poison ivy. He bombed. He did what he had seen John do countless times—set off firecrackers, dropped his pants, shook the paper flower that became a dragon then a bird then a flower again. Polite applause but no big laughs. He didn't have it in him. Susie confirmed it later.

"Since you asked for the truth, Max, you were dead."

He was a young man, oh, maybe forty. Susie loved him. They were outside on the damp grass after dinner. He lay flat on his back puffing on a cigar, watching clouds.

"I know I was dead. But what did I do wrong?"

"Nothing in particular. You just weren't funny. A clown is born that way. Not you—you're no comic." Susie lay down on the grass beside him. She had red hair that circled her face like a halo of fire.

He was too tired to make up his new double bed. Drowsing, he lay back and instantly slept. He dreamed he was on the wire, climbing uphill to Susie waiting for him high on the platform, her public smile a gleam of red and white. She wore blue spangles, glittering, glittering, and pretended for the crowd to be smiling encouragement at Max, while they both knew he cared for nothing but the pressure of the air around him, the feel of the wire beneath his foot, the core of white light inside. Susie beckoned; he glanced around. Faces in the crowd burst on his eyes like exploding rockets: Miss Velasquez, Miss Tilley, Mrs. Cameron, his older brothers who died in their beds after a lifetime working in the delicatessen. Then he lifted his foot expertly, pointing and reaching for the taut wire. That central place in the cushion of the big toe had to touch first, for an infinitesimal fraction of time; toe, ball, heel. Perfect alignment or there was trouble. He looked up to Susie: her blue spangles reflected the bright light inside him. He took another step, shot a glance at the crowd. Their faces were tense and anxious. Mrs. Cameron, Miss Tilley, all of them were shaking their heads. No, Max, no! Susie waved, leaning towards him and stretching out her long slender arms, the drumroll ascended around his ears, somewhere an elephant trumpeted gloomily, and the center of his toe mistook the wire, touched a sixteenth of an inch to the left. He teetered like Freddie Case used to teeter, swung the balance pole, got ready for a hop in the air to try again, better this time, but before he could hop, a fiery pain cut through his chest and upper arm. Susie reached out her arms, her painted smile shriveled to a small O. The crowd rose, gasping mightily. He lost the wire. He fell, and fell and fell.

He woke in a sweat and switched on the light. Where was he and what for? What was this cheerful bedspread for? Susie was dead of leukemia. Freddie Case was dead. John Todd lived retired with his son in Montana. It was a quarter to five in the morning. When he stood up—surprise—he felt better. The weakness had passed and there were no aches anywhere. He ran a hot bath, and while he waited lit up a Corona Corona. He stepped in cautiously, holding an Agatha Christie, since Susie's death one of his favorite nocturnal companions. The water was as hot as he could stand it. With his pores absorbing the numbing heat, he dropped ashes in little clumps on the rim of the tub. One fell in—he flicked at it with a finger and watched it darken, disperse, then disappear, graying the water.

He had to get out, do something. Start something, a semblance of life. But the schools didn't open till nine. He had no appetite, nor any inclination yet to deflower that kitchen. To kill time he finished his mystery and watched an educational TV program. Great Ideas of Western Man. It was possible to register by mail and take a test at the end for course credit, he was informed. On the elevator down to the lobby he noted for the first time the chrome rails, vertical and horizontal, also a great idea. Necessity the mother . . . He nodded toward the front desk. "Good morning."

"Good morning, Mr. Fried," she sparkled. A top row of false teeth already, alas. "You're out early today. Did you have a pleasant night?"

"Full of adventure, Mrs. Cameron. Full of romance and high jinks." She turned her pained dark eyes back on her work. "Will you be asking that each morning? Because a man of my age, you know, can't be expected, nightly, to. . ."

"Mr. Fried," she said, setting down her pen. "We must have started off on the wrong foot somehow. Before things get any worse, why don't we . . ." Her valor was exhausted, her face a silent appeal for aid. Max stood his ground, unmoved. "I'd like to help make your stay here a comfortable one. That's all I'm trying to do."

"Why do you ask such foolish questions, then?"

"I've got to ask," she said querulously. "I've got to . . . keep track, and then let people know if anything seems . . . not right."

"Ah, you report to a higher authority. I should have known. Tell me, Mrs. Cameron—I know it's impertinent, but how old are you?"

She got pink and began ruffling her fingers through her hair. "Fifty-seven."

"Are you married?" He had noticed yesterday the wide gold band embedded in the flesh.

"Yes."

"In other words, you leave here and go home to the waiting . . . to a companion, right? In that case, Mrs. Cameron, do not ask me whether I had a pleasant night, and I will not ask you."

Her blush deepened to near purple, spreading behind the squarish gold-rimmed glasses. He had a twinge of remorse but ignored it.

"Where is the junior high school, please?"

She told him, with her head bent over the papers on her desk. Max swooped to the door, twirling the cane like a baton.

"Adult education?" she called out.

He had to admire her tenacity; silent, he turned to wave and incline his head in an angle of mock benediction.

It was only a ten-minute ride on the bus. Without her directions he could have walked it in less, and recognized it easily. Fresh brick, rimmed with a broad green lawn, the building struck him as another version of Pleasure Knolls. Institutions for safekeeping, both, and engineered by a committee, to satisfy all and please none.

He was directed to a smooth-faced young man with longish blond hair, wearing snug denim pants and a plaid shirt with the top three buttons undone. Ted Collins was powerfully built, almost as broad as Henry Cook but hardly apelike. Taller than Max by a head and straight as an arrow, he practically vibrated with energy. The fellow had quite a good grip, too, when they shook hands. Sitting down at his desk, he lit a cigarette. Max took out a cigar to fend off the filthy smell, and said, "It's close to sixty years since I've been inside a school."

"Well, I'm glad you decided to return," Collins said affably. "Where did you happen to see our notice?"

"I don't quite recall. Supermarket, drugstore, one of those places."

"I see. And you're interested in working with children?"

"I'm interested in working."

Collins cleared his throat formally, darted a quick look at Max, and relaxed. Smiled, man to man. He leaned back in his chair with his arms behind his head and stretched out one long leg, resting it on the edge of the desk. "Well, let me tell you, first of all, Mr. Fried, what

9

we're looking for. We're very understaffed, though most people think these suburban schools are rolling in money." Absently, Collins stroked a bicep. "We need help in shop—woodworking, carpentry, electricity—with math, especially business math, if you've ever run a business, for example. Science—setting up lab experiments and seeing that they don't blow themselves up. Really everything. We can't pay, and we can use as many hours as you want to give. If you're around at noon, though, you can get a free hot lunch in the cafeteria. Now, maybe I've overwhelmed you, throwing all this out at once. Why don't you tell me something about yourself, what you'd like to do." He took his leg off the desk and leaned forward to stub out the cigarette as he might hammer a nail.

"I am rarely overwhelmed," Max replied. Yet he was, dammit, not by the information but by the appalling vigor of the man. He had forgotten. All that strength to spare. Had he ever? He must have. Susie said. He looked over at the lithe, animated hands, itching to grasp, and had a momentary flicker of hatred for this decent boy who probably fucked up a storm every night.

"I was hoping there might be some remuneration."

"I'm sorry. Believe me, I would if I could. Are you—uh—in a bad way? Because you could go down to—"

"No, no." Alarmed, Max scanned his clothing—tweedy and, yes, conservative, today perhaps even archaic, with vest and watch chain, but certainly not shabby? He never skimped on appearances. Appearances were everything. "It's the principle of the thing."

"I understand." Collins slapped the desktop regretfully.

"I can do most of what you've mentioned. I've run a business, too. Bicycles. But tell me, could you use a juggler?"

"A juggler?"

"Yes. Or how about tumbling? You've got a gym, haven't you? Mats? I could set up a trapeze."

"A trapeze?" He tilted his jaw upward, squinting slightly.

"The daring young man on the flying trapeze? Remember?"

"What daring young man?"

"What is this, an echo chamber?"

"Sorry. I—I didn't expect this. Most of the senior citizens volunteer for cooking, reading stories, you know. Can you really do all that? Where did you learn it?"

"Circus. A life of glamour and magic."

The cigarette Collins was starting to light dropped from his lips and rolled along the floor, past the corner of the desk to Max's feet. Max picked it up. It disappeared up his sleeve. He retrieved it from behind his ear and handed it back.

The young man gasped and smiled with hesitation. "Thanks. How did you do that? Oh, I guess everyone asks you that."

"I don't do it for everyone."

"Look, I'm sure the kids would love it. I've got to check it out with the gym teachers, though, to see if they can work it into their program. Everything's got to be checked out around here, you can't imagine. . . . Could you—uh—possibly do that again, with the cigarette?"

Max lost it in his pants pocket and found it behind his lapel.

"Amazing! One other thing, Mr. Fried."

"Yes? You can call me Max."

"Okay, Max. We need a couple of character references. Just a formality—to check on who's working with the kids. I'm sure— uh . . . Can you give me the name of any local people to contact?"

"You mean to see if I'm a decent person?"

"More or less. Nothing personal, you understand."

"You can start with my neighbor, Lettie Blumenthal. She will vouch for my decency." He wrote down her name as well as his own, and their street address.

Collins studied the slip of paper. "Oh, isn't that Pleasure Knolls, out past Broad Street?" The zeal faded from his face. "Are you—are you sure you can do this sort of thing, Max? I mean, healthwise? It can be strenuous, with the kids and all."

He peered intently at Collins, caught his eye and held it fast. "Would I offer if I weren't well? Why, I could walk the wire today if I had the chance. I've never felt better in my life."

"Walk the wire?"

He paraded two fingers along the desktop. "The tightrope."

"That's fantastic! I've never met anyone from the circus before. Maybe you could come over sometime and tell me about it."

Max stood up and held out his hand. "Gladly. I'll even give you an autograph."

As he stepped out of the office a mob of youngsters roared past, long-haired, blue-jeaned, and of indecipherable sex, a scary flurry of life like the lions let loose in the ring. He leaned up against a wall till they had gone by, jostling each other with a manic delight. When their noise diminished, he could almost hear his heart, roused and knock-

11

ing. Those were the children, his raw material. He felt a twinge of panic in his gut.

Back at the apartment he fixed his first breakfast, the honeymoon breakfast: black bread with cream cheese, topped with a slice of red onion. Black coffee. He ate it in what Mrs. Cameron had called the dining area. He used to eat breakfast in a trailer. John Todd, the born clown—though what Susie had meant by it he wasn't sure, because John out of the spotlight was a rather somber, though lovable, fellow—John Todd used to fix sausages and eggs, biscuits with honey, for him and Susie, Henry, Freddie, and a couple of the others, on rainy weekday mornings. They curled up in corners of the trailer waiting for the hot plates, the smell of mud on their boots mingling with the aroma of sausages and coffee. He could smell it now. When he was in a good mood he juggled the coffee mugs and tossed them over to John, big and sober at the stove, an ugly face that turned mobile and beautiful under the lights, a giant who had to bend his head under his own roof. John's pet monkey, Joanna, sat on top of a cabinet, its wizened face screwed up with attention as John caught them by the handles, every one.

John had always liked Susie but tried not to show it. Once after a wretched fight, Susie took her pajamas and toothbrush and moved into John's trailer. Max felt like dropping her from the trapeze. How long? he wondered. Days went by. When he caught her by the wrists he muttered things.

"Are you having fun, Susie, you traitor?"

She would never stop smiling for the crowd.

"I'm going to let you go, next swing. See how much fun that'll be."

When she flew back she stuck out her tongue, quick as a flash; that intimate malice nearly broke his heart.

She came back one night a week later with the pajamas over her arm and the toothbrush in her fist, and began immediately picking up old newspapers and emptying ashtrays. "Look how you let things go," she said.

Max was sitting at the table, reading. "Oh, so it's you." He got up to face her. He thought over the fine speeches he could make, and then his arms were around her. The whole thing had been his fault anyway; he was an arrogant brute, as Susie had pointed out. What mattered was that she was with him. He never said a word to John Todd either. He liked John, he liked the breakfasts, and he liked harmony.

When he and Susie got too old to jump and fly, they juggled,

12

dressed in tramp costumes. He loved the way she looked in the baggy brown pants and suspenders, the striped shirt and the floppy hat with flecks of fiery hair escaping. Twirling and tossing balls and pins, they were perfection: after so long, their blood pulsed to the same beat. On a tandem bike, no hands, they flipped cups from front to back till Susie gathered them into the folds of her big plaid jacket and Max steered them out of the ring, waving a battered hat at the crowd.

But that wasn't enough—they knew it and so did Brandon. They had outlasted their skills. One overcast day in early November, end of the season, they left. No good-bye party, Max insisted, but after the last show they sent him out on a fool's errand—drive into town and settle the bill at the saloon—and they set up tables in the tent. John Todd danced with Susie. Max danced with Tania, who did ballet on the wire, and with Gina, an acrobat who was an Apache Indian. And he marveled at the tricks of time and space: that his parents should have fled the fires of a Ukrainian village and traveled westward across an ocean so that he might end up with his arms around an Apache Indian, doing a fox trot. In the trailer, when they packed their bags, Susie held up the blue spangled costume. "Now what should I do with this?"

"Keep it, what else?"

"I thought I might give it to Tania or Edith."

"Keep it."

It fit her till the very end—she never got fat or shapeless. They opened a bicycle shop in Greenwich Village with his name and hers in gilt letters on the window, a shop crammed with bikes and accessories, shiny with chrome, and heady with the smell of grease, a shop that drew the neighborhood cyclists, who hung around discussing the lubrication of their gears and the deterioration of their brake shoes, while Max and Susie quietly made repairs. It got so crowded that finally they moved things around to set up chairs, and they brought in a coffee urn. He attracted customers, Susie said; he had an aura. "I never realized I married a magnetic personality." Not at all, he protested; it was the sight of a good-looking woman covered with grease, changing an inner tube. "Max, baby," said Susie, "you've forgotten I'm fifty years old." She was beautiful almost to the end, and then she broke apart in fragments. She grew paler each day until her skin was the gray underside of white. The medicine made her red hair fall out, flame by flame, and one evening when he sat near the bed holding her hand, thinking of the hair haloing her face on the grass outside the trailer, she whispered, "You know, Max, I used to dye it. This wasn't my natural color."

He sat up with a start. He had thought she was asleep.

"You never knew, after all these years. Isn't that something? It would have been all gray by now anyway."

"It makes no difference."

"I know. I just thought I'd tell you. No secrets. Isn't that so?"

There were no secrets. Only that he couldn't stand to watch her get ugly, and he was ashamed. The sparse white hair and bony cheeks, not to mention the tubes they attached all over, made her a parody of the woman she had been. She didn't drag on long. He sat by the bed till they led him away. There was no one around to grieve to; however magnetic, he had kept everyone else at a distance. Alone and dazed, he judged life's offense against him beyond the powers of acceptance. He cursed and condemned and yearned for the feelings of a stone. He nursed his long grievance; its energy kept him alive.

CHAPTER 2

I T WAS THE LAST PERIOD and she had the quick-exit seat. When the warning bell jangled she almost made it out the door.

"Alison. Come here a moment, please. I'd like to talk to you."

She turned and walked sluggishly to the teacher's desk. Miss French was one of the better ones: she spoke like a human being, not a robot, and let her light-brown hair fall in a careless fluff on her shoulders. She was not quite over the hill yet, maybe around thirty-one.

"About this composition you handed in . . . I asked you to choose three kinds of work people do and discuss the nature of their social contributions."

"I remember." Alison had a ready stare of passive resistance.

"But you didn't." Miss French removed her blue-tinted glasses. Her eyes were perturbed. Today she had on black tights with a wrap-around denim skirt and a work shirt without a bra. Why couldn't she act her age? She was always talking about social responsibility, wasn't she? "You wrote about race horses, oxen, and Indian elephants," Miss French said.

"Yes, well, they work, too."

"They're not people, Alison. There's a difference."

"That's my whole point. That's why they don't get any respect."

"But the assignment was . . . Okay, after you describe their work you say it's unfair for animals to be put to work for people. But how do you think farmers in other ages would have managed without oxen and mules and horses?"

"Do you think we need horse racing? Do you think the horses enjoy it?"

"Come on now," said Miss French. "Of course we don't *need* it. But it doesn't harm the horses. Those horses happen to be very well cared for. But that's not the point. Look, throughout history people have

15

learned to master what's available in nature, for their basic needs. We could never have progressed to the point we are now without the use of animals."

"And hunting dogs," said Alison. "They're trained to prey on their fellow animals. It's gross."

"I'm aware that you're clever." Miss French put her blue glasses back on and smiled with a kind of melancholy. "But you'll never learn anything until you start listening to what's being said to you. I don't think you've really heard a word I said."

Alison gave the impassive stare again.

"And besides, if you're so interested in animals and fairness, haven't you grasped that different species prey on each other? Not with any evil intent—it's the way the cycle of nature is set up. Take a look around. It's not one big happy family." Miss French held out the assignment.

"Do I have to do it over?"

"Yes. People, this time. How about scientists, newspaper reporters, bricklayers? Really work up an essay."

"That doesn't grab me, but okay."

She walked home past the shopping center. Groups of kids clustered around the pizzeria and the movie theatre. Traffic thinned as she turned down a side street; the neighborhood became residential, with low, broad houses set far apart on sloping, mostly vacant lawns bearing the October remains of flower beds. There were no sidewalks. In fifteen minutes she reached her own lawn, where Josh's flower bed was overgrown, faded and waiting for spring. Also waiting for him to come back and do some weeding: he was away in Arizona for two weeks, visiting and checking up on his company's trailers like an itinerant country doctor. Arizona was trailer heaven, Josh said. He had been there many times.

She shut the door of her room tightly behind her, opened the window over her bed, and reached to touch the leaves of the maple just outside, before taking the notebook out from under the mattress. The heroine of her newest story was called Alice. Alice was going on fourteen, just a year older than she was. Fed up with ordinary life and in quest of adventure, Alice runs away to lead a life of crime in New York City.

She soon gets hooked on drugs and mugs people in the subways with an innocent-looking tennis racket, to support her habit. After a painful withdrawal period, a stunning test of will, she triumphs, but

16

goes on to become a teen-aged alcoholic. A member of Alcoholics Anonymous stationed outside a bar tries to save her, but she will have none of their corny, God-fearing methods. Once again she saves herself, emerging from a sodden stupor with renewed will. She moves into an abandoned building (till then she has slept in doorways and on park benches) and assembles a gang of younger runaways, whom she directs in a series of robberies. The young policeman who finally traces her falls in love with her. "You are the rarest creature I have ever encountered," he tells her one night in the police car. Unable to bring himself to turn her in, he wants to reform her and keep her for himself, but since he symbolizes law and convention, Alice laughs in his face. When he tries to kiss her she spits in his eye. "You little tiger," he whispers, undaunted. His hanging around becomes a drag, so Alice pushes on, hitchhiking to Ohio in a truck whose driver lost both hands in the Vietnam war and had them replaced by hooks. The truckdriver, named Hal, is drawn to her too, and for the first time in her life Alice has some feeling for a man. Even though Hal's vocabulary is very limited compared to hers, she can see beyond the surface to the spirit within.

Today Alison needed to find a way out of Alice's dilemma: part of her wants to accept the mutilated truckdriver's love, but another part of her is repelled at the idea of those cold hooks caressing her naked body. She stood up to take a break first, and pulled her blue T-shirt over her head. It was by now unmistakable—she had breasts. Some of the other girls had had them for more than a year, but she was skinny—maybe that slowed things up. The nipples protruded as if puffed with air, and they were surrounded by a soft fleshiness. She touched one breast with a forefinger. It felt tender. Looking in the mirror, she twitched one eyelid and her upper lip very slightly, a faint expression of disdain that had taken weeks to perfect. Soon they might begin growing at a shocking speed. She had seen it happen to Franny Grant, her ex-best friend, and to Hilary and Karen. When they jumped for the ball on the volleyball court, the breasts bounced. It must feel strange, soft bumps on your body, flopping uncontrollably. The cycle of nature, as Miss French said. A portent of things to come. Pimples next, on her high forehead. But pimples could be covered up, and eventually they pass away. Breasts are forever.

Unless you got cancer and had to have one taken off. Like Lou, her mother's best friend, a few months ago. Wanda went to visit her in Parkvale Hospital and came home murmuring, "Poor Lou, poor

17

Lou," as she drifted around the kitchen fixing herself coffee. While the water heated Wanda put her head down on the kitchen table and cried. "A young woman like that."

"Lou's not so young. She must be thirty-five at least."

"That's young, Allie, that's very young. Listen, sweetie, make yourself a hamburger or something. I'm not hungry. I'm going to lie down."

It was odd to see Wanda cry, because most of the time, when she wasn't being moody and silent, she was silly, like people on TV acting slightly drunk. And yet Wanda hardly ever drank—it made her too dizzy, she said.

When Lou came over she looked the same as before, on both sides. Alison could hear the two of them in the living room, talking softly against the sound of coffee cups clinking on saucers.

"But what does it look like?" Wanda sounded eager as a child.

"Ah, well, Wanda," drawled Lou, who came from South Carolina. "What's the point? Better not to know. I don't look at it myself."

"Listen, Lou, it's like an epidemic—you're lucky they caught it so soon. Think of it that way." "Sure, hon. Easy to say." She couldn't imagine anything that would make her mother weep and moan, "Poor Alison, poor Alison." Oh, no. Wanda stared at her sometimes with those daffy green eyes as if she were a creature from another planet. An alien. It was true, she certainly didn't look like any child born of Wanda, who was blond and pink. She had her father's coloring. "Olive, sweetie," Wanda said when she was in a good mood. "Olive is nice." And at other times she said, "Why do you stay cooped up in your room all the time! For God's sake, you're positively green." Her eyes were good, though—tiger eyes that gave a clue to the real person inside. Staring at the mirror, she raised her head and straightened her shoulders. Miss Hanes, the gym teacher, was always telling them to straighten up and let the world see who they were. The world would not see any better who she was this way, though. Who people were was the greatest secret on earth; they guarded it with their lives.

She put her shirt back on and returned to the bed and to Alice's dilemma. Alice feels sorry for Hal and is grateful for the long ride through the Midwest. Also, she wants to see what it's like—everyone talked and wrote so much about it. But still, those cold hooks . . . She postponed the decision by making the truck fall in a ditch. In the complicated rescue operation the hooks come in very handy. But she

18

would have to look up the names of the parts of the truck and fill them in later. She was too tired and hungry now.

As she knocked on Wanda's door a low, steady murmur came from inside—Wanda on her Princess phone.

"Alison? You can come in."

Her sneakers sank into the lavender carpet. The master bedroom, it was called, because the master and the mistress slept there. It was spacious, hung with purple and green velvet curtains and full-length mirrors; in the center reclined Wanda, rolled in a pink satin quilt on the king-sized bed, the telephone cord around her wrist like a bracelet. Her face was flushed from sleep and her short yellow curls were mussed. Magazines lay open around her. A cigarette butt smoldered in the ashtray and the odor of the burning filter spread through the room.

"What is it, Alison? I'm talking to Lou."

"Is there anything to eat? It's almost six."

"Oh, Christ. Already? I never got to go shopping. Look, honey, take ten dollars from my bag over there on the dresser and run over to the A & P and get a couple of steaks. Okay? Be a good girl. Honestly, I haven't felt like myself for days." She made a pleading face.

"Can't we just have spaghetti or vegetables or something? I'll make it."

"Just go, all right? I'm talking on the phone. Get some ice cream too, any flavor you like."

She took the money from Wanda's purse and walked to the door.

"Wait. Wait a second, Allie." Wanda took her hand from the mouthpiece of the phone. "Lou? Let me call you back in five minutes, all right?" She hung up. "Come here, sweetie. Sit down by me, that's right." She put her hand over Alison's. "I really am sorry about dinner. I feel extremely lousy. Try to understand."

"If you'd tell me in advance I'd plan it myself. Last week you sent me out once for pizza and once for barbecued chicken."

"Did I really?" Wanda raised her eyebrows and smiled. "That's shocking! I guess I'm not the most efficient person in the world. Let me look at you. It seems like I haven't seen you for days. How's school? Do you know, you're finally getting something up on top? How do you like that! Let Mamma see." Wanda made a grab at her shirt.

She leaped away and crossed her arms over her chest. "Cut that out! For Chrissake!"

"Oh, you're sensitive about it." She laughed, reached for a cigarette, and fit it into a plastic holder. "Well, all right. I must say it's about time."

"I think I'll go for the steaks now, if you don't mind."

"Alison, before you go, would you bring me up a glass of ginger ale, please? Lots of ice. Five ice cubes! Maybe it'll help my stomach."

"Yes, Miz Markman. Right away, ma'am."

"Oh, go on. Don't be such a tough customer."

When she returned with the soda, Wanda was on the phone again, giggling with Lou. She sounded as bad as Franny and Hilary and Karen giggling in front of the pizzeria, waiting for the boys to notice them. They weren't speaking to her now because she had told them how stupid they looked chasing Bobby and Elliot around the parking lot to get their books back. Well, tough shit. She got her bike out of the garage and coasted down the driveway.

Steak. Slabs from a cow, soft and porous, sliced off its body. Meat. There was the same kind of meat in her. Squeezing her thigh, she could feel the muscles move as she pedaled, and she shuddered. In less than an hour she would be holding the slabs of cow in her hands, with the red blood dripping into the sink and making pale pink stains. She would pat them dry with a paper towel, like drying a baby after its bath. Lay them out on the broiler and salt them, like powdering the baby with talcum. And then eat one—she was so hungry she would love it. She was an animal that preyed on her fellow creatures. Part of the cycle of nature.

She slid her bike into the rack outside the market and tested the automatic In door to see exactly which point on the rubber mat made it open. Inside, she took a Hershey bar with almonds from a front rack and tore off the wrapper—if anyone asked, she would promise to pay on her way out—and at the encyclopedia display, looked up Vegetarianism. Many eminent and talented people, it said, such as George Bernard Shaw, a playwright, and Mohandas Gandhi, an Indian leader, had been vegetarians. It wasn't so weird after all. She had heard of that George Bernard Shaw recently. Yes, Miss Patten had read them something two weeks ago from a play he wrote about Joan of Arc. Next week she would look up Puberty, and the week after, Breasts.

The meat bin was stacked with dead flesh and bone wrapped in plastic. Once they had all walked around on four legs, peacefully eating grass. A few packages were labeled "Hearts." So they took the very heart out! "He's eating my heart out," their next-door neighbor sometimes said to Wanda, about her husband. Right in front of the sirloins, blocking her path, an old man was bent over with his eyes closed. He was lean and muscular, and his large hands gripped the edge of the counter. From under a dark beret white hair showed straight and thin. He had a large bumpy nose and a cleft chin, and his face was crinkled with tiny lines. It was a sharp, almost harsh face, with the full lips pressed firmly together, but the expression was remote, as though all his concentration had been withdrawn from the world to some tremendous sensation within. She hesitated. "Excuse me."

He opened his eyes, black and glittery, but didn't move.

"Pardon me, I need to reach the steaks."

He shook his head, a minuscule arc.

"Are you all right?"

"No."

"Here, sit down." She dragged over a huge carton of paper towels and he slumped onto it, leaning an elbow on the meat bin and supporting his head on a veined hand with very long fingers. Miss Belling, the art teacher, once showed them photos of artists' hands; they had become tools, she said, the fingers stretched and articulated from work. His hand was like those artists'.

"Should I call a doctor or something? Are you very sick?"

He shook his head again.

"Well . . . when are you going to feel better?"

"Why, is there any hurry?"

His voice was low, with a slight rasp to it. She edged off and chose two steaks, the least bloody-looking she could find, then returned. "I don't think I should just leave you like this. I'll get the manager."

He lifted up a hand weakly. "No managers. It's going away. It's nothing."

"Are you—you're not going to . . . pass out here or anything?"

"Not at the moment. But the prognosis is grim."

"Do you have any pills? I could get you a glass of water."

"The pills are in a suitcase."

"Oh, I have an idea. Have one of these cans of orange juice. There are little openers on top. See? Here, drink it."

He drank. "A resourceful girl. Thank you. That's better. How old are you, if you don't mind my asking?"

"I'm almost thirteen. How old are you?"

"Seventy-four."

"You don't look that old. That's quite an advanced age."

"I think so too. Sometimes I even think, enough is enough." He took a red bandanna from his jacket pocket and wiped his face.

"Would you like me to walk you home?"

"Thank you, no. I'll be fine. I'll have them deliver it. Go ahead with your shopping. Your mother will worry about you. Doesn't she warn you not to talk to strangers?"

"I don't think she cares who I talk to."

He shrugged. "Well, that can have its advantages."

"I don't know. Lately she just stays in bed and talks on the phone all the time."

"Perhaps she's not feeling well."

"She looks okay to me."

He spread out his palms and tilted his head. "An enigma, then."

He couldn't be from around here. He spoke differently and he thought differently. Possibly from very far away, somewhere exotic.

"When I was younger I used to think I was adopted," she said. "In fact, I once wrote a story about it, a few years ago. There was this changeling. Her mother was a gypsy princess and her father was a Turkish lion-tamer. But it turned out to be not true."

"You asked?"

"Well, not exactly. But whenever I got mad I would tell them that when I grew up I was going to search the entire globe till I found my real parents. My father got disgusted and dug my birth certificate out of an old carton. And then my mother found these ancient pictures of herself pregnant. So that was that. I was very disillusioned."

"Yes, I can imagine. May I ask . . ." He closed his eyes for a moment and ran his hand slowly over his face. "Why are you telling me all this?"

"Because . . . I don't know. I really don't know. I don't usually tell people things. Am I bothering you?"

"No, that's quite all right. I'm indebted to you for the juice and the carton."

"Really? Do you think I saved your life?"

He smiled. "I suppose it's a possibility. But you shouldn't go about telling your private fantasies to strangers, you know."

"Did you ever think you were adopted? It's a common fantasy, I've read."

"Oh, no," he replied. "No, that would have been a great luxury. Look here, I'm really not up to a serious discussion. And I'm sure your mother's waiting for you."

"You're sure you'll be okay?"

"Yes, yes. Go on about your shopping now."

She paid for the steaks and dashed outside to her bike. At last, someone! He was like a messenger in a play who bursts in with news of the outside world. So there really were people like that out there. He had traveled and seen life, as Alice was going to do. And she herself had saved a life. She longed to tell someone, but the only one who could possibly understand was Alice. She raced towards home, the sentences spinning out to the rhythm of the wheels. She had the dilemma all worked out now. Alice could save Hal's life when the truck falls in the ditch, and he would be so grateful that he would look upon her with awe and reverence. He wouldn't need to run those chilly hooks all over her. "His hungry eyes took on a look of trance as he gazed down at her slender, lissome body. Instead of brute craving, his face portrayed infinite gratitude. He reached out to touch her, but quickly drew back his hook. 'No,' whispered Hal. 'I have gone beyond that. You must remain untouched by crude passion.'" She pedaled up the driveway and took the package of dripping steaks out of the basket. Lissome, or lissom?

A week later it happened again, like an omen. Late as usual, she pushed open the gym door, to be assaulted by a clamor of voices and bouncing balls. Four volleyball games at once. Four gray balls smudged with years of finger marks flew over the four droopy nets while dozens of arms flailed in disorder. Shouts rang through the air, which was already damp with sweat. Over in the left-hand corner, away from the games, Fats Fox, one of the gym teachers, stood high up on a ladder, threading a length of thick rope through big hooks in the ceiling. And there below him, on a wooden stool, sorting lengths of aluminum tubing and calling out instructions—she could see his full, old lips moving but couldn't make out any words in the din—was that man, the one whose life she had saved! From the grim reaper. The icy grip of death. Cold fingers clutched at his throat but were thwarted just in time by a youthful . . . Okay, enough! she whispered fiercely, and in her head a black curtain dropped on the parade of phrases. Skirting the games, she strolled over. The navy-blue beret lay on a black attaché case near his feet. He looked like the photo of Picasso that Miss Belling had hung in the art room—head thrust forward like a large cat about to spring, hard dark eyes glinting rays into the camera. This man might be a foreign painter too. From Paris, maybe. She could see him seated in front of an easel, on a bridge over that famous river, what was it again? Except he had had no accent.

"Hi," she said.

He swung around on the stool to face her. His eyes were dark and glinting also, and seemed to penetrate behind her face.

"Don't you remember me? We met at the meat counter."

His brows contracted and the eyes narrowed, as if searching in a cluttered place for the memory. "Ah, of course! The young lady who gave me the orange juice. The nonadoptee. Allow me to thank you once again. Pardon me for not getting up, but if I move I lose the exact measurements." He was marking off spaces with a pencil on a length of tube.

"What are you doing here?"

"I'm helping Mr. Fox set up some equipment. Obviously. And you, I take it, are a student?" He looked briefly toward the volleyball games; there appeared to be a touch of scorn in his face.

"Yes, but I find volleyball barbaric. It comes at you so suddenly. I'd much rather play basketball—at least it's not so disorganized."

"It's true," he said, glancing again at the nets. "Volleyball is a particularly chaotic game."

"I can get it in the basket every time. It's my one skill in life. I really like that curve the ball makes, you know, when it goes over the hoop and slips in? I can feel that curve in my hand while I'm still holding the ball. It's like magic. It's all controlled and beautiful."

He had stopped penciling the tubes and was looking at her curiously. "You have the curve in your hand? Yes, I know what you mean. Fox!" he called out all of a sudden. "Hold it right there! That ought to be firm enough. Try sliding down. Your weight will test it."

Fox, red-headed, wide-shouldered, and pudgy, pulled his gray polo shirt over the strip of pinkish belly above his sweat pants and stared down. "You mean slide down the rope?"

"Sure. You don't propose using the kids to test it, do you?"

Slowly Fats transferred his body from the ladder to the rope.

"Put your feet on the knots. Attaboy. Swing a little, be a monkey. There you go."

The rope swung tentatively in a small circle. Fats curled his body around it, his shoulders and arms tense.

"Oh, if I had an old freind of mine here now," the man whispered to

24

her, "you'd see a real monkey. This fellow looks like an ape but hasn't got the bounce."

She grinned back at him as Fats, rather pale, reached the floor. "Do you think that's all right now?" he asked, rubbing his palms together.

"Fine, Fox. We'll put sturdy mats underneath. No need to fear."

"What kind of new torture is this?" she asked Fats.

"Mr. Fried is going to teach rope climbing and trapeze skills. Why is your attitude so negative? And aren't you supposed to be in a game anyhow?"

"Oh, all right. See you around."

The old man nodded his head in farewell. "A pleasure running into you again. *Hasta luego.*"

The river was the Seine, but she doubted now that he was a painter.

At three o'clock she saw Hilary and Karen headed for the pizzeria. They waved and beckoned—so they weren't mad any more—but she only waved back and continued on her way. Hilary shrugged as she walked off, fluffing out her long loose hair with one hand. On the left back pocket of her jeans was sewn a broken red heart with an arrow going through it. The heart was for Bobby Cavale, on the swimming team. Karen, plump and a head shorter, chattered and walked fast to keep up with her. They would find the boys there and most likely chase them around the parking lot again. The few times she had gone along she had felt completely hollow inside. Even her voice sounded phony, and her mind stood somewhere apart, watching, judging every word she spoke. Wanda had warned her. "Do you think they'll keep asking you forever? Do you want to be alone all the time? You'll be sorry, believe me." But she wasn't sorry yet.

On the way to the library she stopped off in Bamberger's to go up the down and down the up escalators, and so it was near dark when she finally got home, her knapsack bulging with books. Wanda was busy at the stove, stirring something in a big pot. She wore a long flowered robe in a silky fabric, and her lipstick was a frosty pink.

"Set the table in the dining room, would you, Allie? And take out the salad. He ought to be here any minute."

"Yes'm. Right away, ma'am." She opened the refrigerator. There was a bottle of champagne next to the salad bowl. "What are you two celebrating?"

Wanda squeezed her frosted lips shut, as if something might slip past them. She bent to open the oven. "Just his return, I guess. Use the good silver."

She couldn't get a clear picture of Josh's face. It happened every time he stayed away more than a week: she kept only a blurred outline with dark curly hair and a square jaw. Days went by when she hardly thought of him, except now and then some image would flash through her head like a lingering bit of dream: in his white tennis shorts, going to work out at the gym—tanned and muscled like the tennis pros he watched on TV. Going over the bills at the dining room table, so concentrated, with his shirt sleeves rolled up, a sharpened pencil in his hand and a cigarette between his teeth. She wished he wouldn't smoke, yet that cigarette in his teeth gave him an air of . . . she couldn't think of the word. Or the way he used to hold her on his lap, with that funny lopsided smile, and she would put her arms around his neck and feel . . . But that had not been for a very long time. You couldn't force people to keep loving you in the same way, and anyhow, she was much too big. Only babies got petted like that.

As she finished setting out the plates she heard the car. In a moment he was opening the front door, suntanned, his dark hair rumpled, his jacket and tie slung over his shoulder, a suitcase in his hand. When he saw her he gave that same lopsided smile, one corner of his mouth crooked as though something were secretly funny, and he dropped everything to reach out his arms. He was firm and warm, and for a moment she let herself relax against him, wrapped up snug like an infant. Almost too cozy. She drew back before the hug seemed really over.

After he hugged Wanda, Josh picked up his jacket and took a tiny white box from the pocket. "I didn't forget to bring you something this time, Allie."

It was a silver ring with a narrow double band and a blue stone in the center, a rare blue, bluer than any skies or flowers. She put it on her middle finger. "Nice," she said, not looking at him.

"It's Navajo. Silver and turquoise, and made by a real Indian. I got it at a trading post."

She held her hand out and gazed doubtfully. Too brilliant on her hand, or she was too pale. A person should be beautiful and glittery, to wear that ring.

While she ate she twisted it and moved it up and down over her knuckle, watching the stone catch the light of the globe above the table. Wanda poured tomato juice. "Aren't you two going to have your champagne?"

"Oh, that's for later." Lowering her eyes, Wanda began to eat quickly.

"Don't let me stand in your way."

"Oh, don't be so silly, Alison," said Josh. "Now tell me what you've been doing these past three weeks. Read any good books?" He gave her the broad empty smile, the smile that looked ready to become a laugh whatever she might say.

She hesitated. *"Tess of the D'Urbervilles."*

"What's it about?"

"Oh, this girl. She gets into a lot of trouble. Her illegitimate baby dies."

"I don't know where she finds these books," Wanda groaned. "But you can count on her. They're either pregnant or alcoholic or both."

"It's a famous book! I found it right in the school library. Oh, and by the way, I saved a man's life last week."

"You never told me that." Wanda stopped chewing and stared across the table, her green eyes wide. "How?"

"I was in the A & P—that night you forgot to cook dinner, remember?—and he was sort of stretched out over the meat counter. I got him a box to sit on and I gave him a can of orange juice. I guess he was having heart failure or something, but after a while he seemed to get a little better. He was really old, seventy-four. I offered to walk him home but he said no."

"Well, I'm glad of that." Wanda went back to her rice. "You never know, with strangers. Better to call the manager."

"He didn't want the manager. Anyhow, he must be all right now. I saw him at school today."

"At school?" Josh shifted in his chair. "Was he hanging around outside?"

"Oh, no. He wasn't *that* type. Putting up some equipment with the gym teacher. He seemed rather interesting. Well, anyway, how was business?"

"Business?" He smiled over at her. "Business is not bad. Everyone's interested in mobile homes these days—with the market so high they can't afford houses any more."

"Did you see anything exciting this time?"

Josh cocked his head and slid two fingers up and back along his jaw. "Same old thing—desert, cactus, canyons. Grumpy Indians. They certainly seem to have it in for white people. Oh, I did finally stop in to have a look at the Grand Canyon. It was grand, just like they say. I got

27

some postcards I'll show you after dinner. It's amazing," he said, turning to Wanda. "They've got motels, buses, even supermarkets. You can practically live there."

"But how did you feel on the edge of that huge thing?" Alison cried. "I mean, it must be . . . I don't know . . . overwhelming."

"I felt mighty small, baby. Wouldn't want to get lost down there, I'll tell you."

She pushed the slice of roast beef around on her plate. It lay in its puddle of lukewarm gravy like something dead. The first moment he returned was always exciting, but after that everything remained exactly the same. She would try to get behind that lopsided smile to its source, while he, like a dumb camera, would produce whatever had passed before him: deserts, cactus, canyons. Never what any of it meant to him, what he really thought about it. Maybe it meant nothing and he had no thoughts. The hollow space opened inside her again, floating up through her like a bubble.

"I'll clear," she said. As she circled the table gathering plates she studied them, pretending she didn't know them: a nice-looking couple from a TV commercial for dishwasher soap, maybe. But those people on TV were not real; they were actors. Everyone knew they didn't behave that way in real life.

"I'll look at the postcards tomorrow," she told Josh. "I have a lot of homework."

Curled in a corner of her bed, she wrote quickly on a fresh sheet: "Social Contributions of Three Professions. Scientists do experiments in laboratories to find cures for the dread diseases that plague humanity. On the other hand they also invent nuclear weapons and napalm that destroy humanity. Therefore they sometimes strike an objective observer as seeming to defeat their own basic purpose." That was logical so far, only it seemed to be a dead end. Move the main idea along, Miss French always said. And it was supposed to be objective, which meant no private opinions. All she could do was another half page of specific examples—on the one hand and on the other hand— to get it up to a decent length. But specific examples were so boring, and the main idea had been stated quite clearly. It did lack an introduction, development, and concluding paragraph, yet it had a certain neatness. Definitely not wordy. The bricklayer and reporter were simple; she could do them during lunch tomorrow. She dropped the school notebook to the floor and got out the other from under the mattress.

28

Alice decides to leave the truckdriver, Hal, after four days. Being idolized is too much of a strain, and besides, she feels unworthy, remembering the crimes she has left behind her in the city. As a matter of fact, Alice seemed to be undergoing some peculiar change. Between the lines, almost, she was getting closer to the kind of person she was destined to be, a person neither she nor Alison knew yet. The words came out as if dictated by a creature partly herself and partly Alice, a creature just beyond her control. With an eerie curiosity, she watched what appeared on the page. "And so an instinct told Alice the time had come to move on. The unknown stretched before her and the call of adventure sounded in her ears. As she left the kindly truckdriver sleeping peacefully in the back of his truck, his wallet lay exposed before her, bulging with bills. She touched it, but no. Although it would certainly be helpful in her future life, whatever that might be, she could not do that to Hal. It would weigh too heavily on her conscience." She read the paragraph over and crossed out the last sentence.

Alice resolves right then to give up the life of crime. For a moment she even thinks of turning herself in, but no, again: her spirit would be broken in prison. Alice feels exactly the same as Joan of Arc, in that scene Miss Patten read aloud at the beginning of the term. It is not bread and water I fear, but to be shut away from the light of the sky. Do you think living is nothing but not being stone dead?

She hitches a ride with an older girl with long strawcolored braids who offers her a joint, but recalling her past addictions, Alice turns it down. The girl tells about the vegetarian commune in Nebraska where she is headed, and Alice agrees to go along and do her fair share of the domestic work. In Nebraska the bearded boys and the girls in long peasant skirts are friendly, but since they smoke a lot of dope and are very involved in their non-exploitive relationships, Alice pushes on after a week. The next driver who picks her up, an elderly white-haired lady in pink-rimmed harlequin glasses, catches on immediately that Alice is a runaway; meaning well, she plans to turn her in at police headquarters in Laramie, Wyoming.

Her hand was aching; she stopped. She could hear them downstairs, still murmuring and laughing. She pictured them sitting together on the coffee-colored sofa: Wanda, her furry slippers off and her feet tucked under her, sat sideways leaning towards Josh, one arm resting across the back of the sofa. Her long flowered robe swirled around her in folds. She was smoking. They were both smoking, and their words and laughter drifted up in mists of smoke. Josh had his shoes off too, and his long legs were stretched out to the oval coffee table. He leaned his head back against Wanda's arm and blew smoke rings up at the ceiling. They were drinking their champagne and talking of . . . what? It was not possible to imagine how they spoke when she was not there, the real selves underneath the faces, as impossible as it was to picture the other things they did together, when they were upstairs, under the quilt of the huge bed. Unthinkable but true that they touched each other everywhere. That was normal; she had read about it in books. Wanda and Josh were normal.

She lay in bed reading *A Member of the Wedding* till midnight, then turned out the light. Like a cat, she ran her tongue over the silver ring Josh had brought her from Arizona. It tasted like metal, bitter and sharp. Feeling her way in the dark, she put it back in its box.

CHAPTER 3

MAX WAS FEEDING LETTIE this time. In three weeks he had consumed quite a few bowls of her distinguished soups; it was no more than proper to reciprocate. But he had to admit, besides, that he was lonely and he liked her, more than he had foreseen liking anyone again. He had chosen a menu appropriate to her bountiful nature— plump sweet Italian sausages with green peppers, beefsteak tomatoes doused in oil and oregano. Lettie ate it slowly, with a muted ardor.

"You should be teaching them cooking over there at the school. This is delicious. Don't get up, Max, I'll get myself some more from the kitchen. How about you?"

He shook his head. Relaxing in the chair, he sighed over the soothing flavor of garlic. He was a good cook indeed, by instinct. The better of the two—Susie, who could fly with the abandon of a swallow, had been cautious in the kitchen. She used to work with a book propped on the table, always worried about the measurements, while he would let himself go, tossing in whatever he could find. "How bad could it be?" he teased her. He drank Scotch neat as he cooked; the more he drank, the finer the results. Afterwards, often, they spread blankets on the floor and made love. He saw his dinners as a prelude.

"I'm glad you like it," he said to Lettie, returning with her plate refilled. "I've cooked since I was a young man."

"There aren't many men who do. I bet your wife appreciated that."

"Oh." He poured more red wine for them both, and looked away. "It seems like another life," he muttered. "Goddammit."

"I feel the same way," Lettie said calmly. "Twenty years. Would you believe, a fellow who used to come to the club for a drink after work. He saw the show and came backstage. How do you do, et cetera. Like in the movies."

"Yes? And you were happy?" He drank more wine and took the cigar from his shirt pocket. Better to listen than talk. Let her, if she was able to.

31

"We were. I don't usually tell people about it. It gets me down. . . . He was killed in an accident. He drove a truck for a bread company. This is good French bread, by the way. I know bread. Where'd you get it? The bakery, not the A & P, I bet?" Max nodded. "I thought so. He drove at night. It could be he fell asleep, I'll never know." As she spoke she ate, with an air of meditation. "Anyway, he was crushed to bits. Bits. They called me at five in the morning. I was wide awake. I used to stay up all night then, even after the second show, and sleep in the day, with him. Oh, I wasn't still dancing, I was too old. But I did things at the club—I sang a little, I fooled around with the customers, taught the girls the new routines. So, they called me at five in the morning." Mechanically she broke off a chunk of bread and rubbed it in the oil of her salad, a small, obsessive motion, like an absent-minded caress. Max kept his eyes down. "You know why I can talk about it like this? Because I've said it to myself so many times—those same words, crushed to bits—that they hardly mean anything any more. I don't feel anything much when I say them. It's peculiar. Oh, when I first met him, Max, you should have seen me." She gave him a faint smile. "I was a knockout, if I say so myself."

"I don't doubt it."

"Yes, I was. I was just a chorus girl, and the place was not exactly the Copa, but it wasn't too bad, either. I was never ashamed of it. I did a good job, I earned a living. I didn't need to go to bed with every customer who got an idea in his head. People think. . . . A few here and there maybe, you know how it is, but that was not my way of making money, never."

"No need to apologize."

"No, I know that. I just want you to understand that it wasn't like he rescued me from a terrible life or anything like that. I could pick and choose. I chose. So"—she sighed, and stopped eating at last—"they called me at five in the morning, after twenty years. I was cooking a meat loaf for the next day. I remember I had to wipe the chopped meat off my hands to answer the phone. . . . He was a real nice-looking man. A gentle type. Soft-spoken. He was satisfied with how things turned out. So was I. I didn't imagine anything like that could ever happen to me. I mean, not many women can say this, Max, but I had an easy time. Not as a kid, but later, with him. I suppose I expected it to just go on forever. I didn't expect a tragedy. We had it real nice and easy."

He had an impulse to reach out and take her large hand, spread out

32

flat and still on the tablecloth, but he held back. The way she absorbed her grief put him in awe.

"All alone now," Lettie went on. "I didn't have the right kind of life for children. And I think I never had that instinct they say a woman is supposed to have. I liked being out and working. Can you picture me with a baby? I mean, I would have been good to it, God knows. But I guess I was too selfish then."

"Do you regret it?"

"No." She shook her head. "I don't regret much of anything I've done. Except that I shouldn't have let him go on driving the truck at night. He was getting older. Fifty-nine. I should have noticed and not let him. That I regret. Didn't your wife ever want a child?"

"She—" Max began. His throat tightened with the effort to say something, anything, about her. He couldn't see Susie contorted in childbirth or trudging behind a carriage. Though for all he knew, that was his own lack of vision. To him she was always a flier, with an urge in the blood and a skill in the bones. His skill was laboriously learned. He was there to catch her, and she had seemed content, more than content, with that.

"She was kind of a light thing. She had red hair. She flew on the trapeze." The words were coming out choppy, one at a time, like a speech breaking in pained fragments before an audience. "We didn't talk about it at the beginning, we were working so hard. And you know how time goes. By the time we left the circus it was too late. I was selfish too. I didn't want to be distracted. It's funny"—he paused and caught her eye, luminous—"that now, over at the school, I'm with them so much. They're like another species to me. But interesting." The ache in his chest subsided, eased away. Fluency returned, and he smiled. "First they feel they have to act very respectful because you're old. As if you've never felt the things they're feeling. Then after a while it dawns on them that you're human, so they become more themselves. Right now I'm hot stuff over there. They've decided I'm, oh, something exotic. But that illusion will pass, I trust. Fortunately I have only eight or so at a time. It's very instructive, listening to them. You should try it."

"Oh, come on, Max. What could I teach? I didn't go past tenth grade."

"I don't know—sewing, cooking. You can read, can't you?"

Lettie drew back her broad shoulders and frowned. "What do you take me for? Tenth grade in those days was like college now. I'm a very literate person."

"I know, I know. I beg your pardon. I didn't mean it that way. How about some coffee? I bought a rum cake also." He got up and went into the kitchen. "You see my new espresso pot?" he called, and held it up. "Comes out black and thick like mud. Wonderful. Do you like it that way?"

Lettie nodded. He filled the pot and set it on the stove. "For instance," he said, returning to her at the table, "there's one girl who's quite a pest. Skinny, stringy hair, she looks like no one inspects her before she leaves in the morning. Of course they all do manage to look pretty sloppy, I must say. They dress like a bunch of gypsies. Anyhow, this one is very bright, very original, and constantly after me—Mr. Fried this, Mr. Fried that. She sounds like she's filling out a questionnaire. She wants enough data to get her through life. Where did I learn everything I know? How many employees in the circus? How many performances a week? How long to prepare each act? Did you ever notice, people who ask a lot of factual questions, especially how many and when and where—that's never what they really want to find out. It's a cover for something else."

"For what?"

"Oh, they want to worm something out of you that they need for themselves. Some piece of you."

"She might just like you, Max."

"Certainly she likes me. But she wants a piece of me, besides. And I—I have nothing to spare, believe me. I'm hoarding whatever is left."

"Hoarding!" Lettie tilted her head at him. "What is this hoarding business?"

"I never spread myself around. I had to be that way. We grew up poor, I was the youngest, and I was the different one. I needed to keep my wits about me or I'd get sucked in. You know, you give an inch . . . But later, with my wife—I never held back from her. She was different, she didn't . . . pull. And then that was gone. I lived alone. You fall into habits you can't break. Especially after I got mugged in the city—then it hit me that I didn't have much strength left. Not even for myself."

She looked at him hard as he took another gulp of wine. "You got mugged? How bad was it?"

"Bad enough. That was the first heart attack, four years ago. I woke up in the hospital. Furious."

The pain he could have borne, but not the mortification. Half a block from his door, up on West Eighty-ninth Street, where he moved after he closed the bike shop he had come to hate without her in it. One boy held the knife to his throat while the other took the wallet from his pocket. As soon as the cold steel left his neck he shot out an arm that hadn't tried its strength in years. It hit the boy in the chest with hardly enough force to make him stagger. The boy struck back and he fell to the pavement, out cold. Soon he heard voices. Where the hell had the voices been five minutes before? He passed out again and woke behind white curtains; men dressed in white asked if he had a history of heart attacks. When he held out his bare arm to look at it, betrayal rose like bitter gal in his throat. First grounded after years of soaring, and now, insult added to injury, hollowed out. The marrow scooped out secretly, while he slept. The bitterness had never left him.

"Of course that wouldn't happen here," he said to Lettie. "Never! That's why we're here, right? Put away, out of danger. Here the kids are rich, they don't need what's in my wallet."

"They're not all that rich," she said. "Some of them—"

'Oh, yes they are! I've walked around and seen the houses. Have you ever taken a good look? Plenty of money, but no taste whatsoever. Plastic boxes." Rage had sneaked up. He heard his voice rising. "At least in the city you could see a real building! People! Here no one is even out on the streets at night. No one walks. When I go out at night I get looks, like I'm a loiterer!"

And there he was, swiftly stalking around the table and waving his arms in a fit of temper—just what Dr. Small had said not to do. What a life, when a man couldn't even rant freely. To top it off, the police sirens began screeching again. When the wail dwindled he wagged a finger at Lettie. "You can be sure that siren's not for any bunch of kids taking an old man's money. No. The kids here are only starving for a little real life. No wonder they get so screwed up later on. At school, you should see, I'm their drug! They get a high from me. A free trip. They can't even tell I'm half dead myself." He stopped pacing to bang his fist on the table; the wineglasses shook. "They could have anything they want, and all they want is to look like bums! They don't know what it's all about. To them it's a—an entertainment, to dress in rags!"

"Oh, for Chrissakes, sit down already, Max. What are you all worked up for over nothing? I didn't realize you were so bitter. These children haven't hurt you. Their clothing bothers you? Styles change."

He sat down heavily, tired of himself. "All right, all right. I'm sorry again."

Lettie's quiet hands broke off another piece of bread. "Maybe that particular girl doesn't have a loving home. That's very important."

"Oh, a loving home, come on." His arm sliced disparagingly through the cigar smoke. The bubbling roar of the espresso pot erupted inside and he stood up. "Overrated. I came from a loving home. It can kill you. Love, my friend, doesn't live up to its reputation," he grumbled on his way to the kitchen.

Liar, he thought, turning off the flame. Treacherous liar. But that was different. And that was dead. Any love he might have left was for the beautiful, not the needy. Not some needy kid. And there was no beauty left for him. Susie in blue poised in air like a solitary bold bird: that beauty had failed. And he, with all his vaunted love, had failed her too. She was hideous, so he hadn't wanted to look. He had run his fingers gently over the line of her cheekbone and turned to look out the window, at vacant sky. But he still kept the curve of that line in his fingertips.

Lettie cleared the plates and brought them to the kitchen. He took an orange from the refrigerator, tossed it in the air and caught it. "This is what I use at school. I'm teaching them to juggle. They bring oranges from home. You should see those oranges roll across the gym floor. It smells nice, at least." He took a deep breath. "As a matter of fact, it smells beautiful." He held it up to her nose for a second, then cut two strips off the peel and dropped them into the coffee cups. His heart quieted.

"I come in, they rush over, they surround me with the smell of oranges. When the lesson is over we eat them together." She was very close. He smiled at her. "I'm not really as nasty as I sound."

There was a hush. Lettie's face had a sudden suspended look, as though she were about to touch him. The instant passed. She stacked dishes in the sink while he cut the cake. It was crowded in the small space—he was bumping into an arm or a hip at every turn. The touch of her revived feelings he didn't think he wanted. Lettie seized a sponge and began vigorously wiping the countertop.

"You don't have to do that."

"Why not? I'm not overworked."

"Come on inside. Let's have the coffee hot." She followed him back to the table. "Why are you incarcerated here, Lettie?"

"Heart condition."

"A fellow sufferer."

"It could be worse."

"Oh, I know that. One of my partners, a big hefty man by the name of Henry Cook, this man, Lettie, who would hold six of us on his shoulders, got muscular dystrophy and shrunk up like a prune. Sits all day in a wheelchair, if he's not dead yet. I lost touch."

"That's a pity."

They sat silent for a while. It was good that she knew how to be quiet. He had always kept the impression that big women talked too much and too loud, because his mother had been big and vocal—her words drove him out to the roof of the tenement, where he perfected walking the ledge. She never knew, so busy scrubbing and cooking, what he did up there. High in blissful escape from his loving home, he juggled soda bottles left by teen-aged neckers; when he dropped them they bounced neatly on the sun-baked tar. He loved it up there alone in the sunshine, above the daily stench and absorbed grime of the building, and close to the sky. But you couldn't make a life's work of fooling around on rooftops. After high school his mother had wanted to ensure his future by installing him behind the counter of his uncle's delicatessen, where his two older brothers were already sinking into a rut of tedium. His father was another warning example: a faded man, thankful for small decencies like the roof over his head, he had never dared expect life to yield much joy, and so never exerted himself to procure any. Max had no intention of aging and dying before his time. Spoiled by books and dreams and sky-gazing, he wanted transcendence. The roof was his jumping-off point. A reticent son, he never quarreled with their plans for him, merely disappeared one day when he was seventeen. With fifty dollars in his pocket earned making sandwiches on Delancey Street, he boarded a train west. Second-generation American, he became upwardly mobile, up and up, till he was scaling a rope to a metal bar hung in cavernous space, swinging wild and exalted like primitive man. He knew he was Urban Jew at play like Tarzan; but defying the social odds, he stayed up there half a life. Now there was no more escaping.

He should have gone back to see them more. He had sent letters, photos, and money. Flimsy paper things. When it was too late, he came to understand that it had been no inspiring business, raising kids in a cramped apartment in an alien country, on a garment worker's wages; if they gave too much anxious love and too little joy it was because the one was all they had to spare, the other a luxury they

37

could never afford. Still, it left him with no taste for family life. He found joy in suspended moments, high above the tug of the world. He would do any amount of labor, training his body to cheat gravity, for those keen solitary moments. He had his transcendence. But once that appetite is awakened, he found, enough is never enough. Even now, the blood raced as hungrily as before, while the muscles atrophied. He lived on, throbbing but motionless.

For an odd instant he looked at Lettie, pouring more coffee for both of them, and wondered if he might embrace that body and find there some remnant of elation. The thought alone made him weak. No, if you need to ponder it first, better forget it.

After the coffee she said, "By the way, Max, you shouldn't be so hard on Vicky Cameron. She means well."

"Meaning well doesn't count in my book. Oh, what the hell. Let me clear this up."

"I'll help you." She insisted on washing the dishes. He stood next to her in the tight space and dried them.

"What did you do after your husband was killed?"

Her chest rose and fell as she rested her hands briefly on the edge of the sink. "For a year or so, nothing. And I mean nothing. I had money, compensation, so I was able to stay in and stare at the walls. It was a pretty bad time. I swore later I would never let that happen to me again—it's like a living death. I ate like there was no tomorrow. Finally I tried to pull myself together. I got a job as a cashier in an ice cream parlor. I tried every one of the twenty-six flavors —I'm sure they lost money on me. After that I did alterations in a fancy ladies' dress shop. The work was not bad; I like to sew—I used to help with the costumes in the old days. But the fittings were hard, all that crawling around on the floor with a mouthful of pins. And they were always in a rush. I'm not a fast worker. I have to concentrate and take my time. One morning at the machine I had a heart attack, and when I came out of the hospital they didn't want to take me back. They were scared I'd drop dead on them, I suppose. I might've, who knows? The doctors said I ought to be someplace with no pressures, so here I am."

"No pressures here, eh?"

"Ah, let's not get ourselves depressed." She handed him the last plate and swished the sponge expertly around the sink. "Do you want to watch something on TV?"

"Why not?"

He settled in the armchair with his feet on the ottoman as she switched the dials. His eyelids drooped. His head was heavy with red wine. He caught a glimpse of a fellow getting hit in the head by a circle of pizza dough. The next thing he knew, Lettie was shaking him gently by the shoulder.

"I'm going home, Max. Why don't you get up and sleep in bed? This way your neck will be stiff."

"I'm so sorry! How rude of me. Did I sleep long?" His neck was stiff already.

"It's nothing at all. Thank you for a lovely evening. Next time I'll cook for you."

"To think that I could fall asleep with a lady. Nothing personal, I assure you. It only shows how—"

"Ah, come on, Max, cut the crap." She bent down to kiss his forehead lightly, and shut the door noiselessly behind her.

As he was undressing, the phone rang: Ted Collins. Would he consider giving an hour of gymnastics instruction, two mornings a week, to a group of six teachers, including himself and Frank Fox? The question was no surprise—a couple of them had approached him the other day; he had told them to get a group together and make a definite proposition.

"Gladly," he said. "Eight sharp, the kids start at nine-ten. Five dollars each per hour. That's a bargain compared to Jack LaLanne."

He folded back the multicolored bedspread. There were other prospects. Yoga was a big thing. He could read up on it, and in nearby Hastings, reputedly populated with Yoga-loving artists and psychotherapists, take a few classes (or—okay, okay, Dr. Small—observe them). Before he knew it, he would be in business. He grunted and plumped up the pillows. Already he was a success, taking the innocent town by storm. And he knew why too. With no good reason, they presumed beneath the ceremonious exterior a heart of pure gold. A curious error, since the heart was not pure at all but an alloy, a heart of steel.

He maneuvered his crackling bones into bed but couldn't settle down; he had slept too long in front of the TV. Frustration coiled his muscles. Everything that infuriated him, that he had expressed so imperfectly and incompletely to Lettie—above all, the vicissitudes of the flesh—streaked through him again with a vengeance. There was no recourse. He twisted and battled with the sheets. At last something occurred to him. Sinking into the pillows, he picked up the phone at his bedside and pressed a button.

"Mrs. Cameron? Max Fried here. I had a feeling this was one of your late nights."

"Yes, Mr. Fried. Is everything all right?"

"Hunky-dory, as we used to say in school. As a matter of fact, you remind me a little bit of my sixth-grade teacher, Miss Eustace. Did I ever tell you that? Her favorite motto was 'Discretion is the better part of valor.' She used to say it when she broke up fights in the schoolyard between the Italians and the Jews. I never knew what that meant until many years later, and then I decided it wasn't. Discretion, that is. Valor is the better part of valor. Only that's a—what do you call it?—a tautology. What do you think?"

"Mr. Fried," she said with a trained patience, "is there something we can do for you?"

"I very much doubt it, alas. I called merely to bid you good night. I know it's hectic down there, I know the joint is jumping, as it were, but still I wouldn't want your anxieties over me to give you insomnia when you go home. I want you to know I've eaten well, put on clean pajamas, brushed some of my teeth and put the rest in a glass of Polident. I'm ready to be tucked in."

There was a heavy clatter at the other end, then a bleak emptiness. Dammit. Again a siren wailed. An action-packed night. He was left holding the phone, a sinewy old man with a crick in his neck. Feeling ancient and stupid, he pushed another button and the light went mercifully out.

CHAPTER 4

"CATHERINE WAS STRUCK with confusion and dismay when she learned of her mother the Queen's pregnancy." Alison shut the door tight and tossed the three oranges over to her bed. "Needless to say," the words continued, "life in the castle would undergo some drastic changes. There would be servants wheeling a perambulator around the palace gardens. And if it was a boy, she pondered as she removed her royal garments, he might interfere with her . . ." With her getting the crown—but there was an exact word for that and she couldn't remember it. There ought to be a dictionary that worked backwards: if you knew the meaning it would tell you the word.

She was too old to do fairy tales anyway. She threw her clothes to the floor, where the jeans, socks, and underpants clung together like a crumpled-up, inside-out body. The blue T-shirt with the anti-nuke slogan hung limply over the back of her desk chair, its sleeves half folded in on themselves. She stood in front of the mirror. Her breasts had not grown much lately; she was almost used to them now—at least till the next spurt of growth. Bodies did things that way, in spurts. They did gross and unpredictable things all by themselves. There were things her body did in bed at night that she didn't decide to do at all. They happened against her will. Wanda's body, with a baby inside, had spread out and opened up for him. But that they had done on purpose. She herself had been in there once too, wet and sticky.

When she had passed them downstairs just now, carrying her oranges from the kitchen, Wanda was lazing on the sofa across from Josh, her feet up and her robe falling open to expose long white legs, her nipples pointing through the thin nylon. "Come here a minute, Alison." They had something to tell her. "The doctor said to stay off my feet as much as I could the first few months," Wanda said, "because I've already lost two. It was years ago, you wouldn't remember, Alison. But that shaky stage should be over now." They hadn't wanted to tell her before, Josh said; in case anything happened, she would be disappointed.

Him on top of her. Putting it in. She stared at her bare body in the mirror. She never would.

Straightening up, she ran her brush through her hair. Wanda kept nagging her about paying attention to her appearance. She tried bangs. The fine brown hair hung down to her chin: a curtain. "The famous star of stage and screen traveled incognito, her lustrous hair shielding her identity." Then she brushed the curtain aside and made braids. The high school girls with thick black hair looked exotic in braids, like Indians or gypsies, but she looked like an overgrown baby. It was no use. She brushed them out and got her pajamas from under the pillow.

She hadn't known what to say to them, so she had stood numb as in a game of statues, clutching the oranges to her chest. "I'm sure you'll be as happy as we are, after you get used to the idea." Josh sounded disappointed. He folded his arms across his chest and stared at her, waiting. "But you used to *want* a baby brother or sister," Wanda said. Then Josh got up and came towards her; she stepped quickly back to the stairs. "We'll still love you, Allie. Is that what's bothering you? We'll still love you the same as before."

The same as before. A hollow space spread inside her. Picking up two oranges from the bed, she began the simplest routine, tossing them up one at a time, not more than a foot in the air. They made a nice smack as they hit her palms, and they smelled good too, sharp and sweet. When you can do that much, he had told them in gym, try to keep both in the air at once. That was easy. She tossed them up together, fast. Then switch hands, he said. See if you can cross them. That's it, very good. Take it easy, keep it going. Orange X's blinked in the air before her. She heard the quick smack against her palms. Faster! Her forehead wrinkled up tight, her eyes darted from right hand to left. Fifteen minutes a night, he said. At least. She caught them against her chest and breathed deeply, sitting down on the bed. "What do you do with those oranges anyway?" Wanda had asked as she was going up the stairs. "Oh, juggle." "Juggle! That same old character?" Josh said. "What next?" And he gave her the broad silly smile.

She picked up a third. Three at a time was much harder. The trick was to keep your mind off somewhere, quiet, he said, and let your hands and eyes do the thinking for you. Her hands and eyes pulsed with the effort: not an instant to rest, endless curves. Don't hang on to them, he said. Send them right back up! And stay in one place. Don't dance around. That's it, keep your balance. It's the oranges that move, not you. Her eyeballs were aching from tracking all three. The moment the head gets into the act you're finished, he said. You kids all think too much! Be a pair of eyes and a pair of hands. Faster! She was doing it: four times round, five times. Her tongue was glued to her upper lip. If she could make ten . . . But as soon as she thought that, one orange dropped and rolled under the bed. A second rolled across the floor to the desk. Well, pretty soon she would get to do it as casually as he did. She would practice every night till she was so good that she could run away and join a circus.

It was midnight on the Raggedy Ann clock on the window sill. Wanda had given it to her for her birthday almost three years ago. The face of Raggedy Ann was gross, with the hour and minute hands radiating from her nostrils. When the alarm went off, a nasty girl's voice whined, "It's time to get up for work and for play, Now get out of bed and start a new day." She glared at it with the look of disdain, then set the alarm for six-thirty and turned out the light. Gathering the quilt around her, she moved toward the wall and slipped a hand inside her pajamas. She knew from friends' houses what babies were like. They took over the household, with their bottles and putrid diapers and plastic toys strewn everywhere. They sat in highchairs doing revolting things with mushy food. They puked on your shoulders—Hilary's baby cousin did it to her last year, when she was over there doing math—sour-smelling white stuff like watery cottage cheese. When they got older they destroyed your property. Franny's best piece of sculpture, a life-sized clay frankfurter in a blue roll, that she had worked on for a week and glazed and baked in the kiln, was smashed to pieces by her two-year-old brother. She would have to keep all her papers under lock and key. They would never look at her once it was born. They hardly did now. Once they had the baby to hold they would forget she existed. Mother, father, and baby—what a cozy little group they would be.

The insides of her legs were hot. She edged her fingers slowly up to the place. That book Hilary showed her last summer at the town pool. They were sitting together, she and Hilary, on the grass near the fence, reading the chapter with the page turned down. Then Franny had run over, dripping wet, to see what was so funny, and the three of them sat in a circle, rocking in hysterical laughter as Hilary read it out loud, stopping at every other sentence to gasp, "Oh, my God!" and clap her hand over her mouth. Later it didn't seem funny any more—she couldn't get it out of her mind. A girl of twelve, not even as old as she was, from a poor family, meets a man in the balcony of the movie theatre she goes to every Saturday afternoon. He gives her a dime to let him feel between her legs. She keeps going back every Saturday, and while he does it she pays no attention and watches the movie—she just wants the dime. But one Saturday he manages to get his fingers inside her. She squirms around and opens her legs wider for him—she knows it's wrong, but she can't help it. In the dark, he wriggles his fingers slowly all over, inside her pants, inside her, while the movie about cowboys and Indians goes on, and meanwhile something is happening, a slow fire creeping through her thighs, her stomach, and before she knows it her eyes are squeezed shut and she cares about nothing else in the world except that feeling, the slow fire. It pushes through and grows and spreads, a fire gone out of control and frightening, but Alison didn't even care, she just had to keep it going till it got so fast and immense it was everywhere and had to burst through. It burst like her insides exploding, and then died away.

Her face was flaming as she pulled the covers back up. She could have stopped if she had really tried, but she always gave in. The books in the library said most kids did it. Years ago people used to think it was evil and gave you pimples and rings under your eyes, but now they had discovered it was natural. Her fingers were wet and sticky—she wiped them on the quilt. Lots of things they said were natural were disgusting. Her eyes felt hot, as though she had been crying. She turned over on her side and burrowed into the pillows. All the errands she would be sent on: shopping for bottles and rubber pants and teething rings. Hold the baby, Allie, while I find a pin. Give the baby his bottle while I get his sweater. Love the baby, will you, for just a second. Her body was heavy, blurry, near sleep. If only Wanda would sometimes . . . But they thought she was too big. Not lovable, like a baby. Must figure out how to act towards this baby. Early June, they said—six more months. She clutched a corner of the quilt in her fist and her open mouth wet the pillow, as sleep came close enough to take her, and she yielded.

It was twenty after six when, waking to the gray light of early winter, she switched off the alarm and reached under the mattress for Alice.

The white-haired woman with harlequin glasses leads Alice down a wide dusty street past a bunch of brawny cowboys lounging in front of the town's one movie theatre. "Hey, kid, how about coming in for the afternoon show?" one calls out. Alice ignores them. Right in front of police headquarters the woman says, "Remember, it's for the best, dear." Alice nods obediently. But then, pretending to have left something important in the car, she runs off and dashes through a maze of side streets till she reaches the railroad station. She grabs a pole and hops aboard just as the silver train starts moving. Although she is tired and hungry and hasn't the slightest idea where she is headed, she feels wonderful. She has her freedom. It is not bread and water I fear. . . . Do you think life is nothing but not being stone dead? . . . When the train stops in Arizona she finds the town filled with Navajo Indians. The women all wear turquoise rings, and many have fat drooling babies tied to their backs. She strikes up a conversation with two of them; they seem extremely friendly, and in fact invite her back to the reservation, where she learns to set up tepees and make jewelry. For a time she is content in their simple village, disturbed only by the nightly wails of the babies, till one evening a traveling circus caravan passes by. The lure of that life is too powerful. Hastily, Alice gathers her few belongings, leaves a note of thanks for the Indians, and hitches a ride; when she catches up with the caravan she hides out in the acrobats' trailer.

It was seven-thirty already. She couldn't be late—she needed to speak to him. She raced to get to the gym before the others arrived.

"Mr. Fried, I have trouble with three oranges. I get all mixed up and I can't keep hold of the inner center, like you said."

"You'll get it in time. It takes patience and practice, and then it comes all of a sudden. Remember to toss them very low at the beginning, and don't think about it too much."

"I was wondering if you would have time for any private lessons after school. I'd like to prepare for a career. All the really great artists started their work when they were very young."

"Is that so?"

"Yes. Mozart, Anna Pavlova, Picasso. I looked them up."

"But this is not an art, Alison. It's a trick, a skill." He tossed an orange high in the air and swiveled around. It passed his left shoulder, went behind his back and ended neatly in the palm of his right hand. He smiled down at her. "Now when you get to the trapeze, that, maybe, is an art."

45

Hilary and Franny and Karen came up and clustered around him, then Bobby and Elliot. Nick, small and timid, hung back at the edge of the circle.

"Good morning, ladies and gentlemen. How is the juggling coming? Are you practicing every night as I told you? . . . Ah, I'm glad to hear that."

He had not answered her question about the private lessons.

"This morning I thought I might show a few intrepid volunteers how to jump off a rising seesaw."

She followed his sideward glance, as they all did. He and Fats must have put it together before class. It was a long plank of plywood on a thick base that stood about a foot high and tapered up like a bullet. He stepped onto the low end of the plank and walked uphill with easy strolling steps. Past the halfway point it tipped beneath him. He strolled down to the other end and then back again, in the same nonchalant way. If she looked only at the upper half of his body she could never guess a seesaw was tilting up and down underneath: he moved as if on flat ground. The balance was inside him, separate from the board. He stepped off and spread his arms in a wide, expansive gesture. "Simple, isn't it? All it is, is walking. You always have the earth under you—that's the thing to remember."

She gazed at him and her eyes slipped out of focus; he became blurred and circled with a fuzzy shimmering aura that made him seem larger. A vibration of light radiated from him. His voice took on a richness she had never heard before. She didn't grasp the sense of his words, but the deep timbre sent a shiver through her. There was something magical about him—he could control things. She had had a feeling that very first day. She needed to get at that power in him. The need was an ache in her throat.

"Okay, Nick," he was saying. "You stand on the edge of the seesaw. No, with your back to it. Now jump off. Yes, that's all I mean. A one-inch drop. Good boy. Not too hard, is it?"

Nick shook his head, puzzled.

"Any of you could do that blindfolded, right? You even think it's funny. Now what if I pushed down on the high end while Nick, or any of you, was standing on that edge. Of course—that low end would pop up. And there you'd be, popping with it. But if you were off fast enough, you'd be on your own, up in the air. Oh, and remember, you always jump up, not down. What you've got to do is use the impulse of the pop, of the surprise, but not let it control you. Once you're up, you're all alone and you're in control. That's the beauty of it."

They listened, entranced. Again he strolled back and forth across the tilting board, and stopped dead center to face them. With the board resting perfectly parallel to the floor, he stood, arms spread wide and head cocked, as though on a pedestal. Then he stepped down.

"Okay, Nick, get back on the seesaw. I'll push down the high end and you jump. Up, not down. And fast. The minute you sense the vibration in your feet. We'll see what happens."

Nick gaped, nervously brushing a lock of sandy hair from his forehead.

"This is not a high seesaw. You can jump a foot to the ground, I'm quite sure."

He pushed down hard. The board flew up; Nick jumped up and out, to land, smiling, on his feet. They all applauded.

"Wonderful!" He patted Nick on the shoulder. "Nothing to it if you concentrate—I've seen some of you fooling around outside doing much trickier things. And remember, the mat is very soft. Once you can do this we'll raise the seesaw. Then you can learn to aim for a specific place when you land. And after that, to land on top of someone else. But they probably won't let me go that far."

Her turn came last. At the first faint pressure under her feet she willed herself up and out. For a glorious instant she soared. As she landed on the mat her legs gave way. Down on her knees—and it had looked so easy!

"That's fine, Alison," he said. "Next time concentrate on your legs. Tell them to hold you straight up, just like you told them to lift you off the board."

"How did you know I told them?"

"I know because I know how it feels. I've been there. It's okay to topple over at the beginning. Then you can—"

"Hey, Max!" It was Fats Fox, trotting over from his volleyball game across the gym. "Are you sure that's safe? We don't want any broken necks around here."

Their voices rose to defend him.

"Calm down, all of you. There won't be any broken necks, Fox, I assure you. This is nothing; it's no more than they do by themselves in the yard, only we're taking it seriously. With precision. Besides, there's a mat."

"But if they miss the mat—"

47

"Nonsense." Max moved to the other end of the seesaw. He held out his palms as if making an offering. "I'll stand here to catch them. Is that enough? Hilary, you push the seesaw down, please. A swift sharp push will do." He pressed his hands together as if in prayer and rocked them slightly back and forth. "I am the net, ladies and gentlemen," he said with a crooked grin. "Pretend I am the net."

"Max." Fats's voice curled with doubt. "Are you really strong enough to catch them?"

"Mr. Fox." He seemed to expand as he pulled back his shoulders and eyed Fats steadily. "I could catch even you. It's all in the legs and the pelvis." He slapped his thigh hard. "Oh, and as long as you're here, help me raise the seesaw, would you? They're ready. A very talented group."

"I don't know," said Fats.

"I told you I'll catch them. Come on, Frank, lend a hand."

Max brought over another foot-high cylindrical block, with a hole in the center. Grudgingly, Fats raised the plank while Max attached the new piece. He placed a long wooden peg through the board and the two blocks. The center of the seesaw stood two feet off the ground.

"Alison," he said, "try again, from this height. Don't worry, I'll be here, if necessary. Up and out, so you clear the plank. Now this time, get an image of yourself, first in the air, and then landing straight up on your feet. A beautiful image of how you will look, so precise that you could bring it out again, any time you need it. Hang on to that. Become the image. Do you understand? Become your own image."

But standing on the plank, she saw no image. She saw nothing except the familiar faces of the others, watching her with expectation. The coming leap was out of her control —it was Max controlling her, and she was in his power. Maybe she would fall, and find out how it felt to be caught in his arms, blue-veined below the rolled-up sleeves of his work shirt. Suddenly she felt a vibration tremble through the board. She flung herself up and out, flying. One keen instant of suspended joy, unconsummated before it was over—and she hit the mat and fell to her hands and knees. No pain, only a soft thud shuddering through her, to ripple outward and settle, ringing, in her ears. Max bent down to help her up. He lifted her by the shoulders and pretended to dust her off. He smiled at her, encouraging, his face a benevolent, god-like blur.

He worked till twelve on Fridays, she found out from the schedule

48

on the gym bulletin board. She didn't go down to the lunchroom at noon but leaned against a tree outside, keeping an eye on both the front and the side doors. It was chilly, with a soft feel of coming snow in the air. She zipped up her down jacket and unwrapped her sandwich. At ten after twelve he came out, wearing a dark-green corduroy jacket and carrying a brass-tipped walking stick, along with the black attaché case. Except for the beret, he could be any ordinary person on his way to an office. No one would guess that the case contained not papers but plastic pins and colored rubber balls. He set off down Broad Street with a quick, intense stride, the stick tucked under his arm. Crumpling her paper lunch bag, she followed.

After a block and a half he got on the shoppers' jitney. It stopped at every corner and she jogged alongside, jostling ladies with shopping bags and strollers. It felt like the sort of weird thing Alice might do. In a few minutes he got off and entered the large Rexall drugstore next to the supermarket where they had met. Keeping a safe distance, she saw him pick out Gillette razor blades (Josh used a noisy electric razor), a small package of cigars (good; less cancerous than cigarettes), and an economy-sized box of DiGel tablets. He left a prescription in the back section. As he swung through the revolving doors she grabbed a Hershey bar with almonds and slammed a quarter on the counter, then trailed him around a corner. He walked fast and turned into the flagstone path of a four-story brick building that looked like school. She paused. It was the old people's home. She had passed it often in the car with Wanda and Josh. "Pleasure Knolls, my foot," Wanda once said, rolling her eyes. "What kind of pleasure, I wonder?" It couldn't be! Maybe he was visiting a sick friend. She sat down on the curb and ate the Hershey bar. After a while she tucked the wrapper in her knapsack and went inside.

The woman at the desk held her head drawn back, as if she wanted to be far away from things. Her nose and chin jutted out sharply. She had on a gray dress with a pale-green scarf and a cameo pinned to its knot. "Can I help you, young lady?" Her voice was reedy and nasal, like Franny's brother's oboe, and as she spoke she ran her fingers nervously through her hair.

"I'm looking for a Mr. Max Fried. Does he live here?"

"Yes. Is he . . . expecting you?"

"Oh, sure." She headed for a glass door on her right.

"Not that way. The elevator is to your left. And it's 319. Press three."

"Oh, yes. Thanks." Plainly visible through the glass door was a lounge. How could she be so dumb?

"Are you a relative?"

"Yes, his great-niece."

The third-floor corridor was all straight lines and had carpeting the color of stale grass. The walls were peach, hung with paintings of trees drooping over ponds. There were brass numbers on the doors; she found 319 at the far end and knocked before she could lose her nerve.

"I'll get it, Max," she heard. The door opened. This woman was large and grayish-blond, dressed in a scarlet pants suit, with loops of gold chain on the broad slope of her chest.

"Hello there," she said kindly.

"I'm sorry. I didn't realize . . . I mean . . ."

"Are you looking for Max?"

She nodded.

"Max, you have a visitor," the woman called over her shoulder, then turned back. "You must be one of his pupils. Come on in, it's all right."

Max appeared, a dish towel tucked in around his belt. He was holding up, like a magician's wand, a long wooden spoon coated with a dark sauce. "Alison?"

"Obviously." She tried to laugh. "You look shocked."

"Well, Max, let's let the girl in, for heaven's sake." Alison entered and the woman shut the door.

"I'm sorry. I didn't know you were married. Excuse me for . . . just barging in." His aura was swiftly evaporating. She felt weak with disillusion as he seemed to shrink before her eyes, still holding up the spoon in his stern grip.

"I'm not married," he said. "My friend, Lettie Blumenthal. Lettie, this is Alison, from school. Alison what?"

"Oh, plain Alison is okay." She breathed with relief. They might be living together. Living together in an old people's home—yes, that was neat, just the sort of thing she would expect of him. "Glad to meet you," she said cheerfully to Lettie. She knew how Wanda spoke in delicate situations.

"Same here, I'm sure. Would you like to sit down?"

"Thank you. What a nice apartment."

"Yes," said Lettie. "It gets a lot of sun."

"I can see from how well your plants are doing," she replied.

"Are you cutting classes to visit me?" asked Max.

50

Wanda's tactics felt too silly here. "Uh-huh." She nodded. "It's almost one. I should be in—let's see, Friday—math in six minutes." She slid the knapsack from her shoulders down to the carpet, and walked over to the window.

"How about some lunch as long as you're here?" Lettie asked. "We were just about to eat. Max made chili early this morning."

Max glanced at them both, gave a disapproving grunt, and withdrew to the kitchen.

"I've had my sandwich, but I guess I can manage a little more. Does he put an awful lot of meat in it, though?"

"Meat? Well, I don't know. I never had his chili before. Max," she called, "Alison wants to know, does your chili have a lot of meat in it?"

"It's because I—"

"Sure, it has plenty of meat," he called back. "I'm not that hard up yet."

"Are you allergic to meat?" Lettie asked.

"Oh, no, that's all right. Do you live—uh—nearby?"

"Right next door. It's nice to have an unexpected visitor. Excuse me, I'll get an extra chair. He really shouldn't strain himself."

She followed Lettie to the bedroom. "In school he said he'll catch us if we fall. He said that he would be the net."

"Good Lord!" Lettie whispered. "He really gets carried away, doesn't he? Well, tell the others not to."

Alison took the chair from her and brought it to the table.

"Ready, ladies," Max announced. His chili was delicious. She must remember to ask for the recipe before she left. She could substitute some soybean product for the meat. Wanda would be amazed.

"Alison," Max said, "it is most flattering to have you as a luncheon guest. I have few guests, except for Lettie and some cronies from my poker game. But if an inquiry would not be too blatant, to what do I owe the honor of this call?"

You didn't have to answer questions directly. He hadn't, this morning before class. "You don't talk that way in school."

"Ah, true. There I have my ingratiating pedagogic manner. Works like a charm. I'm much less engaging in actual life."

"Max, talk to the child in plain English. It could be she doesn't even understand what you're saying."

"Oh, I understand perfectly," she said to Lettie. "I'm verbally precocious, at least that's what they told my parents the problem is.

51

He's saying he acts friendly when he teaches so that we'll want to learn. And he wants to know why I came."

"Not bad, not bad," said Max. "So why did you come? But as long as you're here, have some more chili."

"Thank you. I came because you're an interesting person."

He set down his glass of wine to stare at her. Okay, let him. Let him find her out, if he could. It was satisfying to sit quite still under that gaze.

"You followed me home," he accused.

"How do you make the kids do those things? Do you use hypnotism or something?"

He burst out laughing. "Hypnotism? But I just told you, and you said you understood—it's a manner. A method. You think I'm some kind of Svengali?" Lettie laughed at that too. The name sounded exactly like what she meant, though, so she nodded. She would look it up in the encyclopedia, next shopping trip. Svengolly? Svengaly?

"There's another reason, actually," she said. "I think I might like to join a circus sometime. Fairly soon, maybe. I thought you could give me some advice."

"I'll advise you another day," said Max. "Right after lunch you're going back to school where you belong. It's not my ambition to inspire truancy." He rose and went into the kitchen.

"No, I'm not planning to go back to school today."

He moved fast: in a moment he was back, bringing three dishes of strawberry ice cream. "So be it. But you'll have to go somewhere, because we're going to the movies. When you're old and superfluous you'll have the luxury of afternoon movies also."

"What's playing?"

"*Children of Paradise,*" said Lettie. "It's an ancient French movie. I saw it years ago. It's full of romance and passion."

"Don't tell me you fell for that," said Max. "The romance is a crock. It's the pantomime that's worth the price of admission. Now, there's something beautiful to see."

"Oh, I wish I could go. I've never seen a French movie—they hardly ever come up here."

"Well, come along, then. You don't mind, do you, Max? Otherwise she'll have to wander around till school lets out. I remember how it is. I used to do that all the time. And it's December."

"Yes, and besides, I need to take my mind off my problems."

"Your problems?" Max asked, pushing back his chair.

"My mother is pregnant."

"I should think that would be her problem."

"I don't care much for little children. Didn't you ever hear of sibling rivalry?"

He got up slowly, staring at her once again, with a slight groan. That was all right. He would change, after a while. She would work on him.

"I'll clean up later," he said. "We're late, and I don't want to miss the coming attractions. Alison: the knapsack, the Hershey wrapper on the floor, and the tomato sauce on your shirt. Come on, hurry up, both of you."

CHAPTER 5

THERE WAS SNOW on the ground. The air was bitter and stung his cheeks like ice, and the wind, tearing through his black parka, knocked against his heart. Rounding blowy corners, he thought about how cold all of them must be in their graves now. But he had endured; he had to go out—he had promises to keep. His rumored talents were in great demand. The parents of young schoolchildren invited him to entertain at birthday parties. He gave spectacular, if highpriced, magic shows, and the rich bastards forked it over without a whimper. Some curious teachers from the early-morning gymnastics class invited him to dinner: as a guest he was an excellent commodity—he could sing for his supper. And at school, since they had discovered he could tell a good story they had been trying to persuade him to do it weekly for the kindergarten across the street. At this rate he would become an institution. There had not even been time for Yoga. He was saving Yoga for the spring, if he lived that long. Meanwhile it was nearing February, worst of months. He dreaded like a recurring bad dream the month she died. He used to feel, when he closed the door of their apartment in the Village, that nothing could intrude. They even took the phone off the hook. Death, as it turned out, was the only intruder to be reckoned with. Slipped in with Susie, her shadow.

Now he answered every call. His phone rang more in a week than it had in months, those last years in the city. Alison, for one, had taken to calling late at night. First there were reasonable pretexts, questions about the tumbling he was teaching in the gym. Then as she gained confidence she began closing in, like a fly buzzing around its chosen crumb, in narrower and narrower loops.

"Max, say a kid joins a circus and works around the place, you know, doing odd jobs—how long would it take before she could get into an act?"

"That depends, on how fast she can learn, what kind of physical shape she's in, what their situation is. A lot of things."

"Well, suppose she's very agile and a fast learner and all that."

Max frowned into the phone. It was midnight. It had been a long, cold day, and he was in bed, yearning to curl into oblivion with Hercule Poirot. "If you're thinking of trying it, Alison, let me warn you, you'll be sweeping up an awful lot of elephant dung before you become a star."

"Oh, it's not for me."

"Who is it for, then?"

"I can't tell you . . . Oh, all right. I'm writing a book."

"You're writing a book. I see."

"It's an adventure story, about a girl. But please don't tell anyone at school."

"I won't tell. Look, it's rather late. Why don't we talk about the book another time?"

"Okay. But listen, there's just one more thing, Max. It's about the juggling. I saw these three jugglers once, two boys and a girl, at Rockefeller Plaza a couple of years ago. It was New Year's Day—my parents took me in to see the tree. They were so fantastic—they had these tramp costumes and their faces were painted all white with green eye shadow, and a big crowd gathered around. It had just snowed. It was all cold and sunny, and they tossed these big black pins back and forth and kept cracking jokes and laughing while they did it. It was so weird, Max, I mean, right in the middle of the city and all the big buildings, to see this. So anyway, what I wanted to know was, how can a person join an act like that? Because I am getting pretty good at it, and maybe if I could get in touch with people like them, who do it for a living . . . Max, are you still there?"

"I'm still here."

"So how do you think I should go about it?"

"Alison, I haven't the vaguest idea. But why don't you finish junior high school first, then maybe try high school?"

"You're being sarcastic again. All right, I'll let you go to sleep. But you want to know something? Guess what happened to those jugglers that day."

"What?"

"A cop came along and chased them away. Isn't that just typical?"

"Typical, yes." His eyelids were drooping. "Good night."

But when he hung up he could neither sleep nor concentrate on the whodunit. It had begun hailing outside, and the brisk tapping sound on the windows was exactly the same as on that night he could never forget, when she brought home with her death the intruder. In his head it was like yesterday, keener than yesterday. She had been feeling weak and had an appointment the next morning for some blood tests. He was home from the shop first; she had stopped to buy new boots. Her old ones were letting in the snow. When he heard her key he went to take her coat and packages. He kissed her. He brought a towel to dry her hair, gleaming with bits of hail. She stood leaning against the door. Without a word, with a slow, numbing authority, she unbuttoned his corduroy vest, slipped it off his shoulders, and let it slide to the floor. She did the same with his shirt, then started to unbuckle his belt.

Confused, Max submitted with a silly grin. "What are you carrying on? You're a totally abandoned woman."

"Assault," she whispered, and continued.

He delighted in every touch of Susie's, but this touch made him uneasy. She wasn't playful. Dead serious.

"Do you still . . ."

"What, Susie?" She was tugging awkwardly at the zipper of her new boot. He bent down. "Let me do that."

"Do you still want me like when I was young?"

"There you go—it was caught. You know you're my unbridled passion," he teased. It was all wrong that she should ask.

She made love to him wildly, on top of him on the couch, to the sound of the hail pelting the windows. He felt seized and taken and devoured, but he yielded completely, for Susie was possessed by something that had to be placated. She cried out with pleasure but her face above him was sorrowful. When it was over she collapsed on his chest and sobbed.

"What is it, for God's sake?"

"Don't you know I'm dying?"

"There's nothing wrong with you! You're tired, that's all, run down. It's the weather. Please, Susie. Please."

"Oh, I am so scared," she wept.

She was right. She had found out long before him what dying felt like. He knew a little bit now, but far from all she had known when she lay flat with the tubes in her arms. Sometimes he felt a shiver of knowledge, not understanding but more like a tainted breeze passing over him. And at those moments, he wanted to follow right into that barren wind and away.

He wanted out, but they wouldn't let him go. They called with their

56

offers. He might feel like a wall around dark space, but it appeared a beam was still visible from outside, as when one leaves a room but forgets to turn out the light. He accepted the offers, and though his heart wasn't in it, he did his best. It was no use living in the past, Dr. Small and Miss Tilley had advised. But with all due respect, where else should he live? That he had no future his fluttery chest informed him every time he walked up a flight of stairs.

Even Vicky Cameron had strategies to whip her charges out of depression. On one of her late nights she phoned him at eleven-thirty.

"Mr. Fried, I know you keep late hours so I'm not going to apologize. And you don't like it when I'm polite so I'm not being polite: I want you to give a little performance Friday night for Mr. Rakofsky's birthday party. He'll be eighty-four—you can't refuse."

He had no one but himself to blame that she was so well acquainted with his skills. How many times had he juggled her paperweights, conjured her stapler and Scotch tape off the desk, slid her ballpoint pens into his pocket and out his sleeve? The bill for those indulgences had fallen due.

"All right, all right, I'll do it. But I must say, you puzzle me. Is this the Victoria Cameron I knew?"

"You do bring out a new side of me, that's quite true."

"There's hope for you yet, Victoria."

"Never mind the prognosis, Mr. Fried. Just see that you're in the lounge Friday in time for the dinner. Seven o'clock. It wouldn't look right to come in afterwards. I trust you'll put together a really fine act. Nothing too risqué, please. Thank you and good night. I say that as a formality, not as a wish."

"Well done."

He entered the lounge Friday evening with an arm linked through Lettie's. The high-ceilinged room was laced with red and blue twined crepe-paper streamers. People in small groups stood about chattering. On the far wall, between the picture windows with beige curtains drawn across them for evening, hung "Happy Birthday George," in big red letters. Ten white-clothed tables set for six were arranged in a circle, each with a bottle of wine in the center. Across the room he spied, wearing a green and white striped party hat, the birthday man in a wheelchair. The place was brightly lit by overhead fluorescent beams; light bounced off spectacles on the faces that turned to examine Max.

He had never faced his fellow residents *en masse*. The tableau, in the harsh fluorescence, made his heart hurt. Voices from all sides called out greetings to Lettie—it seemed he had latched on to the most popular girl in the dorm. With so many friends, why did she need him? Pity? Aloof from her, he let himself be propelled among the tables and introduced. "My good friend, Max Fried." He shook a dozen aged hands. "Happy birthday. Congratulations." He clapped George Rakofsky carefully on the shoulder. Surely he could not say "Many more"?

The soup was brought in. At the next table a man's head, wobbling, bent to meet the bowl a woman raised to his lips. Parkinson's. Max averted his glance. The last time he ever saw his father, a touch of it. A man opposite said, "I'll be sixty-seven next April, and I've never felt better in my life."

"It's since you retired, Joe. For thirty-five years, I told him, take it easy, slow down, but who listens to a wife? Up every day at six and in the store by seven—that's no way to live!"

Later they all gathered around to watch George cut the cakes, one huge and tiered like a wedding cake, frosted with pink roses, and one small and less ornate, baked by Lettie with ingredients, she explained to Max, safe for George and the other diabetics.

They were his own people, but he wished he could disown them. All right, so morally he was some kind of monster, warped by a lifetime defying the laws of nature. Still, his own undeniably: they had shared the century, together undergone the Depression, two world wars and lesser skirmishes (which of them had lost their children or husbands?). Together watched hemlines go up and down, prices go up, and Presidents go from bad to worse; watched foreign enemies become friends and friends become enemies, immigrants assimilate and new immigrants arrive; watched their own bodies go from weak to strong to the final weakness. The ones with walkers and in wheelchairs had known freedom of movement, like himself. Their bodies concealed a history of moments of elation, passed. They could speak of all these passages in a language shared by those who shared a lifespan.

Still, if he had the chance he would defect without a qualm from the common history. Were a stranger miraculously to appear at the door, scan the group, and point to him—"You! You over there! There's been a mistake. Come away."—he would go without a backward glance. Rejuvenated, he would return to the hardy. To her. Yet gazing around, he could see he was no different; no one would single him out.

And Susie, of course, nevermore.

Vicky Cameron came in during dessert to announce a Social Hour, after which Max would provide entertainment.

"A Social Hour!" he moaned under his breath.

"Shut up and socialize," Lettie whispered back.

He had a second cup of coffee and wandered. In a corner, alone and motionless, sat two women. The larger one, solid and smooth-skinned, held the hand of the other, who was spare as a bone and shrinking into her chair. The yellow-green hollows of her eye sockets shone as if oiled. Her hair was sparse white tufts; her eyes, set deep in a pallid face, stared darkly, neither curious nor critical, but profoundly indifferent, as if from beyond the grave. He was about to walk over, to give them—yes, with condescension, he admitted it—the facile gift of his charm as he gave it to the children. When he recognized the look in those eyes, both charm and condescension failed him. He found Lettie in a cluster of men and pulled her aside.

"That woman over there in the corner—don't turn so much—in the dark-blue dress. What's with her?"

"Oh, Mrs. Jordan." Lettie lowered her eyelids. "She has leukemia."

"I knew it. I knew it."

"What are you, a doctor all of a sudden?"

"I just knew."

She watched him for a moment, then touched his arm. "Oh, I see," she said softly.

"Okay, you can go back to your admirers." He walked off.

Except for the momentary distraction of a police siren, the act went flawlessly. He made coins and balls multiply and disappear. He turned a big paper flower into a parasol and turned the parasol into a top hat, which he presented to George with a deep bow. Behind a handkerchief he transformed a crumbled piece of birthday cake into a perfect slice. As a finale, he played "Happy Birthday" with a spoon on an octave of glasses variously filled with water, then made the glasses vanish behind a scarf. His audience clapped and cheered.

"You're the hit of the evening, Mr. Fried. What a marvelous talent." A woman in velvet décolletage and an ash-blond wig bore down on him.

Max took a step back.

She advanced. "But you can't really trust a magician, can you? Who knows what kind of tricks he might play?"

"With someone like you, my dear lady, a lot of tricks." He leered

59

just a bit too overtly down the bosom of her dress and she retreated.

The guest of honor came over to thank him personally. "Drop in to visit me sometime. I'm right below you." George had had a toy store, he told Max. He was familiar with games and tricks.

"What happened to the business?" Max asked.

"It's still there, in Suffern. My sons are running it. Hey, maybe you could give them some ideas."

He could be a business consultant. The nation was in a frenzy over unemployment, but for him opportunities were rampant. Soon he would need an appointments secretary, like the President.

He remained till the party broke up. At their adjacent doors, Lettie said, "How about coming in, Max, for a cup of coffee?"

He looked at his watch. "I don't think so, Lettie. I've had about all the coffee I can take. Thanks anyway."

"Well,' she sighed,' "the show was fun."

"Good."

She came over to his door. "Max, it's no use being depressed. You have to make the best of it."

"Who's depressed?" He forced a show of spirit. "There was a good-looking woman down there running after me. Are you jealous?"

"Ha!" She threw her head back haughtily. "Me, jealous! What on earth for? Anyway, that one gives every new man the eye. It's no special honor."

"Do you ever think about getting married? You seem younger than a lot of these people."

Lettie hesitated. "Do you mean in a general sense or a particular?"

"General, general!"

"Of course not! Lower my Social Security and cook three meals a day for some old bastard? Never."

"You're faking."

She went back to her own door. "Good night," she said coldly.

He was limp with remorse. "I'm sorry, Lettie. That's how I get."

"Forget it."

He started towards her. "I want to kiss you good night, for once."

"I don't need any favors, Max. And keep your voice down when you make that kind of proposition. The walls have ears."

"You're refusing me?"

"Go take one of your hot baths instead."

"You have to admit I'm the cleanest dirty old man around."

She shut the door firmly in his face.

60

When the phone rang as he was setting down his bag of tricks, he was hardly surprised.

"Max, I've been meaning to ask you—what made you set out on a life of adventure?"

"Alison, do you know what time it is? I'm an old man. I've been out partying all night. I need my sleep."

"I'm sorry." Her voice sank, deflated. "What party?"

"A birthday party for an octogenarian. Oh, it's all right, I was up. But why always so late? What about all the other hours in the day?"

"I can't fall asleep. I'm sitting here in the kitchen, and there's no one else I feel like talking to."

"What about your parents?"

"They're impossible. All they care about is being normal, like everyone else. You can imagine what a disappointment I am. Anyway, they're in bed. My mother is supposed to get a lot of rest. I told you she's pregnant."

"Yes. I remember. When is she expecting it?"

"Oh, who the hell cares. June. Max, I am really in a fucked-up mood. Can I come over and talk to you? You don't have such a provincial attitude towards life."

"At this hour? Don't be silly. There's not a soul out on the street. Why don't you talk to the guidance counselor at school?"

"Are you kidding? You've seen her."

She was right. A formidable, heavily powdered woman, Miss Wharton had once stopped him at the door to the men's room, loudly demanding his credentials.

"Find someone better, then, Alison. I have my own problems."

"Really? Tell me about them. I can be very sympathetic."

"I'll see you in school Monday."

"Do you want to have lunch together? I'll bring you a sandwich. We can take a walk if it's not too cold. Okay?"

"Okay."

"What kind of sandwich would you like? I'll make you anything except meat."

"Anything at all. Please, let's hang up now."

She took to dropping in, late afternoons.

"Hi, Max," she announced. "I wasn't sure you'd be in—you're so busy lately." Striding into his living room, she yanked the knapsack and jacket off her shoulders and dug out her oranges. "Watch this." She juggled all three in pure low arcs and an easy, steady rhythm.

61

Then she caught them expertly, with a flourish. "Isn't that good? I've been practicing a lot."

"That's remarkable! You're a hard worker, I can see. Next thing is to get them up a little bit higher, and then you can start going behind your back. Is that what you came to show me?"

"Well, partly. It's also a social visit. Can I take a glass of milk?" She was already in the kitchen.

"Help yourself. There are some brownies that Lettie baked, on the counter."

"I found them, thanks," she called. "How is Lettie?"

"Fine, as of yesterday."

Alison returned, carrying the milk and brownies. "She's a very close friend, isn't she?"

"Right now, the closest I've got."

Her eyes were downcast. "So you're not lonely?"

"I didn't say that."

"I understand about feeling lonely. I find people my own age very limited."

"Is that a fact?"

"Yes. There are things a person really can't talk about to a thirteen-year-old. I mean, they don't have the experience." She settled in his armchair. Max poured himself some Scotch and took the couch.

"Like the future, for instance. They don't have any concept of it; they just drift along from day to day. I have to get my plans organized. I don't like to feel . . . aimless. Remember you said, about leaping in the air, that you have to feel in control—you can't let surprises control you, like when the board pops up? I want to control where I'm going."

"But you're confusing things. I was talking about a feat of skill, a— a performance. A performance is a planned thing. No one can control the future, or what happens to them. The best you can hope to do is control your own balance. And sometimes even then, a surprise will knock you over."

"Not if you're prepared for it. What I mean is—a couple of years ago I used to stop at Bamberger's every day after school to ride the escalators—I mean in the wrong direction, up the down and down the up. The guards get to you pretty fast, but still, you can have a few good rides. I figured out how to do it. You have to race against the pull of it. First it seems like you'll never get there—you keep going and going. But you have to go a lot faster than the stairs go, or else you just stay in the same place. And then suddenly the floor is coming up to meet you, and the only way to reach it is a sort of flying leap. It was scary at first, because as you get ready to leap you're being pulled back the opposite way. But then you get used to it, and it's fantastic. Do you see what I mean? If you figure out a technique, no matter what . . ."

Max smiled. "It might be fun for an escalator, but it's a hard way to live. Do you really want to race against the pull all the time?"

"I don't know. I want to be able to do things. Someone like you—you know exactly what you're doing all the time. You can even make people do things they could never do before. Like Nick. You picked him at the beginning because he was the most frightened."

"I've told you before that I don't make people do anything. It's a common teaching method. Socratic, since you're so smart. I used to train the new kids when I was on the road. They had the ability but they didn't always know where to look for it. How to bring it forth. It's simply helping people find things in themselves that they didn't know were there. Drawing it out is very different from putting it in."

She pondered for a moment. "Not really so different, if you think about it. Because if you can't feel something it might as well not be there. So then it's like the person who found it almost made it. Right?"

"Wrong." He laughed and finished his drink. "But interesting."

"Well, anyway, Max, can't you tell me how you got to have—I don't know, it's like an aura. It's just there—nobody has to draw it out. You know things."

"An aura? There's no such thing. An aura is in the eye of the beholder. As far as knowing things, I'm as much in the dark as everyone else, believe me." He got up and paced the room. "Only older. Older."

"But at least you had the kind of life you wanted. Did you run away from home?"

"In a manner of speaking."

"Did they send the police out looking for you?"

"No, I left a note explaining. And I was past seventeen. People went out on their own much earlier then—they had to earn a living."

"How did you know where to go?"

He sat down opposite her. The recollection made him smile. "I didn't. But I used to read a lot. And in my books all the adventure was west, so I took a train west."

"That's funny—in my book, too, she goes west. She hitchhikes, mostly."

"I had a little money. I went up to Penn Station about six or seven in the evening and sat in the waiting room trying to look casual, as though I did this every day and knew exactly where I was going. Chicago, Des Moines, Denver—the names sounded so exotic over the loudspeaker. It seems comical now. I sat there a long time. I remember I bought a candy bar and ate it very slowly while I read a newspaper. With a newspaper, I thought, I wouldn't seem shiftless. It wasn't long after the war—everyone still read the papers religiously."

"Was that the First World War?"

"Of course. What did you think, the Civil?"

"I wonder if I would have that kind of nerve."

"You don't need it. Your parents will send you to college and you can choose whatever field you like. Things are altogether different now. Here."

"But I don't want that," she cried. "I loathe school! I want to be out in the world. I want to get on a train like you or like Alice, and ride and ride for a long time, and then get off in some strange place, and know that I'll manage to get along somehow, no matter what."

"Who's Alice?"

"The girl in my book. She's—she's a person who does what she feels like. Do you have any children, Max?"

"No."

"But you were married?"

"Yes."

"I thought you might have had children. What was your wife like?"

He shook his head warningly at her. "Don't you have any friends you sit around and talk to?"

"Oh, a few. No one special. Is she dead a long time?"

Astonished, he stared: bony, hungry shoulders, sharp chin, green eyes digging in him. "I don't discuss it."

"Oh, well. Do you have any circus pictures?"

"As a matter of fact, I do. I have quite a few." Maybe they would appease her. He never bothered with them—two-dimensional things, no feel or texture. He had dragged the albums from place to place, unable to toss them out, because they were precious to her. "Su—my wife took them; it was a hobby of hers. I'll show you. You'll see it's not so glamorous as you think."

He fetched the two large albums from a shelf in the bedroom closet. They were heavier than they used to be; his muscles slumped with the weight. "I haven't looked at these in I don't know how long."

"Oh, this is great! I love old pictures." She swallowed the last bit of brownie and came to sit close to him on the couch, pulling the album over so it rested on both pairs of knees. She had a funny child smell—chocolate, sweat, pencils, rubber-soled sneakers. "Who's this? He looks like some kind of animal."

It was Henry Cook, standing on parched shaggy grass in front of the tent in an absurd muscle-man pose, arms held out L-shaped and biceps bulging. Somebody—Brandon or Susie, he couldn't remember which—had stuck a clown's small dumpy hat on his head. Off to the left, a banner suspended between two poles rippled in a forgotten wind. It was Henry Cook all right, but also nothing, a weightless image no one looked at, a moment no one alive could locate. Without this evidence, that moment, that wind, might never have existed.

"Henry. He was the man on the bottom, who supported everyone on his shoulders."

"I thought you did that."

"Oh, no, you need those shoulders and legs. Look at the size of the fellow."

"Where is he now?"

Max shrugged.

"What's this?"

He peered. It was in color, faded and indistinct. "Oh, yes, I remember that now. We were having a party, New Year's or something. See the balloons? We took it with a flash—that's why it's so blurry. You see this fellow over here on the side? John Todd. He was a wonderful clown. This was his trailer. I can't make out the others too well, there're so many crowded in."

"Is that a monkey he's holding?"

"Yes, she was his pet. He called her Joanna. I never cared for her myself. She used to sit up on a kitchen cabinet sometimes, while we ate breakfast."

"Which one is you? And where's your wife?"

"She's taking the picture. Let's see if I can find me." He bent nearer to search. His finger wavered, then rested on the dim image of a young man with a broad chest, thick dark hair, and a wide grinning mouth. A patter of light hollow thumps ran through his chest. So his youth was extant, preserved in plastic coating. How forgetful—he had been lugging that image around in a suitcase for years, a jittery monkey on his back.

"That's really amazing! You don't look that different, Max. You had more hair, though. Why do you have your arms up in that weird way?"

"A few of us worked up this little number, sort of a parody of the girls doing ballet on the ropes. Just for laughs, in private."

"You must have had a lot of fun."

"Fun! Half the time we were exhausted—getting up so early and rehearsing. Two shows a day sometimes, and then we had to pack it all up and move on. You get to hate the sight of a road. Eight, nine months of the year, traveling. Plus the smells, the animals, always shitting all over the place. Oh, pardon me."

"Do you have any pictures of the acts—you know, during the show?"

"No, this is all personal stuff. We were small, no fancy programs or publicity shots. Mud show, it was called. But in the back here, I think there may be an old poster. Ah, yes." As he opened it the paper, yellowed and blotched, crackled. The words "Brandon Brothers" in red honky-tonk lettering made an arc in the center; above and below were pictures of bespangled women and haughty men in silver, elephants and dancing bears decked out in costume. The border was a chain of flaming hoops. "The usual thing," he said.

Alison studied it and turned back to the photos. "I'd rather see some of your wife. What was her name?"

"Here's our trailer. We never really had a chance to fix it up the way they do nowadays. We were always on the move."

"My father sells trailers. Mobile homes, they're called now. Out west people buy them because they can't afford houses any more—the market is so high."

Max turned a page and got a thud behind his collarbone. Blots before his eyes. Susie stared straight up at him—thirty-five years vanished and he was there, pointing the lens down at her on the blue shag rug. She sat leaning against an armchair wearing lush velvet slacks, knees drawn up to her chin and arms hugging them, curly head slightly tilted. Her lips were parted—just before he snapped she ran her tongue over them to make them shiny. Her eyes were huge and deliberately seductive—as if he needed to be seduced. Susie playing provocative. After he took the picture he sat down on the rug with her and they played a game, touching fingertips only, till they couldn't stand it any more. Then her eyes gave up the teasing glance, darkened and shone. In the picture now they looked pained, asking why he

66

hadn't rescued her. Up in the air, he had never once let her fall.

"Oh, Lord," he whispered. She wore a black turtleneck sweater; her face was pale next to it. It was December. She had always hated the cold; they both did. At night she sneaked her icy feet between his to warm them, and he would jump and groan, "Jesus, Susie, have a little consideration."

"Oh, that must be her," said Alison. "She's really pretty. What was her name again?"

His skin felt like a net drawn tight. Blood beat down every pathway, while outside him, as the pages turned, Susie was everywhere, framed by those silly black tabs she used to paste the photos in. She did that soon after they left the circus and opened the bike shop. For a week she sat each evening at the kitchen table with her jar of glue and her shoebox full of photos, patiently organizing and pasting. Her hair was long then, fluffy and restless on her shoulders; her hands strong and bare—she didn't like rings. She wore big horn-rimmed glasses and one of his plaid flannel shirts over dungarees, and as she worked she sipped from a mug of tea. She was fifty, overwhelmingly sexy at the kitchen table under the strong overhead light. Max laughed at her industriousness.

"Why are you spending so much time on that, Susie?"

"I like to."

"It's not as if we were going to pass it on to our grandchildren."

She gave him a severe look through the glasses. "What is that supposed to mean, Max? Isn't it enough that it's for us?"

"Yes, yes. I feel neglected, that's all."

"Act your age. I'll be finished in a little while."

"I have this terrific idea, Susie."

"Well, you just hang on to it."

"You're so strict. Come on, put it away and come to bed. I'm more fun. I'm flesh and blood."

"I'm aware of that," she sighed. "That's why it's strange you don't seem to tire out like other people." She removed her glasses and took a last gulp of tea before she stood up and came towards him. When he touched her she started to laugh, and said, "You twisted my arm."

"You didn't even answer me," said Alison. "What are you thinking?"

He had forgotten she was there. "Don't ask that! It's a rude question."

"All right! You don't have to snap like that." She tossed her head carelessly. "I know anyway. You're thinking about her. I bet you think about her a lot."

He moved away from her. His back was stiff from leaning over the album, and stiff words were on his tongue. He held them back: it would be cruel to hurt a child, nothing yet but a mass of possibilities. In anger, he doubted if the possibilities in this one would ever radiate out to reality. She was certainly going about it in the wrong direction: involuted and curled in on herself, smothering the craving flame. He knew all about latent powers, about urging what was inside to beam out and glitter. What she needed was someone to recognize her; unrecognized she didn't trust her own reality. Recognize and take her on. But it was too taxing. He was in retirement. He sat silent.

"You can tell me about her," she said earnestly. "I can keep a secret, I swear. Tell me how you met."

He would throw her a scrap to make her stop clawing. "I had a job there, cleaning up, setting up the acts, and so on. She was the girl who swung on the trapeze, with some big fellow called J. B. Jones. He was a bum."

It wasn't Susie he had wanted at first. He wanted the flying. Brandon said if he could get someone to teach him in his spare time, it was okay with him. Max picked Susie simply because she was the best; her moves appeared effortless. Fluid. "You don't have the right body," she said when he asked. "Never mind about the body. Just teach me." She was surprised by his progress. She gave him all her free time and worked him without mercy, but it didn't even occur to him. He was a sweeper of dung and she was a star, to the manner born. Her parents had been circus people all their lives, till they were killed in an auto accident. Brandon, an old family friend, had always looked out for her: the orphaned princess. Then one night Max had to go on because J. B. Jones, the bum, was sick, and the next man in line had a torn ligament. They cut the act to a minimum, trusting him with a few simple routines. When they were done she kissed him on the cheek. "Max, you were terrific! You caught me!" He could still hear the delight in her voice, the guardedness in his. "Of course I caught you. What did you expect?" "I wasn't absolutely sure." "And you went on anyway?" She smiled, a clever, wry smile. "Someone had to take a chance on you." Still he didn't see what she was getting at, until she took hold of his hand and squeezed it. "Hey, Max," she said in a funny, questioning voice, and flashed the clever smile again. Then he understood. With that look she had him.

"I'll tell you: she coached me," he said to Alison. "I don't remember all the details, but to make a long story short, she coached me, and somehow we got together."

"Did she like you right away? I mean, did she tell you?"

"Well, naturally she let me know, one way and another."

"I would never have the nerve to tell someone I liked them. Someone my age, I mean. Unless maybe they told me first."

"It's not a question of nerve at all. It's more being ready to reach out and take what comes your way. If it's what you want."

"Are you ready to reach out and take what comes your way?"

"Me! Now?" He laughed grimly. "Certainly not. I'm ready to be finished. Anyhow, things don't come your way unless you're ready. It's kind of a paradox. A paradox is—"

"I know what a paradox is. I looked it up once. But can't you let me be your friend? I came your way."

"You are my friend," he said, slamming the album shut and drawing back from her. "You come over to see me, don't you?"

"That's not the same thing and you know it."

"I feed you, I take you to the movies, I show you pictures. What more do you want?"

"Do you think about me when I'm not here?"

"Well . . ." Max said.

"You certainly don't think about me like . . . you know . . ." She dropped her head and put the tips of two smudged fingers between her teeth.

He rose. The unpleasant tightness was still in his back. His left eyelid began to twitch. "Let me try to . . . enlighten you," he said carefully. "Whatever it is you seek in me is not available, for the simple reason that it does not exist. It may never have existed—I don't know myself any more. But"—and he shook his finger at her—"you are operating under a delusion. You have placed your eggs in the wrong basket."

She stood up too, her body loose and dangling like a garment on a wire hanger. "See!" She stamped her foot. "Now you're talking that way again! You throw words at people like they throw knives at girls in a—in a side show. You're a real case, Max."

"I can't recall soliciting your opinion of me. No wonder you have trouble finding friends."

"*I* have trouble!" she shouted. "*You* can't be friends with anyone because you're still back with— I bet you think about her all the time, don't you? Only you're not dead yet. You know what Joan of Arc said? That living is not simply not being stone—"

"I don't give a flying fuck what Joan of Arc said!" Max roared. He grabbed the album from the couch and held it like a shield against his chest. "Go home, will you? I've never invited you here, have I? So go home to your own parents!"

"All right, I will!" She hoisted up her knapsack. A clump of chewed pencils fell out and rolled along the carpet.

"Oh, shit!" cried Max. "You're a messy kid." He spun around and fled into the bathroom, slamming the door shut. What madness had he sunk to, howling back and forth with a child?

For maybe ten minutes he sat on the closed lid of the toilet, waiting for a slice across his chest. Now, with his secrets all bared by her, his life fingered like a raw wound—now would be a good time to go. Strike, heart. He was ready and willing. But nothing. Never suited your convenience. This child was gratuitous. This extra time, borrowed time, also gratuitous. He had never requested any loan. Thank you very much, but no, thanks. Then a timid knock on the bathroom door.

"Max? Are you okay?"

Not gone yet!

"Max? I'm sorry. I was leaving, but you've been in there so long. Max?"

Good. Let her think he dropped dead.

The familiar dull bang of her knapsack hitting the carpet. She was knocking louder, pounding. "Max? Max! Say something! Should I call Lettie?"

That roused him. He opened the door and raised his arm, ready with the fierceness he had used on roughnecks trying to crash the gate. But her face, bleached by terror, stopped him. The arm lost its impulse; he breathed in and patted her shoulder awkwardly. "Alison, you're a little girl. You see what I am. Go find some other girls who are precocious like you—there must be a few around. Go play, or write books, or do whatever smart girls do."

"Are you sick again, like in the store?"

"No."

"All right, I'm going. I'm sorry. I only wanted to talk to you."

The sharpness of her face had vanished, and her eyes had softened from their lucid green to a murky hazel. She was someone else, someone younger come out of hiding and wholly unarmed in the face

70

of all the world's dangers. Somebody ought to rescue this fragile one from the crude character who guarded her like a dragon. It was tempting. But not him.

"Why don't you take an apple, a cookie, or something before you go?"

"Thanks. But you know, an apple is no substitute for anything." Recovered and swaggering again, she got an apple from his refrigerator and dug her teeth in loudly. "Okay, Max. See you in school tomorrow?"

"Right."

At the door, not done yet, not looking at his face: "Can I come back sometime?" Desperate, behind eyes once more cool and green.

"Yes."

CHAPTER 6

Highet's on Broad Street was newly decorated to look old-fashioned, with polished wood floors and heavy oak tables on carved legs. Behind the deep counter up front, rows of tall gleaming glasses were reflected in overhead mirrors, and on the walls hung old posters of ladies in flowered hats and long dresses. The lettering on the cardboard placards describing their ice cream offerings was done in elaborate curlicues. Alison pulled the newspaper clipping from her pocket and spread it out between them on the table. It was their usual corner table, near the window.

"The circus is coming to New York in May. That's only about six weeks away," she told Lettie. "Look, it says 'Order Tickets Now.' I want to take you and Max."

"Take us to the circus? What a sweet idea! But it's much too expensive. Let us take you. I'll speak to Max about it."

"No, my mind is made up. You can still speak to him, though. To convince him to go."

Lettie smiled. "If your mind is made up, I'm sure you can convince him yourself, next time you're there."

"Well, I don't like to be too pesty. One time he got mad and locked himself in the bathroom."

"Oh, but that was weeks ago. You've seen him lots of times since. He just has his moods." She paused a moment. "But all right, I'll ask him, if you like. Here comes our ice cream."

"Enjoy it, ladies." It was their favorite waitress, the friendly one with a long orange braid down her back and a face full of freckles. Lettie dug her spoon into the peach sundae.

"What I would really like him to do," Alison said, "is explain everything to me. All the tricks of the trade. How all the acts work, and how you go about getting a job, and everything."

"Aren't you a little young to be thinking of a job?"

"Not really. Not if I were living, oh, forty or fifty years ago. How old were you when you started to work?"

"Fifteen. But times were different then. I needed the money to live. When my father died I had five younger brothers and sisters. If I had had a choice I would have stayed in school."

"What did you do?"

Lettie laid down the spoon and looked off into the distance. In her flowered dress with the ruffled collar she resembled the posters on the walls. Her eyes were amused. "I was a—a dancer in a nightclub. You know, like a few years ago they had go-go dancers?"

Alison stared. "A go-go girl?" They burst out laughing together. "That's so neat! I've never known anyone who did that. All my mother ever did was work as a receptionist in an advertising agency. Then after she got married and moved up here, that was it." She stirred her soda, crushing the ice cream. "Unfortunately I'm not the go-go girl type. But I could do other things. Did you know that most serious artists began their careers at a very young age? That girl we saw in *The Exorcist,* Linda Blair? She was only fifteen. Also the girl in *Bugsy Malone*—remember you said that type was called a vamp? Fourteen."

"Oh, yes. She was a cute little girl. I was kind of like that."

"I bet." She laughed. "Max thinks I ought to finish school first. Even go to college. He's so particular, he won't even let me come over during school hours. Isn't that odd, for someone who led such an unconventional life?"

"He's probably right," said Lettie. "I really shouldn't be doing this with you. The movies and all. Don't mention it to him, for heaven's sake. I hate to lie, but you know he'd get angry, and it's not good for his heart."

"I wouldn't dream of telling him," she replied. "I have a private life too, after all." She leaned towards Lettie. "Personally, I don't think he gives a damn about his heart. In school he makes a big thing about how strong he is. We're doing complicated stuff now, and he practically encourages us to fall on top of him, just to show off."

"Oh, God," Lettie groaned. "He wants to be finished off, that's the truth." She pushed the dish of ice cream away.

"I'm sorry. I shouldn't have said that."

Lettie waved her hand. "I know it anyway. If it bothers me it's my own fault. Nobody told me to get involved."

"You reach out and take what comes your way, right?"

She threw her head back and laughed, and then patted Alison's hand. "You certainly do have a way of expressing yourself . . . . How would you like to see *The Towering Inferno* over at the shopping center? I missed it the first time around. I love Fred Astaire, even when he's not dancing."

"I have no money on me. I spent my whole allowance on books."

"Oh, forget the money."

"But you always pay."

"Social Security," she said, signaling the red-haired waitress for the check. "Let the government pay."

"Well, I'll definitely buy the circus tickets. Do we have time for a quick stop in Bamberger's? So I can go up the down escalator a couple of times?"

"Sure, why not? I'll see what free samples of perfume they're giving away. But make it a quick one this time. I want to get a good seat."

"Alison, hold it. Before you disappear into your room ..." Wanda called.

She turned at the bottom of the stairs, hugging the four oranges to her stomach. "What?"

"Come over here. We want to talk to you."

Wanda and Josh sat side by side on the couch. They had just finished dinner. Wanda held a coffee mug on her knees, and with her other hand patted her blond curls over and over. Josh was lighting a cigarette, with his hands cupped around the match. They exchanged one of their coded messages, eyes darting, eyebrows quickly raised and lowered, saying something secret and wordless about her. Josh blew out a stream of smoke, shook the match, and coughed. Wanda said, "The guidance counselor, Miss Wharton, called me today to come to school. She told me you've been cutting classes."

She became hollow inside and her face flushed. "You mean you went and talked to that Warts about me again?"

"I had to, Alison. She asked me to come in for a conference. I am your mother, after all."

She could just hear them, discussing her, the problem child. I've told you before, Mrs. Markman, her emotional age lags behind her intellectual age. Is that so? Well, hot shit to you too, Miss Warts. Her attitude is so critical that she has trouble accepting authority. Not that she's disruptive; I would say, rather, passively uncooperative. All those things were inscribed on cards every year—she had read them. Wanda must be tired of hearing them. Well, Wanda would not have to hear them much longer. Very soon she would be gone, and they would have nothing to discuss. And when she came back she would be somebody; they would have to treat her with a little respect.

"Alison," said Josh, "what do you have to say about it? We want to give you a chance."

She said nothing. She had thought it would be fairly safe to leave at lunchtime, because the homeroom teacher took attendance in the mornings. But nothing was safe—they found you out.

"Where do you go? What do you do?" Wanda's voice rose, thin and fast like a record switched up to the wrong speed.

She couldn't tell them about going to Max's at lunchtime and talking to him—and to Lettie, if she was there—of the things she might do in her life: live on an Indian reservation out west, lead archaeological digs in Africa, win the Nobel Prize for her book about famous vegetarians. And how they listened seriously, or if they laughed it was a good kind of laughter, not the mocking kind of the girls in school. Or that Max made her leave in time for her afternoon classes because, he said, he wouldn't abet truancy. The first two times she had walked around shivering with cold, and then she thought of Lettie. Lettie understood that school was no place to be cooped up during one's youth. She couldn't tell them about the walks and the sodas in Highet's and the movies, either, and how Lettie was never shocked at anything she said, but paid attention, as if she were grown up.

"Well, what are you dreaming about? And for Chrissake will you stop fiddling with those damn oranges? We're waiting for an answer."

She put the oranges on the floor. "I go to the library. I can learn more there than in those dumb classes."

Baffled, they sought help in each other's eyes. Josh stubbed out his cigarette and lit another. "Doesn't the librarian ask why you're not in school?"

"They don't care. I tell them I have a special research project. I do, actually. I'm doing a report on—oh, what's the word?—geriatrics."

"Geriatrics!" He leaned forward, one side of his face screwed up.

"Old people, you know. It's a big social problem. They don't feel useful."

"Whatever the hell you're studying," said Wanda, "you'd better study it in the school building. That's where you belong and that's where you'll stay from now on."

It was a strange thing, but as she watched, Wanda's belly seemed to be slowly expanding. She was sitting back awkwardly with her legs apart—it must be too hard to cross them. The belly was just about the size of a basketball; she knew the feel of that size sphere between her

75

palms. She could feel her hands squeezing it. Beneath the red-checked maternity blouse a crescent of white underpants showed through the hole cut out of Wanda's slacks. Three more months. Only yesterday she had caught a glimpse of Wanda in the shower. It was gross. "Do you want to feel it kicking?" Wanda had called out from behind the curtain. "No, thanks!" Now it looked as if it would fill the room and smother everything in it, and finally explode—a shatter of blood and unfinished flesh.

"Take it easy, Wanda. Alison, tell us what's troubling you. There must be something behind this."

"What could be troubling me? I have a perfect life."

"Frankly, I don't see what's so terrible about your life," said Wanda. "Lots of kids would be grateful for your life."

"We want to help you, Alison. I hope you're not—uh—getting into any bad habits?"

"I don't smoke pot, no. I don't like artificial stimulants."

"Is it the baby?"

"Oh, no. I'm thrilled about the baby. Haven't you noticed?"

"She'll get used to the baby," Wanda said. "It's not that. What she needs is to be with other kids more. She's always alone. They call her, but she tells them she's busy. Busy with what, I'd like to know. Franny Grant would love to be friends with her again. They used to be like this"—Wanda held up two crossed fingers—"and then she dropped her for no reason."

"Franny is an idiot," she burst out. "She just had her ears pierced, that's the latest. She doesn't need me anyhow. She has boyfriends now. Real nerds, I can tell you. Elliot Forman—God, I'd rather die. They sit in the lunchroom and throw food and insult each other. I suppose you'd prefer me to be like that."

She could swear she saw Josh almost smile. "Are you having any trouble with your schoolwork?" he asked.

"Leave me alone!" she screamed, and leaped up. Her voice had the mangled sound of someone about to cry—she had to get away fast. "Nothing is wrong! I don't want to talk about it any more! If you say I have to go to school I'll go." She grabbed up the oranges and backed towards the stairs. "But just stop *talking* about it!"

She hurled herself onto the bed, clutching the pillow around her face. This was horrible—to cry like a baby. It was useless pretending no one could hurt her. They trapped her like a tiger in a net, just to humiliate her and prove that she was nothing, nobody. With all her stories, all her work to have something of her own no one could touch, in the end they proved she was nothing. They forced these miserable tears out of her, like cutting her open and spilling her blood. Her life was streaming away.

After a while she sat up, smoothing the hair off her face. She refused to be nothing. She was young and strong, and she would outlast them. She reached under the mattress.

The acrobats are enraged at first to find Alice hidden in their trunk full of old costumes. They are a husband-and-wife team named Lothar and Louise, with a baby named Heidi. But when they see how bedraggled and hungry she is, they give her hot soup and listen to her story. She tells them how much she longs to work in the circus, and they consent to let her stay with them, provided she helps with the baby. For several weeks, crossing the plains of Nevada, Alice barely stirs from the trailer. "Why, you'd think she had years of experience with babies," Louise exclaims to Lothar. "She can quiet her down and make her laugh even better than I can." She feeds cranky Heidi mashed fresh vegetables and yogurt, and Heidi spits back white lumpy stuff. One night while Lothar and Louise are out doing the show, Alice awakes from dozing to find half the trailer a blazing inferno. She grabs Heidi and wraps her in a blanket, and rushes out with the flames practically at her heels. She becomes a heroine. Lothar and Louise are so overwhelmed with admiration and gratitude that they speak to the manager, who gives her a job taking care of the animals. There is a great deal of shit to sweep up, but Alice doesn't mind; she has already decided on her next step. As soon as she can find the right opportunity, she plans to ask a certain young trapeze artist, not handsome but darkly foreign-looking and witty, to coach her in his art.

She stops him one morning on his way to rehearsal, to ask, very politely, if she might climb up to the platform with him for a better view. "Why, certainly," he says kindly, and takes her by the hand.

"Alison?" It was Wanda, knocking at the door. "Can I come in?"

"Just a second." She shoved the notebook under the mattress, and glancing in the mirror, rubbed her puffy eyes and blinked them wide open. "Okay."

Wanda entered cautiously, holding out a small tray with a glass of apple juice and three Oreo cookies. "I thought you might want something."

"Thanks."

She set it on the dresser. "You were crying." Clumsily, Wanda patted her shoulder and tried to kiss her forehead, but she moved off.

"Daddy and I are going to a movie. Would you finish the dishes, please, and not stay up too late?"

"Which one, *The Towering Inferno?*"

"No. The one at the Cameo."

"Oh. *Coming Home.*"

"How did you know?"

"I get around. Can I go along? I can't get in alone."

"It's not for you, Alison. That's why they have those ratings."

"Oh." She took an orange from the bed and tossed it against the wall. "What's not for me, the war or the sex?"

"Both," said Wanda, closing her eyes briefly. "And please stop doing that. You'll break something." She stared at the orange in Alison's hand and shook her head sadly. "You can stay up for *Alfred Hitchcock* if you want to."

"Thrill, thrill."

"You don't mind staying alone, do you?"

"No. You always ask me that. I'm not a baby." She would never tell Wanda, but as soon as they went out at night the floorboards in the hall outside her room began to creak, and then somewhere between eleven and eleven-thirty they gave one tremendous creak that sounded like a heavy foot pressing down. She didn't hear it when they were home.

"Don't forget to write down the message if anyone calls."

"All right."

Wanda sighed, and twisted the gold bracelet around her wrist. "Look, Allie, school is something you have to do. Everyone does it. Is it so hard to be like everyone else?"

"I guess so."

Wanda stood for a moment as if she were waiting for something to happen, then left. Alison broke apart each Oreo and began licking off the cream in slow strokes. The sweetness burned into her teeth. She heard the front door shut and the lock click. The car doors opened and slammed closed; the engine started up. She climbed on her bed to watch out the window as they pulled away. The taillights diminished to two points of red in the blackness. The sound of the motor faded to a faint hum, then the dots vanished around the corner and even the hum was gone. She was all alone. Soon she would go and turn on every light in the house. Already the twitching and creaking were beginning. It was only the wood, aging. She hugged her shoulders.

She might play Queen. Often when they left her alone she became a disinherited queen lost in a raging storm, who discovers the house by chance and takes refuge. She wanders through, touching the unfamiliar objects in each room, wondering what they might be and trying to imagine, from them, what the family might be like. She liked Alison's room, and sometimes she ate an orange from the bowl on her desk; but she couldn't understand what a girl with so many good books and filled-up notebooks around would want with an ugly Raggedy Ann clock, or gym shorts, or lists of spelling words. And where was the finery in her closet, as befitted a child of so well-furnished a house? There seemed to be only wrinkled T-shirts and patched jeans. The Queen couldn't get a clear image of the daughter of the house. But the Queen's favorite place to explore was the master bedroom, where she was puzzled by many things she had never encountered in her own land: nail clippers, boot trees, Princess phone, hair blower, electric razor. These people collected mysterious artifacts, she murmured to herself. Some cold nights the Queen put on Josh's velours robe to keep warm, and once she even lit one of his cigarettes, but she didn't like it—it made her cough. Tonight she went on tiptoe to their door and gazed around. Their bed was unmade: the pillows were askew and the pink quilt in disarray, its upper corners tossed back as if the people had just arisen, although it was evening. Suddenly the Queen felt very tired. She crept into the bed and under the covers, on Wanda's side. The satin of the pillows was smooth and cool against her hot cheek. She turned lazily toward the empty side of the bed. "Darling," she whispered, and stroked the pillow. "Darling, oh darling, I'm so glad I found you at last." She stretched her arms out languidly as if to gather someone in, then leaped up, flinging the covers back.

This was crazy! This was by far the craziest thing she had ever done! Flaming with shame, she ran from their room and into her own. She had to give up these baby games! She had to get out of this house right now, too, or she would do something or think something awful. She was terrified of her own mind—the thoughts it could send. If only a person could think nothing. She had tried, many times, making her mind a blank: a flat empty space, with all the thoughts you couldn't control shoved over the edge. Dark nothing. But it didn't work—it was impossible. How could some of those thoughts even be her own, if she didn't know how they got there and didn't want them?

Some place they could never find her. They would come home and she didn't know how they got there and didn't want them?

Some place they could never find her. They would come home and look in her room to make sure she was all right, and then, how they would suffer! Oh, they would be sorry then that they had tormented her.

The glass doors to his building were locked at night. She had to wait until Mrs. Cameron, peering from behind her desk, pressed the button to let her in.

"Hello there," said Alison.

Mrs. Cameron nodded, with a look of distaste. She realized she should have washed her face and combed her hair. Her orange down jacket was dirty too, and her sneakers streaked with blurry trails of color. Max liked women to look pretty; she could tell from the photos of his wife. Well, it was too late now. She raced up the stairs and knocked. From the other side of the door came Max's voice, jovial as it rarely was for her.

"I have no idea who. Joe Haber owes me ten bucks from last week's poker. Maybe he's come to pay up."

When he saw her his eyes flashed then dimmed, like a bulb flickering out. "Alison. This is a departure from your usual habits. To what do we owe—"

"Oh, please don't start that, Max. I'm sorry if I'm interrupting, but I had to come."

He stepped aside so she could enter. She flopped onto the couch.

Lettie, holding a fan of cards, was sitting at a bridge table set up in the center of the room. She had changed from her flowered dress of this afternoon. In a white round-necked jersey over a long velvet skirt, she looked awesome and beautiful. A chain of amber beads hung round her neck. "But what happened, sweetheart?" she asked.

"I had to get away from there. They're impossible. They want to control every move I make, everywhere I go."

"In that case, do they know you're here?" He was pacing about in his quick, intense way.

"Of course not. They went to see *Coming Home*. But they wouldn't take me. It has sex—I read the reviews."

"Big deal," said Lettie. "That part lasts for all of five minutes. Isn't that right, Max? I'll take you next week if you like. I don't mind seeing it again."

Max gathered up the cards on the table, shuffled, and made a waterfall. One card escaped and the rest fell from his hands, scattering. He shook his head and made a clicking sound with his tongue.

"Slipping, slipping," he muttered, and bent to pick them up.

"Can I play? What were you playing?"

"Gin rummy," Lettie said.

"What do you mean, play? What is this all about? You come here alone at night, it's almost nine o'clock, and you think you're sitting down to play cards? How are you planning to get home?"

He loomed over her, his lips pressed together in irritation. She started to cry, not sobs like before, but slow hot tears that slid down her cheeks. She didn't even try to cover them up: it wasn't bad, crying with them looking on. They were so old, finished with all the struggles and pains. They could watch from a great distance.

"I'm never going home. I don't want to. It's no home of mine."

"Oh, the poor thing." Lettie came over to sit by her, encircling her. Her arms and chest were soft as pillows. "She's so unhappy. Poor baby," she crooned.

She couldn't remember ever crying like a baby in someone's big arms. Crying showed that you hurt, and if you hurt, something was wrong with you. But this felt almost good; she sniffed against Lettie's white sleeve and burrowed into her chest.

"Don't make a fuss, Max. Let her stay awhile, till she calms down."

"I never thought I'd be running a home for wayward girls."

"She'll call her parents later on and they'll come for her. They're out now anyway—what's the harm?"

"Oh, sure. They'll think I kidnapped her for dubious purposes."

"I'm not calling, ever. I don't want them to come for me. I want to stay here."

"Holy shit!"

"All right, all right, Max. We'll play cards for a while, then we'll see." Lettie dislodged her and gave her a handkerchief. "Here, sweetheart, wipe your face. It's enough."

Max dealt the cards in silence, tossing them out with swift flicks of the wrist. Grudgingly, he gave up each reject with a nasty snap of his thumb and index finger.

"I can't get a thing," said Lettie. "This is not my lucky night."

"When is it?" he asked. "You don't keep track of what's on the pile, so how can you win?"

"I win very often, you know that. I do it by instinct."

"Instinct!" he sneered. "Instinct has nothing at all to do with it."

"You two can stop bickering. I have gin." Alison spread her hand on the table. The second time, she said, "You're letting me win."

81

"Me!" Lettie's hand flew to her heart in denial. "I didn't see one thing I could use."

"Well, I am," said Max. "If I wanted to I could win every hand. The two of you would never know what was hitting you. Anyhow, that's all for now. It's time for *The Ascent of Man.*" He switched on the TV and played with the dials until Bronowski emerged, prancing gracefully about a desert oasis, his arms cast wide, marveling at the harmony of the universe. "Now there's someone I wouldn't mind talking to."

"Except he's dead," said Alison. "They told it at the beginning. He died a couple of years ago."

"You see," he said to Lettie. "The good die young."

"You're safe, then." She stood up. "I'll make some tea. Alison, why don't you take your shoes off and lie down on the couch? What happened to those sneakers, by the way?"

"Oh, I drew this abstract design on them with Magic Markers, and then I left them out in the rain overnight so the lines could sort of merge. But it didn't come out very well. It came out a mess."

"Put them in the washer," said Lettie. "At least they'll be clean." She went to the kitchen.

Lying on the couch, hugging a pillow to her chest, Alison heard the mellow rhythms of Bronowski's voice and, dimly, saw Lettie bring in the tea. Her eyelids drooped; she never got to drink any.

And then Max was shaking her by the shoulder.

"Alison, wake up." His voice was hoarse, as if he had slept too. "It's after eleven. Your parents must be home by now. Call them and tell them to come pick you up."

She was wide awake instantly. "Oh, Max! Just let me stay here tonight and I'll go in the morning. I'll never bother you again, I promise."

"Out of the question. Come on, get up and call. They're probably frantic already."

She sat up and cocked her head. "How are you going to make me?"

"Don't you fool around with me. I'm not going to make you. I'll call myself." He went for the phone book on the window sill. "What's your last name again?"

She kept staring at him. It was like hanging on to the basketball and not letting anyone else have a chance, and feeling powerful inside.

"Will you look at her?" he said to Lettie, who was playing solitaire at the bridge table. "She's like a lynx."

"Alison, sweetheart, tell Max your last name."

She sank into the pillows of the couch, stretching out her arms along its back. She filled nearly the whole couch now; nobody could sit on it without being in her power.

"For Chrissake, Max, you've been teaching them all this time. Don't you even know their names? What kind of a teacher is that?"

"For my purposes I don't need last names. I know them by what they do." He groaned. "There's a list in an office somewhere but I never bothered to look."

"Very smart," said Lettie, and went to gaze out the dark window.

"You're the one who invited her to stay. Would you mind turning around and telling me what I'm supposed to do with her now?"

The baffled look they exchanged was very like the one she had seen on Wanda and Josh, hours earlier. "Look, if you'll just let me sleep here," she said, "I'll call up and tell them I'm alive."

"How does a child get this way?" Max queried of the ceiling.

"I'm a freak of nature."

"Go on, go ahead and call. Say anything you please. Tell them I drugged you and tied you up in a closet."

"Could you both go in the kitchen, though, please? I want to talk to them alone. Okay?"

"Maybe she could sleep with you, Lettie?" she heard Max say as they left the room.

"It's you she wants, Max."

"I called to tell you I'm at a friend's house," she said into the phone. But the words were barely out when Wanda began shrieking, and Josh took over. They were absolutely frantic, he said. They had called half a dozen kids from school and were about to call the police. Where the hell was she? he cried. What friend?

"A friend, that's all . . . . I can't tell you . . . . No, I'm fine, I'm really not kidnapped. I just don't—" Something rustled behind her. She veered around. Max, sneaking up! He lunged, but as he gripped her wrist she managed to slam down the receiver.

"That's no fair, Max! You promised!"

"I never promised anything! This is insane! I don't need any more adventures in my life. You'll be sorry, I'm warning you!"

"You sound just like my mother when you say that!" she yelled back. He could walk like an Indian. She would have to find out how that was done. Some other time.

CHAPTER 7

"Y OU TWO WILL EXCUSE ME," said Lettie. "I'm going home to bed."

He didn't like the tinge of amusement in her voice. "Are you actually abandoning me with her?"

"Max, come over here." She led him by the arm into the kitchen. "Let her go to sleep," she whispered. "She's exhausted and upset. Tomorrow's Saturday anyway. In the morning we'll reason with her and send her home. Believe me, everything will be all right."

"But what about her parents? They could probably lock me up for that."

She shrugged it off. "They've heard from her. Who knows, maybe that's as much as they deserve."

"What you are," he accused, "is irresponsible and sentimental."

"She's just one child who feels miserable, and you're acting like your life is at stake. And also, Max, please don't call me fancy names."

He grunted. "I was under the impression that my residence here was for repose, with no undue stress. I call this undue stress."

"We'll repose in the grave," said Lettie, and left.

Alison was curled up sullenly on the couch. Her face and hands were dirty. Her monotonously rhythmic sniffling was intolerable; he could never bear sniffling. He went to get a clean handkerchief. "Here. Blow your nose." Sinking into the armchair, he put his feet up and closed his eyes.

The way she sat, wrapped tight in her suffering, was just like Tania, the ballerina, who used to give way to spells of self-indulgent heartache. After a blow-up with her current man she would come to cry on Susie's shoulder. The two women talked in the tiny kitchen, Tania straddled backwards on the wooden chair, now and then flexing her ankles and pointing her toes absent-mindedly. Susie would bring out a bottle of Scotch and a bowl of ice cubes, and they could sit for hours, drinking and murmuring. The bursts of weeping were followed by heavy silences: Tania wound a lock of long dark hair around her finger till she was ready to resume her account of grief, in a throaty voice. Since he hadn't the patience to wallow in anyone's misery, he went to bed, but through the thin partition he could still hear voices, phrases. Susie wouldn't talk about him, he trusted, although with women drinking you could never tell. After a while Susie could have Tania laughing. The two of them would giggle, borderline drunk in that way women have, a fit of abandoned gaiety. If he called out to shut them up it made them giggle even more. So if he was in the mood and sure that the whining was finished, he would join them in the kitchen in his pajamas and robe, pour himself a drink, and encourage Tania, because with enough Scotch in her she could draw from a huge repertoire the most distinctive dirty jokes he had ever heard, and tell them in her thick Slavic accent. Only she never went home. They would all grow sleepy. Susie would put Tania in a soft chair and cover her with a blanket, then come to bed with Max to make love. The first few minutes, every move he made tickled her. "Oh, no, please, no!" She laughed wildly, and squirmed away. Suddenly, he never knew precisely what did it, she would stop laughing and come into his arms and softly moan. Once after a drunken session with Tania she fell asleep, impervious to all his lures. Horror-struck, Max woke her instantly. "Oh, sorry," she muttered. "Were you in the middle of something?" But it felt like making love to a corpse. When it was all over she unexpectedly came to life, demanding. "Oh, sorry," he echoed nastily. "Louse," she said. "Why did you even bother waking me, then?" And she rolled far away from him. He followed her across the bed and fell asleep with a knee between her grudging but warm thighs. Even the bad was not so bad. Even if he could have her back for one bad night, he would die peacefully.

When he opened his eyes Alison was in the same curled position, dull-eyed and defiant. She accepted the milk and the brownie he brought her in silence, avoiding his glance. While she ate he made up his bed for her. She was nearly asleep—he had to half-carry her in and deposit her on it.

"Don't you want to get undressed?"

She shook her head once and was out. He might as well, she was settled in for the night. He took off the sweaty white tube socks and dropped them to the floor. He slid off the jeans, bending her legs with care. There was almost nothing to her: tiny white underpants over a concave stomach. Her long thin legs stretched out, rough-skinned at the knees. Her shirt had an enormous red sun on it, and the words "Solar Power." She even had the beginnings of breasts. Fancy that. He had never noticed. He stopped for a moment, his hands poised, then left the shirt on her. As he tucked her in she gave a breathy sigh. Startling himself, Max bent over and kissed her lips lightly, briefly. They were soft and cool and smelled sweetly of chocolate. He lingered but half a second, then went to undress in the bathroom. He found an extra blanket, and after a last swig of Scotch from the bottle, put himself to sleep on the living room couch.

It couldn't have been for long. The phone roused him with a nightmarish jangle. His skin leaped. He jumped up to get it, seeing fireworks in the blackness. His heart was clattering like a drum. A gush of words cascaded into his ear.

"Mr. Fried, there's a man on his way up to you. I couldn't stop him, he was wild! He said he's looking for that girl. Should I come up or—"

"It's okay, Vicky, don't come up." He ran a hand over his tingling face. Alison in his bed! Already, fast heavy footsteps sounded in the hall outside. He turned on the lights and threw on his bathrobe before opening the door.

"If you've touched my kid I'll break every bone—"

When his eyes registered Max in the bathrobe, the stranger quieted and lowered his fist. So quickly that it was almost an insult. Did he look altogether played out, a mere old joke of a man?

"How do you do?" He extended his hand. "Max Fried. You are no doubt the father of Alison, my unexpected overnight guest. Please come in. I'm sorry I can't address you by name. Indeed that's the source of—"

But by that speech he had outdone himself. Undone. The wild-eyed man didn't shake his hand. Shoving him aside, he pushed into the room.

"Where the hell is she? What do you think you're doing, keeping her here?"

Max indicated the bedroom door. The man burst through it.

"Alison," he cried, his voice breaking, "are you all right, baby?"

Max got out two glasses and poured Scotch into both. He patted down his hair and secured the belt of his robe before appraising his face in the mirror above the cabinet. Benign enough? Grandfatherly, perhaps?

He could hear him in the other room: "Are you all right, are you all right?" he kept asking her. Carrying his glass, Max went to the bedroom door. Her father had uncovered her and was looking her up and down, touching her on the cheek, the shoulder, the knee. She sat up with her eyes wide and blank, simply a kid awakened in the middle of the night.

"I came here by myself," she said, "after you left. We played cards. I wanted to stay so they let me."

Good girl. Max took another swallow. Her father turned and saw him standing in the doorway. "Put on your pants," he told Alison. Max went back to the couch, from which he could hear the man trying to calm his wife on the bedroom phone. "I don't know yet, but don't worry, I'll find out," he was saying. "I wanted to let you know first. Take it easy, she's all right."

So this was one half of the impossible parents. Well, there was a certain density, he had to agree. Yet the fellow seemed decent enough. He was approaching now, unbuttoning his suede jacket with shaking hands, while behind him, Alison crossed into the bathroom.

"Sorry about pushing in here like that. I came under the wrong impression. But still, what's the idea of keeping her so long without—"

"Have some Scotch." He waved at the ready glass on the coffee table.

"Thanks, I will. Look here, Mr. Fried, it's after one in the morning! Don't you think you might at least have—"

Max explained.

"Shit!" He pounded the back of a chair with his fist. "Markman's the name. Josh Markman. I'm sorry for the trouble. She's such a difficult kid. One hell of a kid to bring up, I'll tell you. I guess I should thank you for—uh—having her."

"Hm." Max poured some more Scotch.

Alison returned, dressed but still unwashed.

"Do you realize what you did?" her father asked her. "This was a terrible thing to do. To everyone concerned."

She looked up from tying her rainbow sneakers. "I don't even want to go home. I'd rather stay here with Max and Lettie."

"Lettie?"

"Never mind that," said Max. "Look here, my dear fellow, she's all yours: remove her, and allow me to get some sleep."

"Oh, Max!" She ran over and grabbed his arm. "Why do you talk like that! You know we're friends, you told me. You know there's a—a connection . . ."

Max disengaged her. On her father's face he glimpsed shock, followed by an array of confused suspicions, sliding over the handsome, bland features like a series of shadows. It reminded him of the stages of bewilderment John Todd and the other clowns used to practice in front of the mirror, refining the delicate shifts of muscle around eyes and mouth. The liquor churned in his gut.

Markman gripped the edge of a chair clumsily, with one hand. His tone was uncertain. "I don't like this business at all. The more I look at it, the more I don't like it. She's mentioned you at home—first it was a supermarket, then you turn up in school with magic, oranges, whatnot." He began to pace in circles, his hand aimlessly thrashing the air. "That's how we located you. My wife remembered something she said tonight—about cutting classes and being interested in older people . . .. Finally we called Ted Collins, from the school, and he thought of you. He gave us your address, but he said he couldn't possibly believe you'd—" Markman gulped down the last of his whiskey and made a wide sweep with the empty glass. His voice rose. "There's something funny going on here! What are you up to— hypnotism, mind control? If I find out you've so much as touched her—"

Mind control! Max had to act. He opened his apartment door, stepped into the hallway, and bellowed: "Lettie!" Like Marlon Brando, he thought, yelling for Stella with drunken, demented passion. Invaluable woman, Lettie, fast on her feet: almost immediately she appeared, running towards him.

"What is it? What happened, Max? Are you all right?"

"Uh-huh." He grabbed her by the hand and pulled her into the living room, slamming the door behind them. In her royal-blue satin robe and her gray-blond hair mussed from sleep, she was splendid. Sexy, but a solid citizen. She would do perfectly. He spoke with forced calm, trying to send signals through her fingers. "Sorry to disturb you, darling, but there's someone here I wanted you to meet."

"Max, for God's sake—"

"It's all right!" He put his arm around her and kissed her cheek. "Let me introduce Mr. Markman, Alison's father. Mr. Markman, Lettie Blumenthal, my neighbor and—uh—paramour."

The cigarette between Markman's teeth dropped into his palm. "How do you do." The lit match burned close to his fingers; he winced and shook it out.

"Pleased to meet you." Lettie extracted herself from Max's hold.

"What's that you called me?"

"Later," he answered stiffly. He turned to Markman. "We elderly folks are trying to lead a quiet life here in our . . . twilight years, mine anyway, doing what we can to serve the community. Now, your daughter, a willful young person, if I may be so bold, has ventured past the line of acceptable behavior. So, if you will kindly . . ." He linked an arm through Lettie's.

With exquisite timing, the telephone rang again. "Yes, Vicky, dear, everything is under control. . . . You've had complaints? I'm very sorry—I guess I was a bit loud out there just now. . . . They'll be leaving shortly. And, Vicky, no more visitors tonight, please! These young people, what can we do? Good night now."

"Max!" From Alison, a shriek of betrayal.

"I'll see you in school Monday, dear. Meanwhile, get some rest and practice your tumbling."

"Sorry again," Markman said wearily. "I guess I was way off base. Come on, Alison. Disturbing these kind people. Awful." He shook his head helplessly and steered her towards the door.

"You haven't seen the last of me," Alison muttered.

Max inclined his head towards Markman. "I'm sure you'll have the courtesy to call Mr. Collins and restore my reputation."

"Oh, righto. Sure. Good night. Good night, ma'am."

Max closed the door on them and poured more Scotch.

"Here, Lettie. You look like you need it."

"Thanks. Jesus, that yell you gave could wake the dead. My heart is still pounding." She sipped her drink. "You're outrageous, you know? And the amount you've been drinking lately is bad for your heart, besides."

"I know, I know it all." He lay down on the couch with his eyes shut, balancing the glass on his chest.

"So what's that word you called me?"

"You mean paramour? Girlfriend. My mistress. My woman."

"I'm no such thing." She was indignant. "You've never laid a hand on me."

"Alas."

"Alas? You mean you wish you had?"

Max raised his eyebrows, and slowly opened his eyes. Lettie sat down on the small space of couch left next to him. The warmth sank into his thigh and seeped up and down his side.

"So do it, then. It'll do you good. If it doesn't kill you."

"You're serious?" He removed the glass from his chest.

Lettie leaned over to kiss him. She whispered, "Take a chance." She was still warm from bed, with the scent of sleep and whiskey on her. Something ancient moved inside and ached badly, a familiar ache whose return nearly brought tears to his eyes.

He swallowed hard. "I'm not used to sleeping around."

"I'll help you."

"In there." He nodded towards the bedroom. "I need room."

"Certainly." She rose, statuesque.

He was reluctant to come alive. And afraid. Not of any mechanical failure, God knows it had been stored up long enough, only afraid that the closeness might kill him, reminding him. He couldn't survive that. Afraid, too, because alive, now with her marvelous hands all over him, was so much more strenuous, pleasure so rich to the famished senses. He put his hand between her thighs and felt his fingers might flame up. His barricades were collapsing; he wanted to hide under the pillow, not to confront himself so bare and unshielded. "I'm scared," he said to the dark. She said nothing, but leaned over him, over-whelmingly present as no one had been for him in years. Her presence, a benevolent shadow in that dark, comforted him, quickened him. He moved into it. And oh, how he had lost the sense of what it was all about! No memory or fantasy was remotely like the real thing, like this real body beneath him and surrounding him. Who did not remind. Oh, no. In every way different, lavish and newly enchanting. His old grievances slid away; only the pounding heat remained, ageless.

"Oh Max, oh Max," she kept saying, heaving. When it was over she even cried. He licked her tears.

"We should have done this before, Max."

"Never mind that, we'll do it again. Sleep now, sweetheart. Stay right here."

He slept late. Waking to the warm body, he felt his heart race in astonishment, and for an instant it was Susie, the years in between a bad dream. When he saw the fair hair and plump shoulder he remembered. Not disappointed, though. Other. And for once, a night with no revivals of the past; no need, for once, to scale dim canyons up to present daylight. That alone a great gift. As he watched her back rise and fall with even breaths, she stirred and turned around.

"Hello, Max." She was smiling.

"Good morning. This is awfully strange, isn't it?"

"I don't see anything strange about it."

She could look good and even smile, first thing in the morning. He was more fortunate than he deserved. Tentative March sunlight seeping through the blinds made pale stripes on her arms. He touched.

"I've been watching you," he said.

"Is that so?" She rolled her eyes. "Well, if you've seen enough I could get up and make us some breakfast."

He put his arm around her. "Not yet. Stay awhile."

"And how do you feel now?" she asked. "Hung over?"

"No, peculiar." He touched her cheek, wanting, in a heat of embarrassment, to thank her, but he couldn't speak those words. He held her a long time.

She kissed his lips. "It was . . . what can I say, Max? Beautiful." She got out of bed. In broad daylight her size and smoothness were intimidating. Incredible that he had been there a few hours ago. And could return. The very prospect generated a mild vertigo.

He watched her enfold herself languidly in the royal-blue robe—ah, she might have been an elegant stripper—then lay back listening to the jiggling of the coffeepot. The click of cabinet doors opening and closing. He did feel peculiar. His body was spent, drained of energy. Not used to it, that was all. He reached out and touched her side of the bed, still warm. Maybe he really hadn't the strength. Maybe, just now, she had expected . . . again. Maybe already disappointed? Ah, shit! Why did he always doubt and destroy? He never used to be that way. Since Susie he had forgotten what a friend was, lost all touch. He had made her happy, for Chrissake! Grumbling at himself, he rose and dressed, to go and be in the same room with her.

Lettie was making pancakes, flipping them expertly and aligning them on the griddle in neat rows of three. Her austere concentration was seductive. Her coffee smelled strong, the way he liked it.

"I wonder how Alison is," she said. "After all, she was the one who wanted to spend the night with you."

"But not like that!" He stroked her rear.

"Max, how much do you know about little girls?" She laughed. "Not much."

"Okay I'll be nicer to her in school Monday. You think I was too tough, don't you?"

"Can she help it if she goes for older men? Here, would you take in the syrup and butter, please?"

"You ought to know."

"Well! There's a difference. And these cups too, if you don't mind."

He liked her taking possession of his kitchen and giving orders. He had always admired an enterprising woman.

After her second cup of coffee she said, "I have to go back to my place and do a few things. I didn't come prepared to stay so long. Do you think I can make it to my door without anyone seeing me? They'll call me the whore of Pleasure Knolls."

"Pleasure Knolls is right, for once. That's exactly what's needed here. They say full services provided, don't they? The staff should provide it for everyone. Oh, but Vicky. Forget it."

"Don't underestimate her. Vicky happens to be married to a very sexy-looking man."

"You don't say."

"Listen, Max, I'm going to get dressed. Should I come back, or maybe you'd rather be alone? I know you like your privacy."

He was contemplating his nearly empty coffee cup while lighting a cigar. He paused to blow out the match, and planted the cigar between his lips. Lettie stood with her hand on the doorknob, waiting. "Of course," he answered, "come back."

"Oh," she sighed, "that I should feel this way again, at my age." She peered down the hall and darted away.

He sat amid the remains of the breakfast, smoking. Only twice while he lived with Susie had he had another woman. It hadn't made him feel guilty, only strange, like a traveler in an alien place. The time she went off to John Todd's trailer for a week he was furious, and in revenge set out to seduce a new girl helping in a dog act. He disliked dogs, especially the small cute kind, and he disliked hearing them yelp as she smacked them around and gave commands in a thin, brittle voice. But she was available as hell, a jittery, hot-eyed kid, so he hung around for a couple of days; it was not hard to impress her. In bed she was angular and bounced around, with a patter of phrases he had a hunch were ready-made to be recited in that brittle, eager tone. At the crucial moment she faked it, he was sure, as if she had learned what to do from a book. It was so unlike making love with Susie that he didn't think of it as making love at all. A screw. He could forgive himself the first time, but when he went back for more it was with self-disgust. At least John was a real person; he envied Susie her good time.

And Lydia. He relit the dead cigar. After all these years, he still grinned when he thought of it. He used to believe it happened only in books, till it happened to him. Largeboned, dark, and sultry, she rode horses with a group of Bulgarians who, rumor had it, kept her happy.

He had never paid much attention. He was close to forty and had enough on his mind. His parents had recently died, one soon after the other, without having seen him in five years. He had sent his brothers money to save the delicatessen, money down the drain but he felt he owed it to them. And there were twinges in muscles that used to obey without complaint. Brandon, sick in bed, asked him one night as a personal favor to go around with a message; the boy who usually did that had influenza too. The illness was devastating the show, making each day a struggle to improvise. When he got to Lydia's he found her in bed under the covers, bright-eyed with fever.

"Oh, you too?" he said. "Sorry to bother you. There's a change for tomorrow. The run-through's at ten instead of nine. Do you think you'll be able to make it?"

She flung back the sheets and got up, stark naked. Her skin was dark, her fingernails and toenails painted forest green. He gaped like a boy. She was the most stupendous body he had ever seen. "How would you like a drink?" she offered.

He was crazy to accept, but how could a man walk out on that? Just a quick drink. He had never been given a drink by a naked woman before. It made all the difference: every common movement, from fetching the bottle and ice to raising her glass and saying, "Cheers," took on a halo of fascination. She began to ramble about things she liked to have done to her in bed—Susie was modest in speech; he had never heard a woman talk that way—and then she lay on the bed, opened her legs, put her hands beneath her breasts, and said, "Give it to me, Max. Come on and give it to me." So he gave it to her. It didn't take more than a few moments. Closing the door behind him, he blinked in the darkness outside and continued his rounds. He felt oddly renewed, as if he had had a vacation from real life.

A few days later, recovered from his own case of flu, he told Susie, thinking she would find it as droll as he did. How profoundly mistaken he was. "But can't you see, it would have been cruel to say no." For that feeble crack she hurled a full ashtray at his head. The sheer needlessness was what got her. Not like her and John Todd years ago, she pointed out, when Max told her she was a spoiled bitch and could pack her bags anytime. He practically sent her over there. And had she ever said a word about that skinny adolescent with the dogs? Okay! But what inspired him this time? Was he nothing more than an animal? she wanted to know. What was he, anyway? Was this—this creature so irresistible? She hadn't a brain, everyone knew that. Just a . . . Susie wouldn't stoop to say it. Max couldn't justify the sudden need, but there had been something, he tried to explain. Some . . . need. That bad a need? Susie shouted. There must be something wrong with her, then; she didn't know about such overpowering needs. When at last—weeks!—she was friendly again, he teased her. "Why don't you ever say, 'Give it to me, Max, please,' in a hoarse voice?" "I'm not so desperate," she replied with her best regal air. Oh, but God almighty, she was, for him. Without the words.

He sighed and reached for his cup, but the coffee was bitter on his tongue. The cigar tasted rotten too; he stubbed it out. He didn't feel like the man who had done those things. Perhaps he wasn't—the memories endured while the body's cells were sloughed away. Lettie's breakfast, like Lettie herself, had been delicious, but it lay dead on his chest like a stone. He was worn out from that business last night with Alison and her father. Foolish to have let her keep coming around— she was really none of his affair. He would go and lie down. But as he moved to rise, a pain like a knife blade ripped across his chest and out toward his shoulder. Heartburn tenfold—the strong black coffee could do that. Dr. Small had said not to. It passed, though. He tried once again to get up, but his legs wouldn't support him; he dropped back in the chair, holding his breath. Something was coming. Ah, there: another slice, up and down his arm; he winced, and then no more pain, just all the juice drained out and his vision fading. Gray clots over everything. So, there it was. What he had wanted, but now he wanted to fight it off. Only his body was useless, stiff with fear. Pills in the bedroom, oceans away, forget it. How ignoble, this dying in a hard kitchen chair in front of a knocked-over coffee cup. And unfair: he wanted to do it with her one more time. Just one more time, Lord— was that asking so much? But already he could feel life ebbing. Ah, now he knew what it was like. Quite simple, really. Cut loose and drifting. No touch. Out of reach . . . His mind scattered, bits of colored glass at the end of a tube. Blue spangles far up, if he could only reach. . . . Amid the debris, faintly, a knocking at the door. Oh if you love me hurry.

"Max! Oh, my God!" Clutched at him and let go in fright. On the phone. Hurry, sweetheart, was all the mind he had left. The white light was racing out of him, and he aching to call after it and demand it back—but as in dreams, from his mouth opened wide to scream, no sound would come.

CHAPTER 8

"HEY, ALISON! OVER HERE!" It was Franny calling above the blur of voices in the cafeteria. The air was thick with the greasy smell of hamburgers grilling. The kids on line in front of her had grayish scoops of mashed potatoes on their plates, the hollowed-out tops filled with brown gravy like little volcanoes with overflowing lava. Franny was at a table near the windows, with Hilary and Karen and the boys from Max's group. Nick, of all people, was standing up waving an arm in the air, doing some sort of routine. She put an apple and a dish of green jello on her tray and went over.

"Nick can do this great imitation of Fats Fox," Franny said, her long feather earrings swaying as she tossed her head. "Watch him, Al. Do it again, Nick. Please!"

Nick had Fats's midwestern accent exactly right: "There will be no run-een in the gym," he said, in a tone that mingled irritation and helplessness. "Do you want to go down to Mr. Barry's office?" Mr. Barry was the principal. Nick even managed to seem chubby, with his hands flat on his slouching hips. When his jaw dropped and his eyes rolled upward in dismay, he looked so absurd that she had to laugh with everyone else. "No more hog-een of that basketball, Alison," and he punched her lightly on the shoulder. Hilary and Franny collapsed in giggles.

"All right, that's enough fooling around," Hilary said. "Alison, we're having a meeting. To decide about Max."

"What about him?"

"Here. First sign this." Bobby handed her a card. "After Fats told us, I cut history to go out and get it."

"A real hero!" Franny pulled a lock of his hair, and he slapped her hand away.

On the front was a cartoon drawing of a man in bed, his legs up in traction, with crossed patches of bandage on his forehead and arms.

95

Inside it said: "Hear you're laid up, Well, don't be blue, Just hurry on back, The gang misses you."

It made her want to puke. Didn't they understand that Max's sickness was invisible? He had no bandages. They had all written their names in different-colored pens, some adding little messages and drawings. Karen had made a stick figure on a trapeze with a crutch, and Bobby's was spelled wrong: "Hope you have a speedy recoverry." The whole thing was a messy scrawl.

"Well, come on, Alison, sign. We still have to decide on the present."

In a small space between the broad flourishes of Bobby's signature and the stiff wiry lines of Elliot's, she wrote "Alison" in tiny block letters, not her real handwriting. Maybe he wouldn't notice it. She could see him looking at the card and shrugging one shoulder. "Aha," he would say with a sarcastic grunt. "It appears the gang misses me." If he lived to see it.

"How about flowers, something like that?" Bobby asked.

"He's not the flowers type."

"Oh, Alison knows all about it, as usual. Why, did you ever ask him?" Elliot sneered.

Karen said she heard somewhere that flowers use up the oxygen in a room. "He might have trouble breathing."

"Flowers are too common. We ought to get something more personal, like maybe a book." Nick was looking at her as he spoke. It was funny how ever since Max had chosen him to demonstrate all the new tricks, Nick had begun giving his opinions on every subject, looking you straight in the eye too.

"A mystery," she suggested.

"Oh, no, Alison," Hilary said. "He would think mysteries are dumb."

"Listen," Bobby said. "If everyone brings a dollar tomorrow I'll cut lunch and go to Korvettes. I'll think of something when I'm there."

"I'll go with you," Franny volunteered. "Boys don't know how to shop alone."

"I wonder," said Karen, "if he dies and they have a funeral, if we'll all get invited. I went to one once, my uncle's. It was really weird. They don't dig the hole while you're there. They have it all ready. And you leave before it's all filled up."

"Yeah. My father says a heart attack in a man his age is no joke. He tried to do too much. He thought he was hot shit."

She stood up. "Elliot, you're such a creepy idiot. And besides, your father is a dentist! He knows teeth, not hearts." Grabbing her tray and knapsack, she left them gaping and ran to the girls' room. She pressed her fists over her eyes till the tears were forced back, and then slipped out a side door and ran home. If Wanda was there she would tell her she felt sick. She did, too—the hollow space had gotten to her head.

There was a note on the kitchen counter: "Went to get my hair done. Back around four-thirty. Mom." Josh was gone too. He had left early this morning for three weeks in the Northwest. When he kissed her good-bye in the kitchen he murmured, "Now no more cutting, remember? And no funny business like the other night, either." She had to think of her mother, he had whispered. Keep an eye on her.

She shut the door of her room. Maybe she would never go back to school again. She could pretend to be very weak, and have a private tutor. She could stay in her room forever, reading and writing—you learned more that way anyhow—and after a while she would forget about how she had gotten him upset and sick, possibly killed him. The people in stories could not really be hurt, no matter what you made them go through. Alice had gone on long enough—soon she would start a new one. It could be about an invalid child, like the boy in *The Secret Garden,* except she would not make her get better in the end. She could sort of fade away, like Paul in *Dombey and Son,* who didn't have enough vital spirits. But first Alice had to be finished; she pulled her out from under the mattress.

Alice follows the dark trapeze artist up to the high platform. From there the wild swoops and swings seem even more glorious. She watches his muscles flex and tighten for the perfect timing of every change, and longs to be suspended, like him, from that bar, feeling her body stretched and taut, the rush of air past her face. To fly is her true destiny. He agrees to teach her, and she learns so fast that after only a few weeks he promises her a small part in a performance. The great day arrives. Warming up, Alice swings back and forth a few times, and each time they pass high in the air he smiles encouragement at her. In a state of trance, she listens to the music for her cue. The moment approaches: she will leap to him and he will catch her. She should be concentrating on the timing, but she is too caught up in the swiftness of flight to think clearly. She leaps a split second early. His arms reach out for her, two inches too far. In a panic, she stretches up towards him, to grasp and tug at his fingers, something she was taught never to do. Never pull, just grip firmly, he always warned. But she can't stop herself. There is no net. She hears the thudding crash of their bodies and the roar of the crowd, then loses consciousness. When she wakes up she has a broken arm, a broken leg, and dozens of bruises. But the trapeze man, they tell her, has suffered far worse injuries. No one will say exactly what. They look at her with cold anger, and leave her alone in her hospital bed. They ostracize her.

She stopped to look up the spelling of "ostracize," then sat rigid with the pen poised. It would be simple to have Alice die in bed, but somehow she could not bring herself to do that. Yet to have her recover completely and go on to a new adventure did not seem right either. There was no place to go from that point. She felt as though a sheet of rock, like the cruel cliffs of a canyon, was rising in front of her. On the wall opposite she had taped Josh's postcards of the Grand Canyon. Depth upon depth. She was lost in a Grand Canyon of empty spaces surrounded by walls of ancient rock, and it was not a thrilling place, as she had dreamed, but more lonely and terrifying than she could ever have imagined. She could not write an ending till she found out what would happen to him.

She raced over on her bike. As she hurried toward the elevator, Mrs. Cameron stopped her. "Mr. Fried isn't in."

"I know. I heard. I was going to see Mrs. Blumenthal."

"She's not in either."

"Do you know where she is? I have to get in touch with her."

"She left early and didn't say. But I imagine she's over with him in Parkvale."

She knew Parkvale. It was way on the other side of town. Once last year while Wanda visited Lou after her breast operation, she had sat downstairs in the waiting room. People were slumped over, reading magazines as if they were in a dentist's office. Huddled in a corner, an old woman wearing a fur coat sat and cried.

"Oh. Do you—" She forced herself to meet Mrs. Cameron's gaze. She had been here Friday night, and knew; she must hate her. "Do you know how Mr. Fried is doing?"

"I haven't heard since early this morning. They said his condition was stable."

"Stable?"

Mrs. Cameron took off her glasses, and for the first time, smiled at her. She was not a witch any longer but human. Her whole face was softer, with soft curving lines around her mouth. There was feeling there. She must keep the human face hidden behind the other, the sealed mask.

"Stable means he's not getting any worse. It's a good sign."

"Oh. Thank you." She turned to leave.

"Alison? It is Alison, isn't it? I can ask Mrs. Blumenthal to call you tonight. Why don't you write down your number?"

She did. "I might see her at the hospital."

"Maybe, but I doubt if they'll let you up. They have a rule about age."

"I know how to get in places. What's his room number?"

The smile faded as the glasses were replaced and the mask was sealed back on. Mrs. Cameron ruffled her fingers through her hair. "I don't think I should tell you that."

She reached Parkvale in fifteen minutes and locked the bike outside. Four stories of red brick with a wide circular driveway, the hospital sat on the crest of a sloping lawn, like Pleasure Knolls, like school. Many of the windows were barred. The woman at this desk had a sealed mask too, but she was dark-haired and younger, about Wanda's age.

"Could you tell me what room Mr. Max Fried is in, please?" A face sealed with wax. Sealing wax. The time has come, the Walrus said, to talk of many things. She and Max . . . Of shoes and ships and sealing wax, of cabbages—

"How old are you?"

"How old do you have to be?"

The woman stared and wrinkled her forehead. "Suppose you tell me how old you are first."

"He's a very close relative. I see him all the time. . . ."

The woman shook her head. There was a row of elevators only a few yards off, but a uniformed guard stood near them, watching her.

"Oh, forget it. Can you tell me how he is, at least?"

She flipped through pages in a ledger. "His condition is still stable."

Her blood gave a sudden rush, and she kicked the bottom of the counter. "Look, all I really want to find out is if he's going to live or die!"

"I'm not a fortuneteller, young lady. This is a hospital. And watch those feet."

On her way out she passed a sign that said: "No Admittance to Persons Under Sixteen." She stood beside her bike, stroking the rubber grips and running her finger over the chilly chrome of the handlebars. She used to ride over to Max's sometimes, before the winter snows—it seemed like ages ago. Once he came down to look at it and said it was a good, sturdy bike; he could fix up a bike like that to ride backwards and spin on one wheel and do all sorts of fantastic leaps. A circus bike. But when she asked if he would, he said of course not, he was only talking; it would be much too dangerous around here. She had been planning to ask again, over the summer. It might never be a circus bike now.

She found a back entrance that opened right onto a row of elevators. Pulling herself up to look taller, she pressed the button. From nowhere, another guard appeared. "Sorry, young lady, we can't let you up." He waited around till she went out again.

The closed windows all looked identical. Even if she knew which room, it wouldn't make any difference; he was probably unconscious. He had wanted to get rid of her the other night, and now he had succeeded. He had found someplace completely safe from her. Very clever, Max. In the gym he had said he would catch them. Pretend I am the net. But he didn't want to be the net any more. Slowly she unlocked the bike and coasted down the driveway. Well, who cared? She had managed all right before she knew him. She didn't need any net.

March was going out the way it came in, like a lion. The wind slashed her cheeks and whipped up her hair. Fighting it, she speeded up on the bike, zooming along the down-grade past stalled late-afternoon traffic. Near the entrance to the thruway, she shifted to a higher gear. There was no special moment when she decided, but all at once she was turning onto the entrance ramp. An instant later she was part of a massive rush forward. She stayed on the shoulder; three lanes of cars raced by on her left, several of them honking at her. Each one passed with a zoom that rose to a roar, and quickly subsided to a dull, distant hum. One after the other, zoom, roar, and hum—her mind slipped easily into their rhythm, while her eyes, dazed, fixed on the spinning of their tires, which raised faint haloes of dust in the sun. She felt her hair stretched out behind her. With the wind beating on her neck and her throat smarting, she switched again to a higher gear. She was flying on the wind.

An exit was coming up. In the corner of her left eye a dark speck appeared, and grew: something was trying to edge over into the exit lane. She ought to slow down, or else speed up and get past on his right. A queer feeling overtook her: why do either? Why not just wait and see what happened? She and that speck were traveling the lines of a V, and they would meet at its point. Still pedaling, she let her mind lapse onto a dark flat plane where all the bad thoughts got shoved off the edge. She yielded to something soft and static at the deep center of her speed. She could watch her own crash. The zoom grew to a roar; as a horn blared long and loud and the speck in her eye became a huge black blob, she snapped out of the trance and tried to get past it, make it shrink again, but the slope was uphill now. She couldn't work up the speed. She could feel it only a few yards to her left, but couldn't stop. She heard a terrible screeching noise that seemed to come from inside her hollow stomach. Standing up on the pedals, she gave a tremendous push and hit the crest of the hill with her eyes squeezed shut, because the blob filled her whole left eye, engulfing her. The screech of brakes ended just behind her, and a second later the driver's rough voice came from off on the right, shouting that she was a crazy bitch and maybe the next one would get her. His words trailed off on the wind.

Gasping, she coasted down the grade. Her heart was knocking in her chest, but the danger was past and she was the winner. She smiled. She could go on forever, no matter what dangers. She was powerful! Way past her second wind now; the pedals were working themselves. There was no future any more, no bad thoughts to think, only this traveling.

When she got home her legs were trembling so hard she could barely stand. Off the highway, all her special powers had vanished; she had never felt so exhausted in her life. She lay down on her bed to think about how she might finish off Alice, but in an instant was asleep.

Wanda's voice woke her, calling her down for supper. Not speaking a word, Wanda sat across from her and read *Cosmopolitan* as she ate. Alison pushed her food around. The pieces of last night's creamed chicken were like raw inner organs floating in a sticky pale sauce. She threw it in the garbage, but Wanda did not look up. She sat down at the table again and stared, but Wanda did not notice.

"Your hair looks nice," she said.

"Oh, do you think so? I thought they ruined it this time. In fact, I had a big fight with them over it. I'm in a rotten mood. I had to pay thirty dollars and it'll take weeks to get the shape back." She flipped through her magazine.

"It's not bad at all." She cleared her throat. "Uh—a friend of mine is very sick."

"What friend?"

"The man who teaches in the gym. Max Fried. You remember."

At this Wanda looked up. "Remember! Are you kidding! Didn't I tell you to leave those people alone, after the other night? Can't you hang around with people your own age?"

"They happen to be my friends."

Wanda sighed. "What's wrong with him?"

"He had a heart attack. The day after I was there."

"Really? I'm sorry to hear it." Wanda paused a moment with her lips parted, and ran a finger slowly down her cheek. Then, with a light smack, she laid her hand palm down on the table. "But look, Alison, what can you expect? I don't suppose he'd be living there if he was well. At that age these things can happen anytime." She bent her head over the magazine.

Alison cleaned up and did the dishes. Wanda kept reading and Lettie did not call. Upstairs she tried her number again, but there was still no answer. She dialed Max's number. It rang and rang, and after each ring was a dense emptiness, like the echoing silence when she rode her bike through an underpass. She listened with a chill, almost expecting that some strange hollow voice might say hello—a voice out of nowhere. But it never came. At the eighth ring she hung up and went back to her room.

She took three oranges from the bowl on her dresser and practiced juggling them, as she had done every night for months, but they kept falling from her hands. There was no point to it, unless she could show him. After she got undressed she tried again—this time would be for him. They did have a connection, and she would make him feel it. She could put power in him just as he put it in others. And it was magic, no matter what he said. As she tossed them, the words rang like an incantation in her head, Live, Max, live. To the rhythm of the blood pounding behind her eyes and the oranges smacking against her palms: Live, Max, live. No misses—a miss would be fatal. Over and over the three beats drummed through her body, while her eyes ached so hard she thought they would burst; at last, one at a time, she caught them to her chest. She dug her nails into their bumpy skins till she felt juice running down her fingertips. He would live. She had made him live.

She opened her window. The trees out back were swaying to and fro

102

in the dark, with the wind whistling through them like icy air in a tunnel. It blew cold against her chest. March wind doth blow, Josh used to read as she sat on his lap, and we shall have snow, and what will poor Robin do then . . .

CHAPTER 9

Hᴉs ᴇʏᴇs ᴏᴘᴇɴᴇᴅ to a flat white surface, but he couldn't tell how far away. They teared, blinked, felt hot, as if from too long a sleep. No pain, only a penetrating stiffness everywhere. He rested the eyes, and when he tried again the white was not as smooth as it had first appeared. There were small grainy bumps and streaks; yards up, a strange ceiling, and he on his back in a strange, unyielding bed. He rolled his eyes to one side and the other and found more white, a rippled surface. Curtains. He understood; he had been in this place before.

An odd drawing sensation throbbed in his left upper arm. No use trying to move it; cautiously, he turned his head to see. A tube was inserted in the inner elbow, leading up to a bottle, of which he could glimpse only the lower half, containing a thickish bile-yellow liquid. They were nourishing him. One more time they were going to piece his heart together and send him on his way. Like it or not, he was helpless to protest—his veins were accepting it.

Slowly, from far off, the awareness of who he was came back to him. The losses he had suffered drew nearer, gradually, like a distant raw landscape approaching a driver on a deserted road. Once he had possessed strength, work, a woman. He was the same man, minus the attributes that had made him that man, which seemed a riddle, but too perverse for now. Looking down, he found more white—his body, swathed in sheets. Gently he tried moving his feet, bending his knees and the elbow of his free right arm, gestures surprisingly not beyond his means.

The white ripples fluttered and parted to admit a woman, also in white. His eyes, hazy, absorbed a halo of red hair, and at once came a pain in his chest. Not the harsh slicing kind, a mere tug. It couldn't be. Weak as he was, he had to keep a grip on reason: he was not dead, this was no afterlife. Yet it was the same hair, and yes, the same narrow

104

slope of the shoulders. She came to him, leaned over and smiled professionally. The coloring was all wrong. The teeth were wrong. The eyes, speckled and sharp, were wrongest of all.

"I see you're awake, Mr. Fried. How are you feeling?"

Her voice in the hushed whiteness was like clattering metal. He squinted up at her.

"Well, let's have a look at your chart."

The chart, as before, was attached to the foot of the bed, where he couldn't see it. She picked it up and held it against her clipboard, running her pencil horizontally over the paper with a mechanical sort of grace. Her face told nothing. Moving his head in a wider arc than he had attempted so far, he spotted a familiar, curious machine to the right of the bed. It resembled a small television set, with a black screen and a bright green line of tiny connected W's streaming across it, coming from an unknown beginning and disappearing into an unknown void. The image of his heart, laid bare and public. The line seemed endless, but somewhere it had an end.

The image was false, though. Those neat, even lines showed an ignorant heart. His heart was jagged, frayed, with swoops and chasms, too unruly for that small screen. "My heart . . ." he whispered.

She looked up from the night table, where she was fussing with jars. "Yes, Mr. Fried?"

He motioned with his head towards the screen.

"Oh, yes. It's doing just fine." She sounded officiously proud, as though his heart were her clever protégé. She sounded like Vicky. All those official ladies, in their innocent pride.

"What's past this curtain?"

"Other patients. This is the intensive care unit. You'll only be here a few days, and then we send you downstairs."

"How long do they give me?"

Her busy hands on the glucose bottle stopped for an instant, as if struck by a spell, then started up again; hear no evil.

He coughed. His voice was coming out very faint. "I said, how much time do they give me? You know."

She coughed too, and whisked into brisker motion, straightening and patting the sheets on his bed. "Mr. Fried, you're receiving excellent care, and you'll be feeling better every day. Just concentrate on getting well. And try not to talk too much."

He had heard that sort of thing before. They were taught the responses in nursing school, needed them down pat to graduate.

105

Naturally they gave individual variations: when he had asked the rosy Carmela Velasquez the same question she had squeezed his hand. "Mr. Fried, I'll tell you what I tell myself in the mirror: *Que sera sera.*" To which he swore at her in Spanish. Carmela hadn't minded; she laughed, twitched her ass, and tossed a copy of *Playboy* onto his bed. But this nurse was a more proper sort, hardened by her experience like mud under an unrelenting sun. After she took his pulse she checked the bottle of glucose one last time and left, pulling the curtains closed behind her.

He slept on and off, the waking intervals so blurred he could barely tell the two states apart. Soon—maybe hours later, maybe the next day—there came loud male voices. A pair of doctors in white coats greeted him by name, and the tall one flung the sheet back avidly from his chest. Energetic and in his prime, he had a painfully booming radio announcer's voice, which pronounced on Max's case in an obscure language. The other one, a younger, diminutive version, tilted his head toward his mentor as if to catch the precious words on his upturned chin. Just so, those yelping dogs used to leap, snout first, for the bits of meat tossed down, so that later, in the spotlight, they would leap high for sticks. Max answered their questions half attentively; his own curiosity had veered elsewhere. Why those dogs? He lay trying to wrest from oblivion how this had happened to him. Alison, of course—with an inner jolt, graceless as the doctors jolting the pole of the curtains, forgetting, in their zeal over his data, to bid him goodbye. The kid in his bed. The entire scene sprang to mind, as a horse opera. That father, in some ways more childish than the child, and the two so radically unalike; he could see why she felt . . . And with the mother expecting. It needn't concern him, though. His teaching career was almost certainly over.

But there was more, something closer to the bone yet out of reach. Like clutching at fog, he teased memory until it came, in vaporous shapes, backwards: the cut in his chest, fragmenting him, half cup of black coffee overturned, fat green cigar poised tenuously on the rim of the ashtray. The hard kitchen chair. And Lettie, soft. That. That quest. Propelled into a woman, looking for something. Oh, and he'd found it all right; yes, how sweet at the time, but was it worth this? Why did she encourage him? What a question, Max—why does anyone? Even now, all wrapped up, wouldn't he like a chance to climb back on her before climbing into the grave? To go down and taste, before going down? Ah, these were no thoughts for a man sick in bed. Medicare would pay the bills, but nonetheless, between the two of them, it had been an expensive evening. Women cost.

He was awakened, he didn't know if hours or days later, by Lettie whispering his name. The moment he saw her he remembered, viscerally, why he had had to do it. After the arid white-clad shapes drifting in and out, she was a welcome sight in deep blue, her color (Susie's too).

"You can only stay ten minutes," a voice outside the curtain warned.

She put her hand over his and searched his face. He could read her hesitation—to kiss or not to kiss? She decided not to.

"Max, I feel so awful about it, it's driving me crazy."

He tried to smile, keep up appearances. After all, a woman he had lured. Or had she? "It wasn't you, sweetheart. No regrets. It could have happened anytime." His voice came out a weak croak.

"Still and all. If you had died I couldn't forgive myself."

"Don't talk nonsense. And if you hadn't come back just then . . .?" He coughed. She plucked a tissue from the box on the night table and handed it to him.

"So how do you feel now?"

"I feel like hell."

Lettie sighed and pulled over a chair. He didn't much want to talk; he wanted her to sit there forever and protect him from the white coats. He tapped her hand with a finger and pointed. "My heart. Take a look."

"Oh, yes, I've seen that contraption before. It's an okay heart." At last, an unofficial smile. "It looks very nice and even to me."

"What do the doctors say? Did you ask?"

"Yes. They say you'll be all right. In a couple of days you'll be out of intensive care."

He peered at her face, but it was not evasive. It never had been. She looked straight at him with her wide-open, sensible eyes, simply herself.

"You wouldn't lie to me?"

"Not about this."

He breathed deep and felt a lump rise, but swallowed it away. "Life is a sewer," he said, and was immediately sorry, for she put her face in her hands and wept.

In a minute she raised her head and plucked another tissue, for herself. "You're not supposed to talk, especially if that's what you have to say."

He gave a limp, impatient flick of the hand and closed his eyes. When he opened them—in minutes, hours?—she was gone.

Scattered over the next few days were more ten-minute visits from her, and then they moved him downstairs as promised, to a real room. His waking hours grew longer; he could distinguish day from night. They detached him from the I.V. tube and wheeled away his heart on its screen, gave him meager meals and questioned him with a less intense concern. Time oozed past; he didn't think about much, not even about Susie. Susie was slipping away, after so long. It troubled him that he hadn't the energy to snatch her back, but he hadn't the energy to be much troubled over it either. Each time he opened his eyes to the white ceiling he felt relief, as well as a minuscule emotion that, if magnified a thousandfold, might be called joy. This will to live—and for what?—was puzzling, and not entirely welcome; it gave him a future, and played games with his perspective; made him foolish and irritable.

"I've read this one already," he complained to Lettie. "This one too." Disgustedly, he flipped each paperback book across the white sheet. "Aha! This one I haven't. Two strikes, finally a hit." He perused the lurid cover, then turned to the sensational preview on the back.

"I'm sorry, Max. They didn't have such a great selection down at the drugstore. I'll exchange these two; meanwhile you have the one."

"I suppose you did your best." He riffled through the pages.

She rose from the yellow plastic armchair and went to stand at the window. From bed Max could see only a patch of smudgy April sky. The day looked warmish, and the wispy mare's-tail clouds gave it a soft feeling of melancholy. Inside, the air was bland. The walls of the room were pale yellow. Jutting into the squared-off space was his bed, far too high, a platform over an abyss. A TV set, above eye level, protruded from the opposite wall like the trophy head of a captured beast. He hadn't used it yet. The old crime movies he favored were shown only in the thick of night, when the house rules prescribed silence.

Twice a day now they let him sit up and dangle his feet over the edge, an activity that discouragingly drained the blood from his head. There was a sagging heaviness in his arms and legs. Orders from the brain were subverted in transit; the muscles, once so eager, were on strike; any movement demanded a sustained determination. No matter: tomorrow, the nurse had told him, he would take a short walk around the room. Mentally he paced out the prospect, which loomed in anticipation like a five-mile uphill stretch.

"What's happening back at the compound? Have they rented my apartment yet?"

Lettie returned from the window and dropped into the chair, her knees, in scarlet slacks, spread wide. Settling back in the stiff plastic, she folded her arms across her lap. The folding was a gathering in and withdrawal. His illness had aged her, he noticed. The lines from nose to chin seemed deeper. Her eyes were bloodshot and her hair didn't shine.

"Max, I can live without the nastiness." She arched her neck and looked off into the corridor. "I watered your plants last night. Your Wandering Jew is thriving, you'll be glad to know."

"I don't know what possessed me to keep plants. They were my wife's thing, not mine. I can't seem to throw them out. Thank you."

"Don't mention it." She paused. He could see her summoning patience, resources. "Alison phones me every other day to ask about you. She's very concerned."

"And what do you tell her?"

"She feels guilty. I tell her it wasn't her fault. . . . Don't give me that crooked look, Max. She's just a child. Anyway, you said yourself that these things happen, who knows why? She's afraid to call you, I think. You might give her a ring one day, when you're feeling a little stronger." Her eyes wandered to the tan phone near his bed. "I have her number."

He sat up straighter on the pillows. "I take it you mean that in all seriousness?"

"I do. Are you so busy you can't spare the time? She'd like to hear your voice. . . ."

He gave his dismissive flip of the hand, with an incredulous frown that could have shriveled a weaker petitioner. A fine woman, but marred by an excess of sentiment.

"You seem a little tired," Lettie said. "Do you want to rest? I'll come back in a while."

"Rest! What do you think I've been doing?"

"Maybe you'd rest better alone. Frankly, Max, I've had enough for now." She came over to pick up the rejected paperbacks.

"Just think," he said, catching her hand. "Less than two weeks ago we were in the sack."

She raised her eyebrows wryly, then smoothed down his hair like a mother. "That's not all there is to life."

"Go already, philosopher."

But when she was in the doorway he called to her. "Tell me, Lettie, when I get home—if—are you going to seduce me again?"

"I don't know, Max. Probably. Ask the doctor about it, why don't you?" She laughed at the mock horror on his face. "What's the matter, are you too shy?"

"No. Pride," he said.

"I see. Well, take care of yourself, just in case. It's an incentive, I hope."

Without a doubt. Only how could she suggest calling Alison? Hadn't the kid done enough for the moment? She had her dense places, Lettie did, and he needed her perfect. It irked him that she was imperfect, but before he could brood on that, he was asleep.

In the dream he had his strength again; he was back on the wire. Illuminated by spotlights, reaching for the sky, and all around, outside the glowing circles, was deep black. His feet dug in with a fine grip, quietly exulting. No urgency, no hurry, he could keep going forever. He felt his center rising straight through his length, fixed to each successive point. The exquisite calm of walking in space seeped through his pores while the encircling air buoyed him up. Suddenly, puncturing his joy, came a scary prickling inside; a second later the premonition was tangible, as the wire quavered, then shook dangerously. Only with a rapid shift of weight could he keep his balance. He turned to look. Way below was someone trespassing, destroying his equilibrium. In her dirty jeans and T-shirt and colored sneakers she was running carelessly up his wire as if it were a broad safe path, and calling, "Max, Max, wait for me." He was stunned with horror; the thoughtless child would kill him, chasing him like that. Already he could barely stay upright. Tottering, gasping, blinking, he was coming apart from the center, from the inside out. He wanted to shout at her to go back, wave her down, but any extra movement was an impossible luxury. He looked ahead to seize a goal, and there, not too far away, spotlighted on the high platform in her blue spangled costume, was Susie, smiling and beckoning. How come he hadn't noticed her till now? In a fierce effort, he gathered his shattered balance, forcing the energy to cleave tight to the center—he had to get up there to her. But Alison was gaining on him. He could see her quite clearly now. And the wire above seemed to be lengthening, stretching inconceivably high off the ground, while from the top Susie, her features grown indistinct, still smiled at him, holding out her arms as though nothing was wrong. Couldn't she see what was happening, or was she blinded by the glare of the lights? He yearned for her so hard he could practically feel her arms pulling him in. The platform she stood on receded. She grew smaller and smaller, unaware. Close behind him came the sneakered footsteps. Desperate, he risked a streaking dash towards Susie, caught his toe in the wire, leaped up to land with better balance but never landed, fell endlessly, down and down. He woke in terror. He was going to die, that was for sure, and his dread was black as the infinite falling reaches of space.

No Susie out there where he was going either, no white lights, nothing at all. He would never have her close again. Over the past months he had been losing her, distracted by daily rounds, ensnared by caring. Her face and voice no longer kept their vividness, and he felt ashamed, as at a betrayal. Yet Susie was bones now; what could bones care about his betrayal? Hers was the worse negligence. He was fully awake now; that shabby defection of hers, to bone, maddened him as long ago, and the skin of his face twitched, tightening against the death's head beneath.

Lettie returned, carrying more books. Two steps inside the room and she went pale. "Max, what is it? Not again?"

"No, no. It's all right."

"What happened, for God's sake?"

"I had a bad dream."

She pulled a chair near him, sat, and took his hand. "You gave me such a scare. Look at you. Your face is gray." She began to cry.

"Don't," he said. The irritation he had felt for her before he slept seemed senseless, a reflection in a distorting mirror. In himself. Each moment had to be lived, or suffered, separately, in its own wholeness, and she was real, and now. He saw her image truly, as she had always been. Only he wished he could spare her. "Don't care so much, Lettie. You know what's in store for you."

"And since when was that ever a reason? Stupid." She blew her nose. "What did you dream?"

He shook his head weakly on the pillow. "It's gone. Forgotten."

"Well, never mind, then." She sat quietly for a long time. "Are you better now? Good. Listen," she said, smiling. "I'll give you something real to groan about. You're not going to like this, but I promised Alison I'd ask. . . ."

He was groaning already.

"Just listen, Max—this is kind of nice. She wants to take us both to the circus in five or six weeks, as her guests, no less. You ought to be all right by then. She wants to know if you'll come."

"In five or six weeks I might be dead."

"So could we all. If you're not dead, will you come?"

"I'll come. Why not? You twisted my arm."

It seemed she had expected more of a struggle, for she leaned back in relief and said, "You know, Max, sometimes you surprise me."

"My infinite variety, huh?" He didn't explain. There was really no need to tell her that he might as well go anywhere now, do anything, that one thing was as good as another since above all something was better than nothing. He didn't want to be dead in six weeks, he didn't want to be dead ever. Life drew him and claimed him, and he was humbled. Mortal and unreasonably hopeful, like everyone else. Alison had overtaken him.

CHAPTER 10

A COUPLE OF WEEKS LATER he gathered his books together and left for home. "Almost as good as new," the bearded intern told him on the way out.

Glancing up at the shaggy, innocent face, Max jerked his head back with a brief laugh. "Listen to the expert! I'm probably your first case. Don't forget, O'Reilly, you owe me forty thousand dollars from gin rummy."

The young man grinned and pumped Max's hand. "You were here at the right time, Max. Next week I go off the night shift."

His arm linked through Lettie's, he hit the warm late-April air. The scent of new-mown grass and honeysuckle rising around him was lushly intoxicating, and for an instant his head swam. He leaned harder on Lettie.

"Are you all right?"

"Fine. The shock of fresh air."

From the window of the taxi he watched the town go by. The low, box-like houses plunked on their tidy lawns were the same, interspersed with shopping centers also the same, the brashly lettered signs still an assault on the eye; yet lit with spring sun, all had an ingenuous glow, and stirred in him a singular compassion. A kinship. It was, after all, where he lived. As they rounded the corner near Pleasure Knolls he braced himself for Vicky Cameron.

"Max!" She rose as if propelled, and rushed to meet him, grasping his hands. He leaned to kiss her on the cheek, acknowledging the honor of the greeting—Vicky used first names only for the happy few. "It's so good to have you back! You're looking fine. How do you feel?"

"Not bad, Vicky. Quieter, is all. You've been carrying on as usual, I trust?"

"Oh, yes, things are about the same. Max, we can send up meals if you like. All you've got to do is call me. Don't hesitate—"

"New hairdo?"

She blushed and ruffled her fair hair, freshly cut in short layers and frosted with silvery tips.

He moved towards the elevator, where Lettie waited with his suitcase. "I'll be talking to you, Vicky."

From back at her desk, her head bent and her hands fussing among papers, she called in a half whisper, "Max, take care of yourself. Really. I missed you."

He waved and followed Lettie into the elevator.

"Another conquest," she said. "You have women of every generation hanging on you."

"But think of the irony of life. Now, when it's too late."

"And after the way you've treated her."

"That's not important. She knows I'm fond of her."

"Fond of her! It's news to me. Are you sure you're all right, Max? You don't sound like yourself."

"I don't feel like myself either. They drained out all the piss and vinegar. I don't even think I could work up a good fury."

"Oh, give it time. Something'll come along to set you off." They got out and walked down the hall.

"No, I think I'm changed. Would you still like me if I were rehabilitated? I mean, the externals would remain the same, but inside, a simple sweet old man? Reconciled to the world? A metamorphosis? You think you could go for that?"

She put her hand in his pants pocket and took out the keys. "I don't know what you're talking about. You're talking above my head."

"Uh-uh. I know you too well for that line, sweetie. You're not sure, that's it. You are having your doubts."

Impassive, she stepped inside and he followed. The apartment looked the same, only neater than the morning he had left. Someone— Lettie, of course—had wiped up the spilled coffee, emptied the ashtray, and washed the breakfast dishes, pancake skillet. Put away the bottle of Scotch, hung up the bathrobe. Also changed the hot sheets. His few plants were thriving—he visited them one by one, fingering the shiny leaves. Only three were from Susie's original brood, a pink-edged flourishing coleus, a philodendron that wound from a high shelf around a lamp to the floor, and an indestructible small cactus she used to swear at when it pricked her. The rest he had left for patrons of the bike shop. Later, to give those three company he had added others, which thrived—he couldn't tell why, since he watered them erratically. A stranger was sitting on his window sill,

114

blooming a brilliant, mournful purple: the African violet the kids from the gym class had sent. Lettie had brought it home from the hospital.

"You took good care of the plants." She was off in the bedroom, opening windows, and didn't answer. He sat down and put his feet up on the ottoman. Lettie returned to study him.

"You look tired. Go to bed."

"A one-track mind."

"Look who's talking. Remember to take it easy."

"I must thank you for everything," he said.

"Please. I can't stand it."

"Okay, okay. I was only trying to be polite."

"It doesn't sound natural."

A siren started to wail, just outside his window. "See, they're welcoming me home."

He settled in to quiet days. He walked, morning and evening, alert to bird sounds and flowering dogwoods, mauve sunsets of the lengthening days, the milder pleasures, innocuous. He cooked and ate too much, Lettie along with him. In the movies they held hands and absently he stroked her leg; they stopped off for ice cream in Highet's on the way home. He felt mellow, like softening, overripe fruit. Those nights he was alone in his bed he read, with a cool relish, mysteries by Dorothy Sayers. They gave him sound sleep and no dreams. Curious, those blank, uneventful sleeps. After a while he ventured farther on his excursions, visiting the local museum, where he found a display on the history of the region that sheltered him. Once it had been dairy farms bounded by thick woods. Way before that, Indians. Now a clutter of commerce. He clicked his tongue in righteous dismay, as though he had a personal stake in the land of the valley.

Then there were the visitors, who in their number and warmth astonished him. People he barely knew, had nodded to in the corridor, came by to inquire about his health. Invited in, they had coffee and expatiated. It was touching; Lettie, at least, was touched. "Charisma," she remarked. "You could have been a politician." But Max said it was mere morbid curiosity: everyone swarms around those who have brushed with death, welcomes the wounded hero home from battle. Human nature; he accepted with forbearance and turned on the charm.

George Rakofsky of the birthday party rode up in his wheelchair one evening. "It's good to see you up and about again," he told Max. "You're too young to die."

115

"From your angle, maybe. But I decided to stick around for your next birthday party."

They talked about business. George had started out in sports equipment, but after the war, he said, with the waves of young families moving to the suburbs, he found he could do even better in toys. "It used to be simple stuff. Lincoln Logs. Erector sets. Dolls that could pee were a big item. But now they've got these little models of McDonald's. Holiday Inns. You wouldn't believe! We were happy if we got a bat and ball."

"A broomstick."

"And a crate on wheels. Remember those, Max? That still beats a skateboard, for my money. I really enjoyed that store, though. I could talk to people as much as I liked—that was for me. I've always been interested in people. The women used to come in, they were bored, pushing the strollers. In my place they got some lively conversation, I'll tell you. It didn't hurt business either. I liked them, and I liked the kids too. That's what I miss here—having kids around. I have five grandchildren, but they're busy with their own things; that's how it goes. And three great-grandchildren. One a new baby I haven't seen yet."

George had a broad resonant voice, younger than his body. A voice vibrant and ringed with calm. Max could understand the young mothers hanging around the toy store.

"Did you ever try living with your sons?"

"You don't have sons or you wouldn't ask. With sons come daughters-in-law. Not that they're not nice girls, both of them. I have no complaints. But what would I do in their houses? Their kids are grown up and gone, and they're out working. All the women, these days. More power to them, if you ask me. But I'm better off where I am. I don't want to be an old pain in the ass living in the spare room."

"When did you move in here?"

"Twelve years ago. After my wife died."

Max got up and walked to the window. How long for him, in this new, bland calm? George at least had a memory, while his own seemed to have evaporated.

"I don't mind it, really. I visit, I listen to music. There are things to do. The only thing I worry about is another stroke—if I lose my speech. When that happens I'll be finished. My wife used to say I could never have any secrets from her. Were you married, Max?"

He turned back to face George. "Yes."

116

"It's peculiar, isn't it? You know how they say if you lose a leg you can still get a pain in it? Twelve years, and still once in a while I wake up at night and reach out a hand. . . . Do you know what I mean?"

"Let me fill these up again." Max took the empty glasses to the kitchen. In deference to George's diabetes he was serving plain iced tea. He poured a shot of bourbon into his own and returned.

George rambled on. One grandson was an orthopedist, another an insurance agent. His youngest granddaughter wanted to be a stockbroker—what did Max think of that? Max gazed with affection at the face webbed with wrinkles and lit by azure eyes. A comforting face, after the females who had moved into his life as if it were an empty house. Men were easier friends—mere guests, not tenants, they asked little of you. Thinking of Lettie and all she gave in return, he felt disloyal. But it was the truth.

"I'm very glad you came," he said at the door. "Come back anytime. It does me good."

George trapped him in a long, shrewd stare from which he couldn't avert his eyes. Thoroughly withered, but how that face lived! And understood. "Pull yourself together, Max," he said brusquely. "Don't waste your time."

The next afternoon was Alison's turn: he had granted permission at last. Lettie was with her, an arm protectively circling the child's shoulders.

"Hi, Max." Pale, hanging back, she extended a hesitant hand. "How are you?"

"Oh, come over here," he said impatiently. He pulled her inside, held her close and kissed her cheek. So smooth and dewy, it surprised him. When she began sniffling on his chest he moved her away. "Sit down. Lettie, do we have a cookie or something to keep her alive? You're even thinner than before. Don't they feed you?"

"Sure, meat and potatoes." She put down the knapsack and took her sweatshirt off. "You're not still mad at me? I mean, you want to talk to me?"

"Of course I want to talk to you. Where else can I find such stimulating conversation?"

"Are you kidding me, Max?"

"Certainly not. Tell me what's happening in the gym."

"Well, Fats is trying to continue the gymnastics but he really doesn't know how. It's very tedious. He has us all walking around on our hands—absolute chaos. Elliot strained his neck from it two weeks

117

ago, a mild whiplash, so his father came in to complain, right in the middle of class. You would have enjoyed that scene. His father is sort of a cross between Dracula and Captain Kangaroo."

"Elliot was always too stiff. I wouldn't have stood him on his hands yet."

Lettie brought in a tray with chocolate cupcakes and milk. "Here, Alison. Eat something. I'll eat with you. How is your mother coming along?"

"Gross. Extremely gross. Just a few more weeks till the blessed event. Max? When are you coming back to school? I mean, it's such drudgery without you."

"Look here, Alison, you want to be treated like a grownup, don't you? So grow up—use your head. My days are numbered. I can't do that stuff any more."

"Oh, no," she said promptly. "If they sent you home you must be better. I bet you could do it if you really tried. You look just the same as always." She bit the icing off the top of a cupcake. "Anyway, Max, do you think you could show me those pictures again, of the people in the circus?"

He had a surge of weariness. So besides the magic powers, she had decided he was immortal. Well, she would find out soon enough. Become the image, he used to tell the kids. But he couldn't play the image she worshipped—it was beyond human powers.

"Pictures?" asked Lettie. "How come I haven't seen them?"

"Oh, they're nothing special at all. What do you care about old pictures?" Always wanting. He went to stand apart at the window, childishly longing for George, who knew enough to see him as he was, a heap of fragments.

"Better some other time, dear," he heard Lettie whisper. Alison made a small, muted sound of disappointment.

He turned round. "No, that's all right, Lettie. This time is as good as any. Those two albums in the bedroom closet—Alison, you can stand up on a chair to get them. I'm going to sit here and read. I'm a little tired."

He couldn't help but listen, though. What an intriguing child, despite everything. She had total recall.

"That one is Henry. He stood on the bottom of the pyramid because of his legs and shoulders. . . . They're having a New Year's party. See the balloons and streamers? . . . Oh, and look, Lettie, that's Max. Isn't that amazing?"

118

"Hold it. Let me get a good look. Aha! Yes, that's him all right."

"That one with the monkey is a clown. . . . The monkey's name is Joanna. Isn't she cute? He let her eat breakfast with the people sometimes. . . . That's Max's trailer."

"Ah," said Lettie.

"And that's Max's wife."

Lettie said nothing. With eyes closed, he heard the pages turn. He heard their breathing. The black turtleneck sweater, the knees pulled to her chin. The teasing look.

"Wait," said Alison. "I haven't seen this bunch before. There's one of them together, with the clown. This is fantastic—they must be holding her up from behind, but it looks like she's floating on air. You know, she was the one who taught him all the tricks. She coached him."

"Mm-hm." Not another word from Lettie, till after many pages the book was shut, and she said, "I think he must have fallen asleep. Maybe that's enough for today, Alison."

He opened one eye a fraction to glimpse her gathering up the knapsack and the sweatshirt, and taking a cupcake for the road.

"Don't forget the circus, Lettie. It's two weeks from Saturday," she whispered.

"I won't forget, sweetheart. Good-bye now."

"I'll see you before then anyway. *Close Encounters of the Third Kind* is coming next week. Oh, shit, I forgot—I can't cut any more."

"Never mind; we'll go for the four o'clock show."

The door closed.

"You can open your eyes now, Max, it's safe."

He did. Lettie was at the window, facing him. He watched her, a firm silhouette against the falling late-afternoon light. She stood extremely still, not a muscle of her face moving, and she looked not at him but into him.

"She was very pretty," Lettie said. "Very beautiful. I see now."

He had thought he knew her, but what she might be feeling at this moment was a mystery. There was more within than he knew. That was the lure of women: more inside than you ever imagined, a dark trail weaving through. As he watched, a burden clotted in his chest. Was she going to trouble him now too?

He had only a brief time to wait. Her eyes relaxed; her face slipped into a sly grin. "You weren't so bad yourself, either. I feel like a stiff drink. How about you, Max?"

The burden lifted and he smiled at her, an intimate smile that already could call forth memories. He reached out his hand. "Come here just a minute, will you?" he asked. "Before you make your stiff drink."

He began dropping in to see George while Lettie was out shopping or at movies with her friends. From outside the door, the first time, he could hear strains of music.

"Come on in. I was hoping you'd be around," George greeted him.

It shouldn't have surprised him, yet it did, to find George's apartment identical to his own. Rooms laid out the same, furniture in the same places but a trifle more worn. Instead of browns and oranges George had greens and golds. He brought out thick green cigars and they settled into a greenish haze of smoke, to talk, that first afternoon, till dinnertime. The cups they drank coffee from were the same, as well as the chrome equipment in the bathroom, which, Max thought with a pang, George must use. There were not many books but there were records. A music-lover, he played harpsichord music for Max. He had once built his own harpsichord, he said, which a grandchild had now; it had taken two years and infinite labor, evenings and weekends, but he was a patient man. Max, abashed at his own ignorance, listened to Bach and Scarlatti, awed at the splendor of form, the balance and precision. This was music that climbed and descended without cease, winding obsessively through lattices like bees humming in a hive. Austere and comforting, it was music with neither fury nor self-pity, transcending the cheaper emotions. He had never known such sounds. And as he listened, going down to George's day after day, he looked out the window and saw things in slightly different perspective from this floor just below his own. The elms' leafy tops were at eye level—you could almost reach out and pluck a twig—and the grass was nearer.

Some afternoons he wheeled George around outside, and they sat in the garden in back. It was mid May; there were daffodils, columns of tulips, a rosebush. The air was sweet and George a safe haven. In his homely long view, life was a steady passage in which everything eventually came to rest in proportion and harmonious balance. Balance, thought Max, was all one could finally wish for.

George wanted to know about the circus. Not the glamor—he had a pragmatic turn of mind and asked for no pictures—but the equipment, the rigging, the nuts and bolts of how it worked. Max felt his memory stir beneath the layer of the present; he scrabbled in the ruins and found shards. He told him how they dug in poles and strung up guys for the tent they would have to dismantle a few days later. Recounting that strenuous pulling on the ropes, a dozen men or more, the tense vigil as the big top caved in and crumpled, he could feel the slack muscles in his arms contract. Sense memory. He told him about getting the wires so taut and securing the nets, about hooking in the bars of the trapeze and erecting the platforms—four men used to the work could do that in no time at all. But then the trailers breaking down, the dreary waiting for new parts in dry one-horse towns. And with a revived, exhilarated weariness in his bones, he recalled how far and how long they used to travel, a straggling procession inching across the map, Florida to Oregon, May through November, then winter quarters down South, for a bit of rest.

"That's just like nomads! No roots," said George. "How could you stand it?"

"We took the roots with us. I liked it that way."

Like any old man, he thought, he was starting to generalize, to idealize what was gone.

"But with all that expensive equipment, plus the traveling, and so many mouths to feed—did it really pay?" George asked. "I mean, in terms of net profits."

"Some seasons we just about broke even, or worse, but other times it wasn't bad. It depended on so many unpredictable things, like weather or sickness, for example. People having accidents. Animals—a pain in the ass, if you ask me. After the war we did better, with the men back and money circulating a little more freely. But it's not the sort of thing you do for money, really."

They smoked for a while in silence. "I had some very good friends there, must be dead now." Max got up. "Well, I've given you an earful. You ready to go back inside?"

The cigar in his mouth, George waved as he wheeled out of the elevator, and Max, left alone, wondered at himself. What had they done to his heart in that hospital? He was getting soft and nostalgic. He was glad Lettie would be out playing bridge tonight; he wanted the solitude. In his armchair, he read till the light faded, and hours later woke there in the dark with a heavy, peaceful feeling. It was new, maybe a different route to death; maybe Susie had known this feeling too. No, he didn't want to think about her; he wanted this peace. He turned on a small lamp and made himself a sandwich, which he ate slowly in the dim living room. He wasn't weak or sick, yet seemed to be moving in a dreamy haze, bewildered, a stranger to himself. Was this what vague old people drifted in, when they didn't answer right away but stared as if some image hung before them in the air, then brought up odd bits of the past out of the blue? He was seized by an urge to order his affairs, correct what was distorted and incomplete. He picked up the phone.

"It's me, sweetheart. Your Friday-night admirer."

"What? Who is this?"

"Oh, Vicky, you're slipping."

"Max! You really scared me."

"So I gather. I called to tell you something." But he fell silent, like a diffident child.

"Well? What is it?"

"This: When I have taken my ultimate leave of these pleasurable knolls, as well as of everywhere else, when I have—uh—crossed the bar, as the poet said—"

"I don't like hearing you talk like this."

"Come off it and listen. Let your hair down, what you have left of it. What did you do that for, anyway?"

"I'm not hanging on to be insulted. What do you want, Max?"

"I want you not to remember how nasty I was to you."

"You are incredible! I can see why little girls chase after you."

"Don't patronize a senior citizen. Will you do as I say?"

"I'll try, but I can't promise. With you it's all part and parcel."

The next afternoon Lettie stopped in.

"You're all decked out," Max said. "Going somewhere?"

"Yes, a bunch of us are going out to lunch, and then I've got a dozen errands. I must get some shoes. There's a sale in Bamberger's. Did I leave my earrings here?"

"Take a look."

She bustled into his bedroom and back. "I found them. Max, it's supposed to rain, so please don't walk for miles. And we've got the circus tomorrow too—save your strength."

"I wanted a woman and I got a mother." And dutifully, barely touching, he kissed her on the cheek.

"Ah, don't make me faint with passion, please. I haven't got the time."

As she walked out the door he missed her. He would have liked some company today, though he would never ask. He had seen all the movies in town and read everything in the apartment, and the view out the window was a bleak gray.

Now might be a good time: he had been fumbling with the idea for days. He poured a drink for courage. And then another. He couldn't tell how long he sat there, trying to rouse will against pride. Surely he could say it to George, who was so old, so beyond strife, that he could listen with serene disinterest, and carry secrets intact to the grave. Susie troubled his peace. She had become a tight, painful knot beneath his ribs. He would wrench out that knot and attempt to unravel it on George's coffee table: how he had had her and lost her, but kept her alive by stealth with his broodings, and then, against his will, lost her again—not like the first time with stark grief, but murkily, absently, through distractions. What could be done? he yearned to ask. What could be done about the unendurable fact that everything a man possessed, even his ghosts, could be taken from him? Words such as those were not impossible, though he had rarely in his life humbled himself to speak so plain. Was it foolish to think that George, his mind content, his body stilled, might rearrange the strands of his knot into some bearable pattern?

At last he went out into the hall. The sirens wailed; he had grown used to them, as Vicky had predicted last fall that he would. Twice the elevator passed him by, so he walked down to the second floor. Two white-coated men were rushing a stretcher out of the elevator; he saw Vicky chase them all the way to the next-to-last door on the right, George's. One by one, other doors along the corridor opened and faces poked out to watch, tense and alert like understudies observing a dress rehearsal. For a brief moment Max stood paralyzed. Then he wheeled around and went back out to the landing, to sit on the steps. But naturally, he thought. But naturally. It was only his shock that was unnatural. He bent over and covered his face with his hands.

As if by fierce suction, the softness of the last weeks was drawn out of his pores; the walls of his body contracted and hardened, like cement settling. Good, this was familiar. This way he could live. The other was sentimental nonsense—how could he have lapsed so far? He rose with difficulty, clutching the banister, and went carefully down to the lobby. He ought to start using the cane indoors as well as out; he was moving very laboriously these days. With her grotesque frosted hair all mussed—ah, that nervous, absurd ruffling—Vicky stood at the door, watching the stretcher being eased into the ambulance parked out front. She was shielding her eyes against the declining afternoon sun, which belatedly and uselessly graced this dismal day.

As the ambulance screeched away Vicky returned to her seat. A few people whispered in small, scattered groups. Max hovered over her, scrutinizing and savage. The doctors were wrong—anger was good for the heart. He simmered with a desire urgent as sex, but its goal was the contrary. He made himself wait.

"What is it, Max? Can I do something for you?"

"Ever ready. He won't be back, you know. You might as well tear up his file."

"He's got a lot of fight left in him. The doctors can do wonders these days."

"Isn't that reassuring. The eternal optimist. Do you want to start planning his homecoming party, maybe?"

She drew herself together and hugged her arms. Her voice faltered, as it used to in his early days. "That's quite unfair."

"Oh, yes, fair play. I keep forgetting. But life is unfair, Vicky. Even our President said so. I suppose you've watched this kind of scene hundreds of times. All in the line of duty, right? Another empty apartment to fill. New faces to greet."

"I have a lot of work to do, Max." She shuffled through her papers.

"I know your time is valuable. So much paperwork. But I'm your work too. I'm still animate. Now's your chance to use a little psychology. Let's see if you can improve my attitude."

She looked up from the form she was filling out, her face wan, as though he had drained from her any possible response. Finally she whispered, "I know you liked him, Max. I'm sorry about it. That's all I can say."

"Speak up, my senses aren't as sharp as they used to be. Oh, and there's something else I've been meaning to ask you, Victoria. You know that Mrs. Jordan who had leukemia? I haven't seen her since I've been back from the hospital. Where's her file?"

She lowered her head. "Mrs. Jordan succumbed to the disease." Her lips barely moved.

"Succumbed!" He banged a fist loudly on her desk. The others clustered around the lobby turned to look. "Succumbed, my ass!"

"You're disturbing people," she said in her official voice.

"Am I?" He parodied the tone. "I wasn't aware." He turned, and with elaborate courtesy, said, "I beg your pardon." Then he leaned over to whisper in her ear. "It's you and your sort, baby, that make it worse."

"Max, please. There's no sort. Everyone lives and dies the same."

"No, dear. Some of us die. Others succumb. My wife died. George will die. Lettie will die. You will probably succumb."

He saw tears come to her eyes. She laid her hands flat on the desk. "I don't understand. Just last night you called me to . . ."

He almost weakened, but the image of the stretcher and George on it, helpless and unexpectedly tall, was too vivid. "Last night? You must have been dreaming."

Upstairs, he had another drink and fell asleep in his chair. When he woke, dislocated in time, Lettie was standing over him.

"I heard. Vicky told me about it."

"Oh. I was just on my way to see him. . . . Did you find the shoes you wanted?"

"They're on my feet."

He peered down. They were dark-brown leather clogs on cork heels, unadorned except for one braided horizontal strip. "Uh-huh. Simple but elegant," he said.

"They're very comfortable. You don't feel the ground under you."

He gave a short laugh. Time passed.

"Max, are you going to sit in that same position forever?"

"Maybe."

"I'll fix you something to eat. It's nearly seven."

"You do that. I wouldn't want to die of malnutrition, with so many more interesting choices available."

Lettie turned on him, eyes blazing. "Don't you pull that stuff on me! I'm not Vicky Cameron and I won't take it from you! You knew how old he was. Jesus, you'd think it happened just to spite you."

He hardly touched the dinner she cooked. She didn't try to speak to him, for which he was thankful. When they finished clearing the table she said, "I'm going now. We ought to leave about eleven-thirty tomorrow. We can take a taxi to the station. . . . What's the matter? Don't you remember? The circus."

"Oh, shit. I forgot all about it. I can't go."

"No? Don't you feel okay?"

"I feel fine. I'm in no mood for a circus, that's all."

"Neither am I, but still, she has the tickets and she's had it planned for weeks."

"So?"

"For heaven's sake, Max, you're an adult and she's a child."

"That is certainly a fact, but I fail to see its bearing on the case."

"Oh, all right. I'm not arguing with you in this mood. Will you call her, at least, and tell her? Tell her you're tired or something."

"You tell her, when you see her tomorrow. You can still go."

"Not without you. You're the one she really wanted. I don't know anything about circuses. It . . . wouldn't work out."

"Don't be absurd. Are we Siamese twins?"

"I don't want to watch her be disappointed! Lay off of me. I have feelings too."

"Well, if you're not going either, then you can call her."

"You're so damned stingy sometimes. It would mean a lot more to her if you called and explained. Such a little thing."

"I don't owe her any explanations! I can't help what anything means to her—I didn't ask for it. She has parents, doesn't she? Why must I care?"

"Here we go again," she sighed, noisily straightening the two chairs at the empty table. "Congratulations, Max, you're your old self. Fully recovered. What will she do with the tickets?"

He didn't bother to answer that. Lettie called. As she repeated the excuses she sank onto the couch with the phone in her lap, closing her eyes.

After a silence she said, "Alison, sweetheart, calm down and listen to me. The truth is, a good friend of his had a stroke today and he saw him go off in an ambulance. He's very depressed. He's old and sick and he has things on his mind. It hurts to lose people. There are times when a person doesn't feel up to going to a circus. You can understand that, can't you? . . . We're very sorry. Yes, of course. Anytime. Oh, and we'll pay you back for the tickets."

When she hung up she stood and faced Max with her hands on her hips, an aging Amazon. "So? Accurate enough?"

"Perfect. You're perfect, I've told you before."

She grunted at him in disgust.

"I mean it, baby. I'm not even being sarcastic."

"Good night." She left him, unkissed, untouched, and with the dirty dishes still in the sink. A cloud settled over him, dense and grim like fog. It cast its weighty shadow whichever way he turned. From his chair he watched out the window as the sun finally went down, and more shadow crept across the horizon to dim the green landscape. He was moving into the valley of the shadow of death, bereft.

126

CHAPTER 11

"I CAN UNDERSTAND," she said to Lettie, "but I still don't think it's fair. I think it's shitty of him. In fact, I think he's a real shit."

She hung up the phone in the kitchen. The house was still—Wanda and Josh had gone out to dinner with Lou and her husband. A shiver went through her, and she rubbed her shoulders, thinking of the long night ahead, with the three green tickets tucked in her notebook under the mattress. As she stood up, a hollow opened in the pit of her stomach and spread wider and wider till it was everywhere. Hunger clutched her, gnawing at her inner walls and screaming for food. She contained a vast cavern, and if she didn't fill it, she might explode from its pushing against her bones.

She flung open the refrigerator and jammed a cold chicken leg into her mouth, crunched the bone and sucked out the marrow. She broke a hunk of cheddar cheese off the slab and swallowed it, then tipped a container of milk to her mouth to wash it down. Three brownies from the breadbox—not as good as Lettie's but it didn't matter—and still the cavern cried out, unsatisfied, so she ate last night's spaghetti out of the plastic container. A sharp pain seared through her lower stomach, on the right side. Appendicitis, it must be. She lay down on the floor and watched the second hand of the wall clock go round and round. Two, three, four times. The pain kept stabbing. How many more rounds till she was dead? She didn't even care. If he didn't give a damn about her after all this time, well, neither did she. If only she had never met him—he had caused nothing but trouble since the very first day. And after everything, he turned out to be not at all what he pretended. Just a mean old man. Wanda and Josh would come home from the restaurant to find her dead on the kitchen floor, with not even a note explaining. She closed her eyes to wait, but gradually the pain went away. When she got to her feet she felt heavy and sick. All the things she had eaten were rolling around at the bottom of her stomach, bumping into each other.

It was almost dark out. She curled up in Wanda's and Josh's bed and turned on the television very loud, so she wouldn't hear the floorboards creaking in the hall. The movie on was *Sybil*, about a crazy girl with sixteen different personalities, because her mother had tortured her when she was a baby, and if Josh were home he wouldn't let her watch it; too upsetting, he would say. But she had already read the book, a year ago. In the middle of the movie she had to jump up and run to the bathroom. Bracing herself against the wall, she held her stomach and threw up.

Hours later she woke in a daze, to feel Josh carrying her like a baby to her own bed.

"And start a new day," the clock's whiny voice said. She slammed down the button of the alarm. It seemed she had tossed all night, while the leaves outside rustled and funny shadows jiggled up and down her closet door. Her head felt swollen and thick, and behind her eyes was a hot sting. She sat up and pushed back the curtains. It was a sunny, still day. The leaves of the maple had a sheen, with the outline of the highest ones cut sharp against a dazzling blue sky. It would be hot later, especially in the city.

She ran the shower as hot as she could bear it, letting it soak her hair. A year ago when she came home from the school beach trip red with sunburn, Wanda had said that a hot shower would take the sting out, and she was right.

With her denim skirt and the clogs Wanda had bought her on sale in Bamberger's that made her look taller, she might pass for fourteen, even fifteen. People in the city didn't bother about strangers. Lots of runaways were never found, even though their parents put pleading messages in the papers—"Janie, come home, we love you." Max had not been found either, that evening after the First World War when he sat in Penn Station eating a chocolate bar and reading a newspaper so he wouldn't look shiftless, waiting for a train heading west. But she might not have to go that far. He had once told her that in the old days a circus could always use a willing kid. If she approached them the right way, no smart-ass stuff, just polite and firm . . .

Or if she could only find those jugglers she saw two years ago, that snowy day when they drove in to the city to see the big Christmas tree. They were a family of vagabonds. Gypsies, like in *The Hunchback of Notre Dame,* and they had made everyone gathered round look so excited and happy. They didn't even seem to mind when the police-

128

man broke up their act—they had just smiled and bowed to the audience, picked up the shabby hat filled with coins, and skipped off in the snow. As they disappeared around a corner she had stared after them, wishing she could go along. And she thought the girl had given her a special look when she threw her quarter into the hat. If she could find them somehow and juggle for them, maybe they would let her be part of their act.

There was one important thing left to do. She had never written the ending. The notebook looked older and more battered than she remembered. When you're with people every day, Wanda once said, you don't notice how they age. But if you don't see them for a while...

The trapeze artist Alice pulled down with her as she fell recovers from his numerous broken bones. She is very relieved—if he were dead or crippled, it would have haunted her for life. But laid up in bed so long, with time to think things over, she decides he was really not such a great artist after all; he was kind of a phony, in fact. Unfortunately, Alice is not as lucky as he is. Perhaps the doctor didn't sterilize his instruments when he set her broken arm—circus life is so grimy. At first she doesn't mention the pain, thinking it a normal part of the healing process. When she finally complains it is too late: gangrene has set in. The arm has to be amputated. Still, she faces she future with determination. Lots of people are worse off. Hal, the truckdriver, with two hooks. That deaf-mute in *The Heart Is a Lonely Hunter,* except he shoots himself. But in addition to this handicap, she suspects that she may be pregnant, which is very puzzling since she has done nothing besides a few kisses and gropings with Hal, months ago. Someone must have done it to her while she was unconscious, under the anesthesia or asleep. A stranger, or maybe someone from the circus. Alice doesn't believe in abortion. Now she will have to become mature and responsible, for the sake of her child. She hitchhikes to San Francisco, where she buys a one-way ticket for a ship sailing to the Orient. And there the story ended, as Alice, one-armed, gazing at the turbulent sea with her long blond hair whipping behind her in the wind, embarks on a new life far away, free and possibly pregnant.

She smacked the notebook shut. She could read it over later— meanwhile she had to finish packing. The last thing to go in the knapsack was the book she had borrowed from Max a week ago, *And Then There Were None.* He didn't know he would never get it back.

She picked up the elephant bank on her dresser, and noticed a tiny white box that had fallen behind it. The ring from Arizona that Josh gave her last fall—she had totally forgotten it! Guiltily, she took it out and slipped it on her middle finger. He would be hurt if he found she had left it behind. In the bank were thirteen dollars and forty-seven cents; that, plus the eighteen dollars she would get from returning the two tickets, should be plenty for a start.

It was time to get moving. She took a few steps towards the door, but her knees felt funny. She returned to sit on the bed, with a hand on the bulging knapsack beside her. The hard edges of books and sneakers jutted from beneath the canvas. Was she really going to do this wild thing? What would she say to people? Where would she eat? Where would she sleep? What would happen at night, when she woke in the dark and saw the creeping shadows in strange rooms? Or in tents, or trailers?

Through the branches just outside her window she could see two houses across the street, identical to her own, each with a car parked in the driveway and a bike lying on the flagstone path. On each lawn, a man sat on a lawn mower. Inside, the women must be in the kitchen, cleaning up after breakfast. The kids would be out soon, riding their bikes up and down the street until they were called for lunch. Then they would play ball and maybe ride some more, till dinner. When they grew up, after countless lunches and dinners, they would have houses of their own, lawns, kitchens, children, and so on, and so on. She could end up exactly like that. She rose and hoisted the knapsack onto her back. It wasn't forever. She would return someday, to see Wanda and Josh and to meet the baby. By then it would not be a baby any more. It might be something like her. She could tell it stories and whisper secrets to it about exotic distant places, and maybe it would want to come away too.

Wanda and Josh lay sunning themselves on beach chairs out in front. Wanda was wearing white shorts and a huge white maternity blouse that made her body look like a pillow on suntanned legs.

"Is this really the same Alison?" Josh looked her up and down. "Wow! I haven't seen you in a skirt in years. Did you grow while I was away?"

"It's the clogs, not me."

"You look like you're going somewhere."

"I am. I'm going to the circus."

"I didn't know about that. Who's taking you?"

130

"It's okay. She's going with those old people from the home," Wanda said in a tired voice. "I forgot to tell you. You were in North Dakota. You're away so much—I can't remember every little thing." She picked up her coffee mug from the grass and sipped.

"Them again! I thought that was all over, after that night."

"Not again. Still. They're her best friends. I hope you took some breakfast," she said to Alison.

"Now, Allie, honey, don't you think it might be better if you—"

"Oh please don't start with a sermon, Josh. I can't bear it so early in the day. If they want to take her, what's the harm? I spoke to the woman about it on the phone last week. Mrs. Blumenthal, I think. She sounded all right."

Alison fumbled with her belt. How ironic that on her last morning, Wanda should be sticking up for her. She watched the belly heave under the white blouse as Wanda sighed and turned her smooth face up to the sun. There was still time to change her mind.

"Well, stay close to them down there, anyway. It's a huge place— easy to get lost." Josh reached up and patted the knapsack on her back. "What've you got in there, bricks?"

"Just some books. I'm dropping them off at the library on the way."

"But the library's closed on Sundays."

"They have a return box out front."

"Books, books." Josh shook his head, with the broad, silly grin. "Maybe you should slow down. At this rate there'll be nothing left for you to read pretty soon. Why don't you call from the station when you get in, and I'll pick you up."

"Okay."

"Have a good time," Wanda said lazily. She yawned and stretched. Suddenly Alison wanted to put her arms around Wanda and kiss her good-bye. But it would arouse suspicion. There was a time, ages ago, when she used to kiss Wanda every morning before she left for school. She couldn't remember when or how she had stopped. A person ought to be able to kiss her own mother without arousing suspicion.

"Here's two dollars extra," said Josh. "You might want to buy a hot dog or something."

"Thanks."

When she was halfway down the front path he called, "Sure you don't need a lift?"

"It's only a fifteen-minute walk."

She waved once. As soon as she rounded the corner she began to

131

run. They wouldn't miss her for hours. Only around five or six o'clock would they begin to think . . . The air was sweet with honeysuckle and roses. She ran faster, as if she were being chased. As if she were chasing herself, and might catch up and drag herself back. A block before the station she stopped.

The trains ran every half hour. There was still plenty of time, enough to try once more. If he would change his mind and come, then she would return with him and Lettie and run away some other day. It was all up to him. If he wouldn't, well, whatever happened would be his fault.

He looked as if he had just gotten out of bed. One cheek kept the pattern of the pillow's creases, and his eyes were watery and vague. A wrinkled white pajama collar stuck out unevenly from the faded blue bathrobe. "Didn't Lettie explain to you on the phone?" Even his voice sounded older. Gravelly and hushed.

"Yes. I just came for a minute. Can I come in?"

He stepped aside with an old man's shuffle, old man's maroon slippers on his feet. "It's a bit of a mess."

She had never seen him this way, his hair all matted, his face gray and drawn. This was how he looked in private. It was how he must have looked to Josh that night, when she had been too miserable to notice. No wonder Josh was so . . .

As she passed the kitchen she saw dirty dishes stacked in the sink and coffee grounds scattered on the counter. The curtains in the living room were still closed. Newspapers, empty glasses, and ashtrays with cigar butts rested on every surface. His shoes were on the floor near the couch, pointing outward, laces hanging limply over the sides. Through the open door to his bedroom she glimpsed the unmade bed, blankets and sheets all jumbled. There was a stale smell in the air.

"Very homey, Max."

"I hate disorder. But . . . There's my coffee perking. Do you want some? Oh, no, you wouldn't be drinking coffee yet, would you?"

"No, thanks. How's your friend?"

"Which friend?"

"The one who got sick and was taken away in the ambulance."

"George. Hanging on. It got to his face this time, though. He'll probably have trouble talking. They can't tell yet how much of his brain was affected."

"That's too bad. Is he a very old man?"

"He's certainly not a very young man if he's here, is he? He would

132

have been better off dead, if you ask me, but these days they keep people alive no matter what. It's the accepted wisdom." He went into the kitchen.

She walked through the living room, brushing chairs and tables with her fingertips. When he returned with his coffee she cleared her throat and looked away. "I thought maybe you might change your mind about going today. As long as he's not . . . dead or anything. You'd still have time to get dressed."

"Why don't you take two friends instead, Alison? People your own age. You'll find the place all right."

"I wanted to take you."

He drank his coffee as if he hadn't heard. So close that she could reach out and touch him, yet he was unreachable. Like hide and seek, and he had crept into a deep, secret place this time; she would never find him. She wanted to grab the cup out of his hands and throw it at him.

"I think it's mean of you not to come. You know I had it planned for weeks."

"I'm sorry. It can't be helped."

"You're not sorry," she burst out. "You don't care at all! You don't care anything about me." She waited, but nothing came. "What are you thinking, anyway? Why don't you say something to me?"

He set down the cup. His hands were trembling. "I am thinking about trying to keep my temper so I don't have another heart attack. That is all."

"Oh." She blushed with shame and fright. "I guess I always say the wrong thing."

"Not always."

"I'll go."

He was up immediately and had the door open for her.

"Maybe I will take a friend. I have lots of friends, actually; I just never happened to tell you about them. Or maybe my father will come. My mother might even come too, if we drove and she didn't have to go on the train."

"Fine. And if for some reason you can't get rid of the tickets, let me know. I'll pay you back for them."

"I wouldn't do that. Good-bye, Max." She had to get out—her voice was shaking. "Say good-bye to Lettie for me."

He smiled faintly. "Surely this isn't *adieu?* I trust you'll be seeing her pretty soon? At the movies, or whatever?"

She started down the hall and didn't reply.

She bought a one-way ticket to New York City; finding a window seat, she placed her ticket in the slot in front, like everyone else. As they picked up speed she watched the river wind by way below, dotted with white sailboats so small and distant that they looked stationary: a photograph. It was hard to believe there were real people on them, maybe laughing and talking, out for the afternoon, or for the weekend, or forever. Some people lived on boats, Josh once told her, and stopped off at harbors for food and water. In thirty-five minutes she would be in the city, on her way to Madison Square Garden. She remembered it dimly from a circus of years ago, an odd-looking low white building with a broad border of concrete. And inside would be the real thing, not some dingy little mud show—scrawny animals in rusty cages, and shoddy equipment. Dilapidated trucks sloshing through the mud; a bunch of freaks and amateurs playing to pathetic dusty towns that didn't know any better.

If you stared very hard at the sailboats on the river you could see them moving. Those people were unattached and free to go anywhere they pleased. They could be seen by strangers at a great distance, but they could not be reached. Like her. No one in the world knew exactly where she was at this moment.

CHAPTER 12

SUNDAY EVENING Lettie was trying to persuade him to go downstairs for once and eat in the communal dining room. Talk to some new people, she urged; be distracted. No, he said. He didn't care to look at dying faces.

"You should have gone with Alison if you like young faces." If it was men he wanted, fine, she persisted. There were several others besides George whom he would enjoy talking to. She even described a few of them in detail.

"How come you know all these men so well?"

"Because I'm interested. A person doesn't have to act dead before they're really dead."

"When I first met you you weren't so full of wisdom. Now you're coining proverbs right and left."

"I won't say another word." She stalked off to his kitchen, where she began rummaging through the refrigerator and cabinets.

He followed her. "I don't like people dying on me, that's all."

"He's not dead yet. How would you like a tuna salad? Or maybe we should order a pizza. There's not much here."

"Tuna is okay with me. Oh, there it goes again." He left her to answer the phone. It was Alison's father, courteous this time. He hoped Mr. Fried remembered him? Ah, but exceedingly well. And might Alison be visiting him again, by any chance? With a diffident, embarrassed laugh. Certainly not. Once more, Max explained.

A brief, thick silence. He could hear Markman draw in breath. "She never told us you weren't going! Jesus Christ! I don't know where the hell she is, then. She should have been back over an hour ago." His voice rising in pitch was an eerily familiar ascent. "I knew I shouldn't have let her. Every time you're involved..." The voice floundered and crackled.

Max broke out in a sweat. He took the phone over to the couch and sat holding his head. Lettie came in from the kitchen and stood watching. "For Chrissake," he told Markman, "stop yelling and do something. Call the train station, for a start."

"I've done that already. I'll go down there myself and find her. Did she say anything to you? Did she have any . . . plans for after?"

Plans? Ah! Did she have plans! He had never taken her chatter very seriously—a big mistake. A failure of attention. No, of perception. As with Lettie, there was more to be known than he had exerted himself to know. "She didn't mention anything. But . . . she used to talk a lot about joining a circus. It could be—"

"Joining a circus! If I weren't almost out of my head I'd laugh. So that's the sort of nonsense you've been feeding her. Is there anything else? Is she in trouble? I know she tells you things she won't tell us."

"Trouble? You mean drugs? Boys?" He could have laughed too. "Oh, come on. With her it wouldn't be anything so commonplace. Look, I'll go down there with you."

"What for?"

"If she's there, I'll know better where to look."

"Okay. I'll be over in ten minutes." Markman clicked off.

He could feel the energy speeding through him as though they had shot it into a vein. He darted into the bedroom and Lettie followed. "Where are my shoes?"

"Max, you're not well enough for this."

"I know." His heart beat fast when he bent over to tie the laces. He brushed his hair in three strokes; a quick glance in the mirror, and he grabbed up his wallet and keys and stuffed them in his pockets. Like he used to.

"I haven't seen you so lively in a long time."

"Nothing like a trip to the circus to pep you up." He hurried into the bathroom.

She handed him his cane when he came out. "I'll go too."

He stopped dashing and very softly laid his fingers on her cheek. "Oh, you don't have to. You've had a bad enough month as it is."

"I'll just go back and get my purse."

He waited outside her door, tapping with a foot. The cane was in his fist but he wouldn't need it tonight. The sluggish machine inside was turned up to peak intensity, whirring like a propeller, parts lost in the spinning rush. He could run for miles. Even fly. It was like stepping into the circle of light, those many years; all excitement and fear and

136

cool control, so meshed you couldn't unravel them, so tangy you could almost taste. The premonition that something transcendent—a spasm like love—was about to take place.

Lettie opened her door. She had put on the clogs that were so comfortable you couldn't feel the ground beneath your feet.

"I'm ready." She took his arm.

Crazy kid. They must have laughed her out of the building. And then? On those seedy streets, skinny prey to anything? He didn't want to think about it. Because in the core of the whirring machine, supplying its brute energy, was a suspicion. Face it: he was implicated all right. He didn't know why it should be, for surely he hadn't wanted it, but if you lived among people you were implicated; what you wanted was irrelevant. Bumper cars, they all were, veering crazily, diverting each other's courses. And whether you crashed or got crashed, laughed or screamed, you couldn't get out of the action till the power was turned off. With Lettie, too, he had diverted a course, but then, Lettie had chosen it (hadn't she? What the hell was choice anyway?). And Lettie could take care of herself. Couldn't she? He held the door open for her as Markman's car pulled up.

In the front with him was a hugely pregnant blond woman whose pretty face was etched with anxiety. Calm, Max imagined, it might have a sort of petulant charm. She had Alison's big green eyes. The introductions were cursory and the silence, while they raced through town, dense and irritating as smog in the throat.

"I don't know, Wanda," Markman said when they hit the parkway. "Maybe you should have stayed home in case she gets back. She might need someone. . . . Who knows what may have happened?"

"How could I sit home alone and wait? The things going through my mind, the things I read in the papers! My baby!"

Max turned to Lettie. She wrinkled her brow in puzzlement; her lips curved in the subtlest of smiles. She put her hand over his, which was drumming on the seat between them.

"Alison can take very good care of herself," Lettie said. "She seems very—uh—advanced for her age, in certain ways. An unusual child."

"You don't know the half of it," her father replied. He was driving at least seventy miles an hour, zigzagging in and out of the left lane.

Her mother was crying. "Why does she always do these things to us? You never know what she'll do next! Just when you think she's settling down . . ."

Markman patted her knee. "Now don't get hysterical, Wanda. She

137

may be perfectly all right. There may be a perfectly reasonable explanation."

"Yes, maybe she stopped for something to eat," said Lettie. "Or to look around. She's so curious about everything."

Max said nothing. He pictured her crouched in a shadowy corner of a dressing room in her solar energy shirt and colored sneakers, her eyes softened to hazel and desperate, as he had seen them once.

"And the way she is about you two," said Wanda, gulping down tears. "I mean, I'm sure you're very fine people and have a lot to offer and all, but it doesn't seem normal for a girl of thirteen." She swiveled awkwardly to face them. "I don't mean anything personal. But it is a little funny, isn't it?"

"It's a little funny," Max agreed.

"I would like to know, Mr. Fried, what is the special attraction? Besides the fact that you can juggle, okay, I understand that. I mean, why. . . . What is it she can say to you that she can't say to us?"

Here was his chance. He could do the righteous thing, return her back where she belonged, even give them a few tips. But he found himself clinging to those hours, almost too swiftly gone now, when she had appropriated his chair to interrogate him, for every story from his past offering a fantasy from her future—not a bad exchange, since the whole world dangled before her like a radiant bubble, though tantalizingly out of reach. Her voice on the phone in his dark hours had been so unripe with infinite longing. And the wispy look of her, half naked under his blankets. Buried treasure wrapped there, for all he knew. He had been unable to take off her shirt. He couldn't betray her.

"Nothing much, really. She eats a lot, and chatters."

"I take her for ice cream sodas," Lettie volunteered.

"That's very kind of you," her father said.

"Chatters," said Wanda. "She doesn't chatter to me. I know she's having a hard time adjusting to the idea of the baby, but still . . ."

"That's enough, Wanda," said Markman softly. "We don't have to drag in everything."

The quiet was worse. Markman turned on the news, and the very air around Max tensed for the horror story, the body, mangled. . . . But there was only the price of gold, a terrorist on a plane to Cuba, the Vice-President back from a global tour. Weather, eternal. Warm, humid, hotter tomorrow. Degrees in Celsius—glad, at any rate, that he wouldn't need to learn all those conversions.

As they swooped round the series of curves that brought them into

138

the city, Lettie's hand in his slid to and fro on the seat. The city air was heavy and damp, and it was twilight. Lights were going on. Lights from both sides of the river rippled on the water with a softness that made him forget, for a moment, their errand. The sun, a hot amber ball poised at the horizon above a dimming skyline of concrete cubes strangely mellowed in the hazy light, was about to sink behind the western shore. They sped past a park along the river, where picnicking families cooked over open grills. The smell of charcoaled chicken drifted into the car, and Max inhaled with a stir of hunger. Below, a rusty barge floated, leaving a slow wake, a ripple of shimmering lassitude. He pressed Lettie's fingers. He looked at her bare arms, and want streamed through him. For her, in the flesh, and for so many things; a spring of wants, submerged, welled up. To have the kid back and lie on the grass in the cooling dusk like the picnickers and watch that amber sun slip down. All simple and all, perhaps, beyond him. But he let them stream unchecked, for the sole pleasure of such keen desire.

The car speeded up. The speed tugged against his growing lassitude, which echoed the foam behind the barge, uncurling now to blend into the river. Hurtling from lane to lane, they provoked a blare of horns. Max snapped alert, to feel the tension about him nearly palpable, drawn in taut lines like the electrical wires that laced the darkening sky. Lettie withdrew her hand and ran it over her face. The road narrowed.

At the Garden the evening show was starting. Max flashed a card—ancient souvenir—from his wallet and stated their business to a guard, who took them through a side door and up a flight of steep back stairs. As they were led through long corridors he could hear the audacious brass of the band from not far off. At last they came to a large open space crammed with people and animals, and his senses were assailed: sequin-costumed bodies whisked by, trailed by attendants carrying gleaming chrome equipment. Dogs in tiny cages yelped; parrots squawked. A juggler in a pink and yellow harlequin suit tossed pins before a cage of morose tigers, watching critically, while farther off, six ballerinas in green satin did warm-ups at a barre. On wooden benches against a wall, the clowns idled, smoking and drinking soda out of cans. Four men in white were leading a chain of elephants across the floor, the great backs heaving under glittery red tapestries. Dozens of painted faces, but nowhere her face, alive with that fragile look of expectation. Suddenly, not three yards away, a thin girl in blue appeared, riding bareback on a white horse; Max trembled and went rigid, till she turned and he saw her face. The same size and coloring, that was all the likeness.

He closed his eyes: the scene pressed too hard. "One minute," he said to Markman. "I have to sit down for just one minute." But from a bench near the entrance he forced himself to look, since it was a rare thing happening, a voyage in a time machine. With a series of small bounces in his chest he had landed back in his own past, in a private warp of history. It was exaggerated tenfold, yet in essence the same. All those heady sights and sounds were dupes, concocted to keep the eye and ear so busy that the heart doesn't grasp the passage of time.

The unseen band rolled to a fine high finish and stopped. A burst of applause broke like a dam collapsing, and a troop of boys and girls in blue came running in, glistening with sweat and laughing. Fugitives from time, like himself; their craving was for the moment, and they learned to swoop after each moment in its flight. They had no idea, poor things, why they flew so high and so fast. It was not his old age that shivered through him suddenly with an aching poignancy, but their youth.

He blinked. He had lost his tolerance for all this; his head hurt. Lettie touched his shoulder. "Are you all right, Max?" He got up. "Well, what now?" Markman asked bitterly. Max spoke to a lean black man checking the locks of the tigers' cages. He had not seen or heard of Alison, but he sent them on to someone else. After the fourth try Markman grumbled, "This is useless. I don't know why I ever listened to you."

"I've got to get out of here," Wanda said. "There's too much moving around. I don't feel well."

"Hang on. Where are the dressing rooms?" Max asked a young blond fellow with a beard, who was leading an elephant. He pointed. "Out that door, to your left, and down the hall."

Halfway through the long corridor they met three girls in red tutus. "Hold it, please." Max blocked their path. The closest one was tiny and dark, scarcely more than a child herself. "We're looking for a girl, around twelve or thirteen, thin. . . ." He could hardly describe her, she was so familiar. As if there were no other way for a child to look. "She was . . . probably trying to hide somewhere."

"Oh, yeah. That kid came in the dressing room for a minute. They got her out, though. I don't know what happened to her. Ask Rick.

That old guy there, at the end of the hall." She darted off with the others.

Clutching Markman's arm, Wanda gave a cry. Max ran, with Lettie behind him, calling to him to slow down. He couldn't slow down. She was very close; he could feel it. Any moment, that fragile, eager face.

"Why the hell don't you people keep an eye on your kids?" Rick grumbled. "That one led me some chase before I got her out. A few years older and I would have called the cops."

"But where did she go?" Markman shouted.

"How should I know, mister? Out the door! Shit, we ain't running no babysitting service."

"Idiot!" Markman yelled after the old man limping off. "You sent a kid like that out on the streets alone? Fucking idiot!"

Max pulled him back. "Cut it out. It won't get you anywhere. He's just a bum."

Wanda was collapsed against the wall, sobbing and beating her fists on the concrete.

Max grabbed Lettie's arm. "Let's get out of here," he said to Markman. "I think I know where she went."

"Another wild-goose chase? Where this time?" Markman's face was creased with exhaustion; his plaid shirt was wet and pasted to his chest. He was twisting the skin around his wrist.

"Penn Station. We talked about it once. I told her about the trains going west."

"Holy shit! What didn't you tell her, I'd like to know. You better be right this time." He scowled at Max, a puerile resentment at the corners of his lips. It made him look like Alison. So he expected wonders of him too. That like a magician, he should produce her. Well, he would produce her, dammit! He would conjure her up on a bench, reading a newspaper and eating a chocolate bar. Hershey's with almonds.

He tried to speak gently to them. "Look, it's worth a try. It's two minutes from here. After that, you're on your own."

He hustled Lettie through another door, into the public corridor and onto an escalator. Tripping on the top stair, he grabbed at her again. "Max, please, take it easy!" she cried. "You'll kill us both." As he steadied himself he had a swift vision of his body sprawled out and carried, brittle and bent, down the moving stairs. Old age was such a bitch. Behind him he could hear Wanda moaning.

141

The station was huge and cluttered too, but its colors were dull, its music piped in and synthetic. Weary weekend travelers hauling golf clubs and tennis rackets streamed from the Long Island Rail Road. Interrupting the Muzak, a booming male voice delivered a litany of arrivals and departures.

"We'll never find her here," Wanda wailed. "It's a madhouse!" Markman was supporting her with an arm around her waist.

"Not here," Max said impatiently. "This is only local." He pulled Lettie by the hand and up the stairs.

"Go ahead, Max," she said. "I'll catch up. I can't run so fast. Neither can she."

There was brighter light in the main waiting room, and less clamor. The space was inhuman in scale, dwarfing the porters pushing heaped-up suitcases on dollies. Around a newsstand, a crowd of kids in jeans, a class outing, played a shrieking game of tag; their cries trailed off in the vast upper reaches. The wail of an infant slung on its mother's back had a thin, spectral echo, while over everything a deep voice intoned: Chicago, Detroit, Minneapolis, Denver, Los Angeles. Max's heart thudded. She might be gone. Leaving Markman and the women far behind, he walked swiftly towards the banks of plastic chairs, where travelers and derelicts, appearing equally enervated, slouched and smoked. He spied the knapsack first, on the floor. Her legs were stretched out in the aisle, crossed at the ankles, and in her lap lay an open newspaper and the candy wrapper. Strands of hair had escaped from her ponytail to drift about her neck and cheeks. Her head was erect and she stared straight ahead, at nothing. His blood seemed to pause in its rush as he stopped to breathe. The others could wait—he needed this sight to himself. He had envisioned, suspended like a portrait within him, streaky sneakers and jeans and the T-shirt. But there she sat in a skirt and blouse—of course, this morning; he had not noticed—a real girl, with shoes like Lettie's, only smaller. His knees weakened; he felt his head begin to nod aimlessly, like an aged man's.

He went towards her. "Alison!" Meant it to be loud, but it came out like nothing. No voice. He called again. She looked up and came running. Behind him, too, they were shouting and running. But she was aiming for him, and she hit with the force of a bullet, a blimp, catapulting against his chest. As he locked his arms around her she leaped off her feet, to hang from his neck like an immense medallion.

The weight drained the air from his body, but that was all right. By will alone, she had staked out this claim, and he ceded; she could have him now. In a kinder world, a longing so great would be a valid claim.

He sat in the middle of the back seat going home, Alison on his left and Lettie on his right. Surrounded, and how very tired. Please, let her not keep chattering. There would be time enough tomorrow to hear it all. Behind the curtains of questions and explanations, he lapsed into a half sleep, half dream.

He is lying on a bed with Susie, not on any bed they ever lay in together, but the one at home, the wide bed at Pleasure Knolls. He has been so worried for weeks now, about losing her. Ever since he woke in the hospital to the deceiving face of the red-haired nurse, he has been losing her, and he cannot bear to lose her again. Of course she is gone, dead, he is not deluding himself. But now he has her back. He can feel every inch of her skin through the silky white nightgown. The lights in the room are bright so he can see her clearly too. Though he is next to her, holding her, through the generous magic of the dream he can see all of her, at the same time: she rests in his arms and in his eyes. She sleeps. He knows the dead cannot speak or see. But she feels. She knows he is there. She lies on her side, breathing quietly and steadily, as she always did, with her back to him. He lies with an arm and a leg flung over her, pinning her down, though there is no need to pin her down, she is not going anywhere any more, ever. He does not even wish to rouse her to make love; that is not necessary. He could not have her any more completely. And he is far too tired for that. It suffices, more than suffices, to hold her with an arm and a leg. Her red curls glint copper in the sunlight on her white neck. The top of her nightgown has slipped off one shoulder and the white curve is exposed. He puts his lips there. Her knees are drawn up: the long, bent line of the legs is an L. He can see the contour of her hip bone, under the light nightgown. She is still slim. She has one hand between her knees and one near her face. Her fingers splay out so he can read her palm. But the lines in her palm are all gone. It is a flat unmarked surface. Her mouth is open and the corners of her lips are wet. He pulls her closer.

He hears the car pushing through the night. Somewhere, he knows he is in a car but has forgotten why, a hurrying car in which a weary peace has settled. Twice, when he opens his eyes briefly to narrow slits, he sees darkness punctuated by quick shots of light. Flesh moves around him, but inside are only the two of them, he dreaming, she sleeping. Outside, voices are querulous, questioning; whines and relief.

Alison says: "Max, when they go up the tightrope with a table and chair, how do they—"

Lettie says: "Shh, he's sleeping." She squeezes his hand. Absently, out of habit, he squeezes back. That hand, that body, an easy, warm place. His. How do they what? He will never know.

Inside, Susie stirs. She turns towards him in her sleep. She will always be there now. He has everyone, gathered round him, and he is grateful.

When he was a boy, he remembers, and learned to swim, he dove underwater and fingered the floor of the river, picking at stones and roots. He liked to see how long he could stay under. Once he stayed too long. He fought his way back up, dreading that he wouldn't make it in time, filled with astonishment and fear and a brilliant excitement like cold fire inside. What would it feel like . . .? His eyes and chest were bulging, he saw green all around, then hit the surface. His mouth burst open for air.

And when he was a smaller boy, he remembers, his mother would sit by his bed and hold him till he was almost asleep, he was so afraid of the dark. When she left him he heard strange creakings and felt he was not alone; something invisible was in the room. He was afraid, and fell asleep in fear, and had bad dreams of falling off high places.

Now the car stops. A door clicks open.

Lettie says: "Come on, Max. We're back. Wake up."

Voices: "Thank you, Mr. Fried." "We can't thank you enough."

His left cheek is kissed softly by chocolate lips. He blinks his eyes open to the night.

Lettie says: "Come on, Max. Get up. Get out of the car."

He does as he is told, gets up and gets out of the car. He leans on her and steps forward in deep darkness. Inside himself, he holds Susie, over on her stomach now, and he is on top of her, covering her. He steps forward again and hits the pavement. Soft under him, still covering her.

He does not hear Lettie's screech: "Alison! Wait!" yelled against the starting whir of the engine. He does not hear the brakes, the car stopping short, the doors opening, the child running to kneel beside him.

144

CHAPTER 13

With enough will power you could control your thoughts and not get carried away. And if you were completely logical you would have to see that dead meant . . . dead. Finished; nothing even to think about. Dead bodies got sealed up in a box; they couldn't feel or know anything or, as in some silly books, send their spirits floating around invisibly, sort of keeping an eye on people. If that were true there would have to be God also, and God was even more illogical—she had figured that out a long time ago. If there were a God who was really good, why would he have made a world with so much wrong in it? And if he made it that way on purpose, to watch people suffer, then he wasn't good, so how could he be God? Either way, he didn't deserve to have anyone believe in him.

It was easy not to think about such things in the daytime. There was school, with finals to study for and lunch with Franny in the cafeteria. During gym they played softball outside, so she didn't have to see the ropes and bars in his corner, which Fats hadn't taken down yet. After three o'clock, if it was hot enough, she went to the town pool and hung out with Hilary and Bobby and the others from Max's group. Nick could do fancy jackknife diving and was teaching the rest of them. They seemed to form a clique, and she seemed to be part of it. It wasn't too hard, once you caught on, to act the way the other girls did—making a lot of noise and splashing, half friendly and half teasing towards the boys, but careful not to go too far in either direction. It was just one more trick of balance, like Max walking nonchalantly across the tottering seesaw. And if that tricky balance made you normal, well, okay, she could learn to do it. Because the other way was too hard. The other way you had wild daydreams that couldn't come true; you looked for work and were ignored and humiliated; you cared about someone and got left with . . .

Become the image, he said. Maybe you could choose what image to become and wipe the old image off the mirror. Maybe everyone had crazy thoughts and feelings but kept them well hidden, and normal was only an act, not the way anyone really felt inside.

In the dark, though, her thoughts ran wild. She woke in the middle of the night with weird ideas fluttering their hideous wings inside her head like bats; there was no stopping them. She saw him lying stiff in the cold ground, earth filling his mouth and nose, and felt the suffocation in her own mouth and nose. Then she would remember he was locked in a box, where each day the air grew more heavy and stale. The walls of her room drew close, and closer, and she stretched out her arms in terror, almost feeling their hard smoothness against her palms. Six feet of dirt above: how could you ever climb out? There was a weight on her chest and neck. It was hard to breathe. Her hands pressed upward against the lid of the box to force it open, and her fingers, curling and stretching like some tangled weed, made clawing motions through the earth. Her throat began to close.

She leaped up to turn on the light, and the walls went back in their place. At the window she took deep breaths, her heart pounding, and gazing into the dark sky, she thought about that Sunday in the city. How it appeared first, from the train: networks of wire spread across the sky, winding over and around the city like string. Rows of dirty brick buildings pressing tight together, holding each other up, the whole thing looking as though it might collapse any minute, like the cities she used to build with blocks and Lego sets. Then it all disappeared, and when the train came out of the tunnel and left her in the huge station, people darting fast as insects sped by her as though she were invisible.

All day she had been invisible. During the long walk across town and during the show not a single soul spoke to her or took any notice. Only later, when she sneaked away from the crowd on the escalators and toward the doors that said "Menagerie," did someone notice. The guard in the gray uniform yelled and chased, but she got away. And for a minute, that was a good omen. But in that big room, no one would answer her questions. Even the blond boy with the elephant, who stopped to talk, would not take her seriously. Would not *see* her. He said she should go home and write a letter to the manager, but secretly he was laughing at her. And the fat man leaning against the wall! His black hat was squashed flat on his head and his face was a pasty moon with a thin cigar hanging from the flabby lips. The moon rotated from side to side surveying the room; he didn't look at her except to wave her away with his fat yellowish hand, till at last, when she kept trying to explain, he bounded off the wall and leaned over close to her face, the smell of sweat and stale cigar enveloping her, and told her to get her little ass the hell out of there before he got really mad. So she ran. And at every door she tried, the same thing. Some of them acted nicer, but not one paid any real attention.

When she finally found Penn Station she didn't care about going west any more, or even about going home. It was a place to be, that was all. She wished she could disappear and not be anyplace. If she sat there long enough she would get weak from hunger and they would come and take her away somewhere, maybe to a hospital, or a home for runaway girls; it didn't matter, as long as she didn't have to work out any more plans. She was so tired of thinking.

But underneath everything was a secret, impossible wish, too impossible even to admit. She had wished he would come and find her. Suddenly to appear, needing to find her: it would be a miracle. And it happened! Exactly that way, so that the whole terrible day wasn't important any more. All that mattered was that he came for her. He was the net, and he caught her.

But then.

If he had really cared, he might have stayed alive just a little while longer. If you had a will to live, a reason. . . . Night after night she ran it through her head like a film, but the ending was always the same, Max lying flat on his face on the pavement.

Then she would read till the first light broke through the leaves of the maple, childish books she hadn't looked at in years: *A Little Princess,* long ago her favorite because of the heroic Sara Crewe, who should have been happy and rich and loved for all her talents, but was exiled instead to the garret of Miss Minchin's boarding school hungry and cold and alone—"You insolent, unmanageable child," Miss Minchin called her; "How dare you! How dare you!"—until the Lascar brings her hot food and kindles a fire in her room, and his master, the Indian gentleman, becomes her friend. But even before her dead father's fortune is discovered, even while she is still a beggar on the outside, Sara Crewe remembers that inside she is a princess. And at the end, when Mrs. Carmichael kisses her, Sara Crewe "felt as if she ought to be kissed very often because she had not been kissed for so long." She read it with shame at the comfort it gave her, for she was too old for that kind of comfort. She ought to know by now that she was not a princess, inside or out.

147

In the middle of the night on Friday she woke, shivering, to the sound of rain. Her nightgown and legs were cold and wet. The curtains at the open window waved back and forth; the wind howled. She got up to kneel at the window. Wet leaves lay scattered on the street. Two plastic chairs on the lawn opposite were overturned. She thrust out an arm: soaked and cold. In the dark and the storm she felt wild, not asleep or awake but in a wild state far from both. It was coming down in torrents on everything—the whole earth was sodden, and the graves. He was wet and cold. He had always hated the cold. If only she could . . . if she were brave . . . Yes, if she were older and brave and wild enough, she would go with an umbrella and. . . . No matter how crazy! She would stand over that patch of earth holding an enormous umbrella.

She shut the window and went downstairs. The grass of the back lawn chilled her bare feet. Wet hair hung about her face. Raising her hands, she made strange shapes with her fingers in the streaming dark. Her arms were like the trees, her fingers like the branches, swaying and twisting in the wind. She lay down on the grass. This is how it feels. The chill. The earth drenched and soft beneath you. The water pouring down on your skin. This. This is what he is feeling.

She tiptoed upstairs. Mustn't wake them, for this could not be explained. It came out of the dark of the night and the dark of her head, and had to be done. Back in her room, she did sensible things— dried herself and put on warm pajamas, hung the wet nightgown over a chair, changed the wet sheet. Wrapped in a blanket, she sat up reading the book he had loaned her, *And Then There Were None.* The people were killed off one by one, but since you didn't care it was very entertaining. Soothing: not real death at all, but a puzzle to be solved. She understood now why he had read them.

When she woke the tree was still against a pale-blue sky, every leaf suspended in a lush quiet, as though a mist had risen and vanished. It would be sunny and hot. On the bathroom mirror was taped a note: "Sat. 7:05. Dear Allie, Gone to Parkvale Hospital. Baby on the way! Will call as soon as there's news. Take care and don't worry. Love, Dad."

It was nine-fifteen; she might not be an only child any more. She wasn't sure if that felt good or bad. It didn't change who she was inside, which was something private and apart from the baby. The baby was harmless. She might help Wanda with it over the summer, maybe, if there was nothing better to do. When they went out at night

148

she could babysit. She would let it stay up as late as it wanted; they could keep each other company in the empty house. She would tell it things. The baby might like her even if she was slightly weird—it would be too young to know any better.

She went out to the back yard. There was the place where she had lain down during the night. The grass was almost dry now, in the sun. No evidence, except in her own mind. She looked perfectly normal—no one would ever have to know. She walked about fingering the leaves of trees and leaping to reach high branches, much higher ones than she could reach last June. What would it be like to feel yourself grow? Like stretching? Being pulled up by the shoulders? Or a slow expansion from deep inside, every cell pushing upward? Wanda's stomach had grown so gradually that you couldn't see the difference from day to day, yet over the months her shape had transformed. Now it would transform again in an instant, back to her real self.

Josh's flower bed was full of weeds; she knelt to yank up a few. The daffodils were all dead and the tulips were dying, but still, the weeds might choke next year's. It was right around this time, two weeks ago, that she had left the house and gone to his apartment. What a mess it was. Yet he hated disorder, he said. He wouldn't go. He was sorry, it couldn't be helped. He didn't sound sorry. He was trying to keep his temper so he wouldn't have another heart attack. But when he did have another heart attack he hadn't been angry at all. He had picked her up in his arms like a child, and held her. As she sat back on her heels to wipe her face, the phone rang. Max! She raced to the door. Oh, but he was dead.

"Allie? It's me. You have a sister, sweetheart! She's just about fifteen minutes old!" She had never heard Josh so excited. His voice sang out like the circus ringmaster's, introducing each new act. It vibrated along the wires, across the distance that separated them.

"That's great." What did Wanda say at moments like this? "Congratulations."

He laughed. "Congratulations yourself! Look, I'll get home as soon as I can and we'll do something really nice to celebrate. I just want to wait here till Mom wakes up."

"How is she?"

"She's fine. It was pretty quick."

"What's the baby's name?"

"We don't know yet. Maybe you can think of a good one. We were all prepared with boys' names this time, remember?" He paused.

"Now, Allie, does this make you feel a little better?"

He was pleading with her, to feel better. If only she could leap across the distance into his arms and stay there, a baby forever. But that couldn't be, especially not now. She swallowed and found her voice. "Oh, yes. It's very exciting."

He gave a brief sigh. "Okay, baby, there's someone waiting to use the phone. Sit tight and I'll see you soon."

"Maybe I could ride over on my bike."

"They wouldn't let you up, though. They're very strict about those rules."

She squeezed her eyes shut. "Wait. What does she look like?"

"Oh, very pretty. Like you looked—long and thin, and hardly any hair. With a loud voice, they tell me. Allie, I'd better get off now. See you soon."

She hung up. Now they could take the crib and carriage and Bathinette out of the garage and put them in the extra bedroom. Wanda was superstitious. Last Sunday, as Josh started carrying the crib across the lawn to the house, she had called to him, "No, wait!" in a strained voice.

"What for?"

"I don't know. It gives me a funny feeling. There's plenty of time for that."

"We don't even have any toys for it yet," Alison had said, watching at the kitchen door.

"Let's just wait, okay? There's plenty of time for toys too." Then, with a surprised stare, Wanda had smiled and spoken more gently. "Once it's born and we see that everything's all right, you can go and pick out any toys you like. How's that?"

Wanda had probably worried the first time too, and been relieved when she came out looking like a normal baby. In her head, though, there must have been something different. . .

She shook granola into a bowl, sliced in a banana, and poured milk over it. While she ate she tried to imagine the baby's crying filling the house. The cries little babies made didn't sound sad, really—babies didn't know enough to be sad. They sounded like angry protests against the world, whatever they could feel of it. Would this one protest a lot? Would it be the kind of baby you could have fun with, or a whimpering pain in the neck? It came from the same place she did, and had the same genes. A blood relation, while Max, actually, was nothing to her. "Blood is thicker than water," Wanda once said. That meant family ties were stronger than friendship: water flowed right out between your fingers, but blood stuck and stained.

When she finished eating she left a note for Josh on the kitchen table: "Be back soon. Shopping. A." On her bike, she sped round the corner.

After a few trips up the down and down the up escalators with the bulky gift-wrapped package under her arm, she stopped at the main-floor counter lined with bottles of amber perfume. They were giving free sprays. She was nudged from behind by a large, soft bulk.

"Alison!" Lettie cried, and threw her arms around her and kissed her, in the middle of Bamberger's.

Lettie's hair was soft and freshly waved. Shiny pearl-drop earrings hung from her ears. Her dress was golden yellow with a low square neck, and on her chest, smooth and creamy, rested a loop of tiny lacquered seashells.

"I thought I'd sample the perfume." Lettie tilted her head down as if with a secret. "Let's see what aromas they're pushing today."

Together they offered their wrists to be sprayed, and went through the revolving doors in an aura of Narcissus Reveries. "It's so good to see you," Lettie said outside. "How about a soda in Highet's, like we used to?"

Highet's was exactly the same: the polished wood floors sparkled, and the glassware behind the deep counter gleamed in the mirrors above. The rosy ladies in flowered hats on the posters looked something like Lettie. At their usual table they were greeted by the waitress with a face full of freckles and one bright-orange pigtail hanging down her back, and when she brought their ice cream sodas she said, smiling, "Enjoy it, ladies," as she always had. Yet it seemed centuries had passed since that other time, before it happened. She didn't feel like the person who used to have ice cream in Highet's with Lettie.

"What's in your package?"

"Toys. My mother had the baby, at last. This morning, in fact. It's a girl."

"Well, congratulations!" Lettie beamed. "That's wonderful! And how is your mother?"

"She's okay, my father said. They won't let me up to see her, you know."

"Yes, I certainly do know. Well, I'm very happy for you. And give your parents my best. Tell them I hope she's every bit as nice as you."

"Oh, I doubt if they'd want another like me." She licked coffee ice cream slowly off the long spoon. "I got her these soft blocks—they're big cloth cubes stuffed with cotton, and they have letters and matching pictures on them. Like an A, with a picture of an apple, and so on. I bet a baby could learn to read pretty early if it gets familiar with the letters. Do you think so? I mean, I might teach her, if she seems smart."

"Sure, why not? But give her some time. The first few months they can't do much except eat and cry." Lettie's face changed. She stopped smiling, and a shine came to her eyes as she put down her spoon and leaned across the table. "You can still drop in and see me if you like, even though he's gone. I want you to know you're welcome."

Alison looked down and sucked bubbles loudly through the straw.

Lettie leaned back. "Only if you feel like it, of course. Maybe you'd rather not." They were both silent. "There is one thing, though. Alison? Come on, look at me for a minute. I thought maybe I could give you a plant. He left me with so many to take care of, my window sill is overcrowded. Would you like to take one home?"

"I don't have any instinct for plants. It would probably die the minute I got it in my room."

"Nonsense. They're not that fragile," said Lettie. "All you'd have to do is sit it in the light and give it water when it's dry, and then leave it be—it'll take care of itself. You can come back with me and get it."

"I don't know. I have this big package to carry home on my bike. . . ." She paused. "You mean have it sort of like a—a souvenir, right? But it seems so. . . He didn't even like the plants, Lettie. He was always grumbling about them."

"You're mistaken—he did like them." She went back to eating her ice cream. Her earrings and necklace gleamed in the sunlight shimmering through the window. The yellow dress glowed golden. "But it's up to you, Alison. Whatever you want."

Lettie had always dressed in bright colors, but somehow they didn't seem right any more. In books, old ladies in mourning went about in black crepe and veils, with handkerchiefs damp from weeping clutched in their pale fingers. Of course, she didn't expect that, but still . . .

As she watched Lettie so calmly eating, a coldness drifted over her. She was sitting with somebody, yet she was secretly alone. All the people nearby, sitting together at tables and talking, might be secretly

152

alone too, and just pretending. They hid their lonely faces and pretended, the way she did with the kids at the swimming pool. All of them two-faced: inner and outer.

Lettie looked up abruptly, with a glance that slid through her like a beam of muted but extraordinary light. "Alison? What is it? What's the trouble?"

Her hands trembled. But it was only Lettie, who had never been shocked by her. "I don't understand how everyone can—how you can look so— Aren't you even. . . lonesome? Don't you even miss him?"

Again Lettie laid down the spoon, and sat back clasping her hands on the table before her, utterly still. "Sure, sweetheart. Sure I'm lonesome."

"But you—"

"It's private," Lettie said almost in a whisper. "Mine. It's too precious to parade in the street."

Alison pressed her fingers to her eyes. She had not cried since that night she slept in his bed, and she would not cry now.

"This has happened to me before, Alison," said Lettie quietly. "I know all about it. For you it's the first time, but for me it's probably the last. You have years and years. . . . This will fade, you'll see. You'll look back with a—"

"Oh, no!" she shrieked. How could Lettie say such trite things? It would not fade! She didn't want a vague memory. What she wanted was him. Now! She stood up and ran to the back.

In the bathroom she splashed cold water over her face and pushed a metal lever for the liquid soap. When she finished washing, there were streaks of blood on the towel—three slashes smeared pale across the grainy paper. On the tip of her third finger she found a slit a half-inch long, an arc drawn fine in the flesh. She looked around: it was the soap container—yes, a razor-sharp metal strip torn away from the lower rim. She put her finger in her mouth and sucked. More blood dripped down to her palm. There was no pain, only a slow streaming out of her body. She watched, mesmerized, as though the blood were someone else's.

It was her own, though, and she couldn't stop it; a part of her self oozing out, as it would all her life when she became a woman, as Wanda called it. She didn't want to become a woman. Bleeding was a little bit of dying, losing your own self. Everyone died their whole life long, then. Even the newborn baby would bleed and die. Poor baby.

She looked closely in the mirror and was frightened: her cheeks

153

were as pale as the sickly soap and her eyes were huge, the pupils, dark and dilated, crowding out the greener part. Her mouth hung limply open. She looked like those photos in magazine ads of faraway orphaned children—abandoned. Is that how I am? she thought. That was her image. He said to become the image. But no, please, not that!

The image in the mirror wasn't necessarily the real you. The real you was trapped somewhere inside with the blood and the muscles. Still, what you looked like, what you saw in the mirror, had to be you, didn't it? It wasn't anyone else. It was the you people saw, at least, and naturally they treated you as if that you were the real. If you couldn't, or wouldn't, show them who the real you was, how would they ever know?

As she stared, the face in the mirror began to pucker and crumple, dissolving. *He* knew! Savagely, she dashed water on her hand, enraged at her tears, her blood. "Max," she whispered, "damn you! Go 'way and leave me alone!" But the words didn't make any difference. There was still only him. Maybe another miracle would happen: he would climb up out of his stifling grave and find her again. When she stepped outside the door he would be waiting. He would heal her finger and see what was behind her face and take her away.

The door opened but it was Lettie, carrying the package of toys. "I thought you got lost in here," she said. "You're pale as a ghost. You don't have to sneak off to a bathroom to cry. You think I've never seen anyone cry?"

"I cut my finger on the soap thing. It's still bleeding."

"Let me see." Her hand was small in Lettie's. "It's a deep cut. Did you wash it?"

"Yes."

"It'll be all right. The bleeding is good for it." She pulled a yellow handkerchief from her purse. "Here, wrap this around and hold it up; we'll get a Band-Aid in the drugstore."

"Thanks. I didn't even feel it when it happened."

"You'll feel it later. Well, come on, you don't want to stay in here sniffling all day, do you? Believe me, you can be just as unhappy outdoors—only it's nicer."

"I'm looking in the mirror."

"And what's so fascinating in the mirror?" Lettie tugged her lightly by the hand. "You'll have plenty of time when you're grown up to look in mirrors."

"Do you think it's all right to. . . I mean, it is really possible to. . ."

154

"To what?"

To be who I am, she meant. But that was too foolish to say, even to Lettie. "Oh, I don't know."

"Why don't you figure it out later, sweetie? Meanwhile the sun is shining. Let's not waste it."

So she went, reluctantly, into the sunshine and among the secretive people. There was no place else.

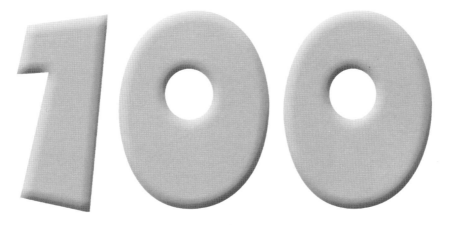

100
things you should know about
WEATHER

Clare Oliver
Consultant: Clive Carpenter

Miles Kelly
PUBLISHING

First published in 2002 by
Miles Kelly Publishing Ltd
Bardfield Centre, Great Bardfield, Essex, CM7 4SL

Copyright © Miles Kelly Publishing 2002

2 4 6 8 10 9 7 5 3 1

Editorial Director: Paula Borton
Art Director: Clare Sleven
Project Management: Belinda Gallagher
Assistant Editors: Nicola Jessop, Nicola Sail
Designer: John Christopher, White Design
Artwork Commissioning: Lesley Cartlidge
Proofreader and Indexer: Lynn Bresler

ISBN 1-84236-115-5

Printed in Singapore

British Library Cataloguing-in-Publication Data
A catalogue record for this book is available from the
British Library

ACKNOWLEDGEMENTS
The publishers would like to thank the following artists who have
contributed to this book:

Mark Bergin
Kuo Kang Chen
Steve Caldwell
Nicholas Forder
Chris Forsey
Terry Gabbey
Shammi Ghale
Alan Hancocks
Alan Harris
Kevin Maddison

Janos Marffy
Rachel Phillips
Martin Sanders
Peter Sarson
Sarah Smith
Rudi Vizi
Steve Weston
Tony Wilkins

Cartoons by Mark Davis at Mackerel

www.mileskelly.net
info@mileskelly.net

Contents

What is weather? 6

The four seasons 8

Fewer seasons 10

What a scorcher! 12

Our atmosphere 14

Clouds and rain 16

Not just fluffy 18

Flood warning 20

Deep freeze 22

When the wind blows 24

Thunderbolts and lightning 26

Eye of the hurricane 28

Wild whirling winds 30

Pretty lights 32

Made for weather 34

Weather myths 36

Rain or shine? 38

Instruments and inventors 40

World of weather 42

Weather watch 44

Changing climate 46

Index 48

What is weather?

1 **Rain, sunshine, snow and storms are all types of weather.** These help us decide what clothes we wear, what food we eat, and what kind of life we lead. Weather also affects how animals and plants survive. Different types of weather are caused by what is happening in the atmosphere, the air above our heads. In some parts of the world, the weather changes every day, in others, it is nearly always the same.

Equator

2 **Tropical, temperate and polar are all types of climate.** Climate is the name we give to patterns of weather over a period of time. Near the Equator, the weather is mostly hot and steamy. We call this a tropical climate. Near the North and South Poles, ice lies on the ground year-round and there are biting-cold blizzards. This is a polar climate. Most of the world has a temperate climate, with a mix of cold and warm seasons.

Mountainous

Desert

North Pole

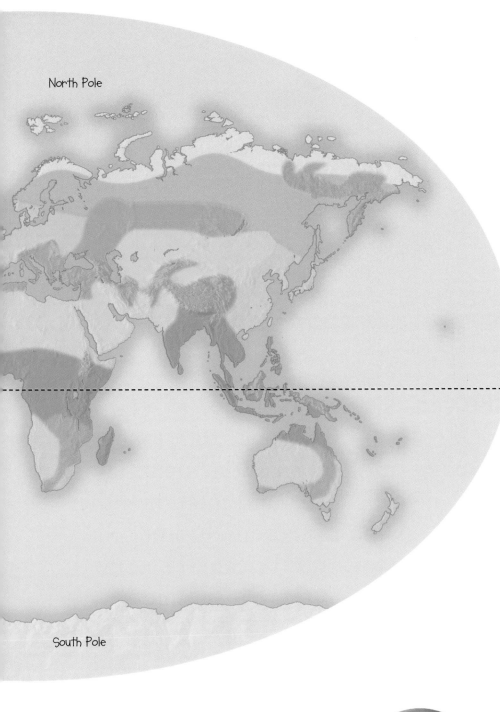

South Pole

Cold temperate

Wet temperate

Dry temperate

Polar

Tropical

▲ Look at the coloured rings to match the different climate scenes to the main map. In general, the warmest climates are found close to the Equator, an imaginary line around the middle of the world. The closer to the Poles, the cooler the climate.

The four seasons

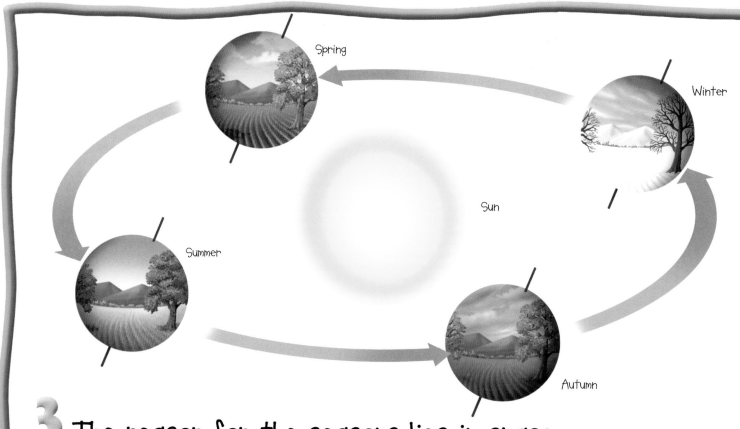

Spring

Winter

Sun

Summer

Autumn

3 **The reason for the seasons lies in space.**
Our planet Earth plots a path through space that takes it around the Sun. This path, or orbit, takes one year. The Earth is tilted, so over the year first one and then the other Pole leans towards the Sun, giving us seasons. In June, for example, the North Pole leans towards the Sun. The Sun heats the northern half of Earth and there is summer.

◄ Northern winter and southern summer happen when the Southern Hemisphere is tilted towards the Sun.

4 **When it is summer in Argentina, it is winter in Canada.** In December, the South Pole leans towards the Sun. Places in the southern half of the world, such as Argentina, have summer. At the same time, places in the northern half, such as Canada, have winter.

5 A day can last 21 hours!

Night and day happen because Earth is spinning as it circles the Sun. At the height of summer, places near the North Pole are so tilted towards the Sun that it is light almost all day long. In Stockholm, Sweden, Midsummer's Eve lasts 21 hours because the Sun disappears below the horizon for only three hours.

▲ At the North Pole, the Sun never disappears below the horizon at Midsummer's Day.

▼ Deciduous trees like these lose their leaves in autumn, but evergreens keep their leaves all year round.

I DON'T BELIEVE IT!

When the Sun shines all day in the far north, there is 24-hour night in the far south.

6 Forests change colour in the autumn.

Autumn comes between summer and winter. Trees prepare for the cold winter months ahead by losing their leaves. First, though, they suck back the precious green chlorophyll, or dye, in their leaves, making them turn glorious shades of red, orange and brown.

Fewer seasons

7 **Monsoons are winds that carry heavy rains.** The rains fall in the tropics in summer during the hot, rainy season. The Sun warms up the sea, which causes huge banks of cloud to form. Monsoons then blow these clouds towards land. Once the rains hit the continent, they can pour for weeks.

▶ When the rains are especially heavy, they cause chaos. Streets turn to rivers and sometimes people's homes are even washed away.

I DON'T BELIEVE IT!

In parts of monsoon India, over 26,000 millimetres of rain have fallen in a single year!

8 **Monsoons happen mainly in Asia.** However, there are some parts of the Americas that are close to the Equator that also have a season that is very rainy. Winds can carry such heavy rain clouds that there are flash floods in the deserts of the southwestern United States. The floods happen because the land has been baked hard during the dry season.

9 **Many parts of the tropics have two seasons, not four.** They are the parts of the world closest to the Equator, an imaginary line around the middle of the Earth. Here it is always hot, as these places are constantly facing the Sun. However, the movement of the Earth affects the position of a great band of cloud. In June, the tropical areas north of the Equator have the strongest heat and the heaviest rain storms. In December, it is the turn of the areas south of the Equator.

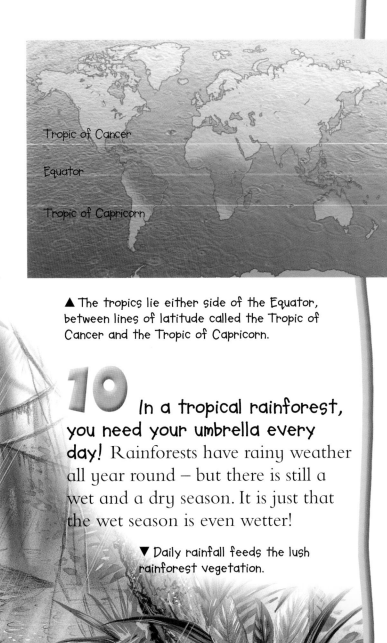

Tropic of Cancer

Equator

Tropic of Capricorn

▲ The tropics lie either side of the Equator, between lines of latitude called the Tropic of Cancer and the Tropic of Capricorn.

10 **In a tropical rainforest, you need your umbrella every day!** Rainforests have rainy weather all year round – but there is still a wet and a dry season. It is just that the wet season is even wetter!

▼ Daily rainfall feeds the lush rainforest vegetation.

What a scorcher!

11 **All our heat comes from the Sun.** The Sun is a star, a super-hot ball of burning gases. It gives off heat rays that travel 150 million kilometres through space to our planet. Over the journey, the rays cool down, but they can still scorch the Earth.

12 **The Sahara is the sunniest place.** This North African desert once had 4300 hours of sunshine in a year! People who live there, such as the Tuareg Arabs, cover their skin to avoid being sunburnt.

13 **The hottest place on Earth is Al Aziziyah in Libya.** It is 58°C in the shade – hot enough to fry an egg!

▶ Desert peoples wear headdresses to protect their skin and eyes from the sun and sand.

▼ A mirage is just a trick of the light. It can make us see something that is not really there.

14 The Sun can trick your eyes.

Sometimes, as sunlight passes through our atmosphere, it hits layers of air at different temperatures. When this happens, the air bends the light and can trick our eyes into seeing something that is not there. This is a mirage. For example, what looks like a pool of water might really be part of the sky reflected on to the land.

15 Too much sun brings drought.

Clear skies and sunshine are not always good news. Without rain crops wither, and people and their animals go hungry.

16 One terrible drought made a 'Dust Bowl'.

Settlers in the American Mid-West were ruined by a long drought during the 1930s. As crops died, there were no roots to hold the soil together. The dry earth turned to dust and some farms simply blew away!

▶ The 'Dust Bowl' was caused by strong winds and dust storms. These destroyed huge areas of land.

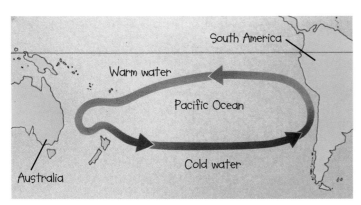

17 A sea current can set forests alight.

All sorts of things affect our weather and climate. The movements of a sea current called El Niño have been blamed for causing terrible droughts – which led to unstoppable forest fires.

◀ El Niño has been known to cause violent weather conditions. It returns on average every four years.

Our atmosphere

Exosphere
190 to 960 kilometres

Thermosphere
80 to 190 kilometres

Mesosphere
50 to 80 kilometres

Stratosphere
10 to 50 kilometres

Troposphere 0 to 10 kilometres

18 **Our planet is wrapped in a blanket of air.** We call this blanket the atmosphere. It stretches hundreds of kilometres above our heads. The blanket keeps in heat, especially at night when part of the planet faces away from the Sun. During the day, the blanket becomes a sunscreen instead. Without an atmosphere, there would be no weather.

19 **Most weather happens in the troposphere.** This is the layer of atmosphere that stretches from the ground to around 10 kilometres above your head. The higher in the troposphere you go, the cooler the air. Because of this, clouds are most likely to form here. Clouds with flattened tops show just where the troposphere meets the next layer, the stratosphere.

◄ The atmosphere stretches right into space. Scientists have split it into five layers, or spheres, such as the troposphere.

▼ The Earth is surrounded by the atmosphere. It acts as a blanket, protecting us from the Sun's fierce rays.

20 **Air just cannot keep still.** Tiny particles in air, called molecules, are always bumping into each other! The more they smash into each other, the greater the air pressure. Generally, there are more smashes lower in the troposphere, because the pull of gravity makes the molecules fall towards the Earth's surface. The higher you go, the lower the air pressure, and the less oxygen there is in the air.

▶ At high altitudes there is less oxygen. That is why mountaineers often wear breathing equipment.

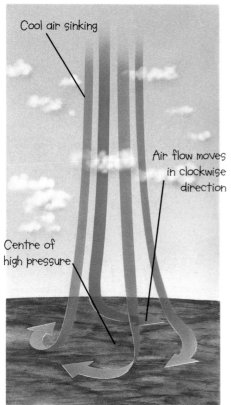

High pressure

Cool air sinking

Air flow moves in clockwise direction

Centre of high pressure

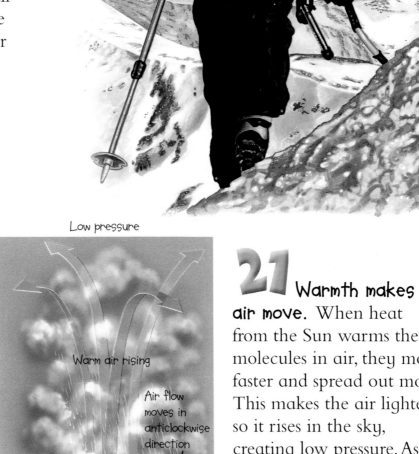

Low pressure

Warm air rising

Air flow moves in anticlockwise direction

Centre of low pressure

21 **Warmth makes air move.** When heat from the Sun warms the molecules in air, they move faster and spread out more. This makes the air lighter, so it rises in the sky, creating low pressure. As it gets higher, the air cools. The molecules slow down and become heavier again, so they start to sink back to Earth.

◀ A high pressure weather system gives us warmer weather, while low pressure gives us cooler more unsettled weather.

Clouds and rain

22 **Rain comes from the sea.** As the Sun heats the surface of the ocean, some seawater turns into water vapour and rises into the air. As it rises, it cools and turns back into water droplets. Lots of water droplets make clouds. The droplets join together to make bigger and bigger drops that eventually fall as rain. Some rain is soaked up by the land, but a lot finds its way back to the sea. This is called the water cycle.

▶ The water cycle involves all the water on Earth. Water vapour rises from lakes, rivers and the sea to form clouds in the atmosphere.

RAIN GAUGE
You will need:
jam jar waterproof marker pen
ruler notebook pen
Put the jar outside. At the same time each day, mark the rainwater level on the jar with your pen. At the end of a week, empty the jar. Measure and record how much rain fell each day and over the whole week.

23 Some mountains are so tall that their summits (peaks) are hidden by cloud. Really huge mountains even affect the weather. When moving air hits a mountain slope it is forced upwards. As it travels up, the temperature drops, and clouds form.

◀ Warm, rising air may be forced up the side of a mountain. At a certain level, lower temperatures make the water form clouds.

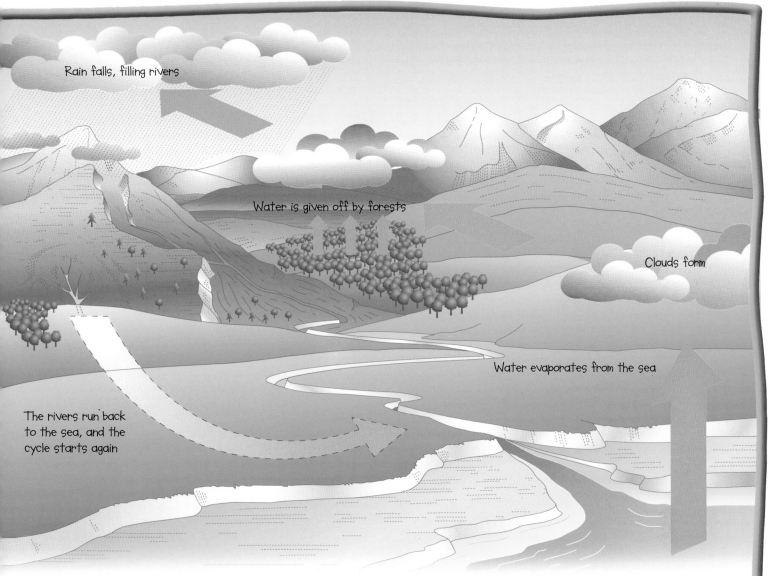

Rain falls, filling rivers

Water is given off by forests

Clouds form

Water evaporates from the sea

The rivers run back to the sea, and the cycle starts again

▼ Virga happens when rain reaches a layer of dry air. The rain droplets turn back into water vapour in mid-air, and seem to disappear.

24 **Some rain never reaches the ground.** The raindrops turn back into water vapour because they hit a layer of super-dry air. You can actually see the drops falling like a curtain from the cloud, but the curtain stops in mid-air. This type of weather is called virga.

25 **Clouds gobble up heat and keep the Earth's temperature regular.** From each 2-metre-square patch of land, clouds can remove the equivalent energy created by a 60-Watt lightbulb.

Not just fluffy

26 **Clouds come in all shapes and sizes.** To help recognise them, scientists split them into ten basic types. The type depends on what the cloud looks like and where it forms in the sky. Cirrus clouds look like wisps of smoke. They form high in the troposphere and rarely mean rain. Stratus clouds form in flat layers and may produce drizzle or a sprinkling of snow. Cumulus clouds bring showers or storms. These huge, cauliflower-shaped clouds look soft and fluffy – but would feel soggy to touch.

Cumulonimbus clouds give heavy rain showers

▶ The main classes of cloud – cirrus, cumulus and stratus – were named in the 1800s. An amateur British weather scientist called Luke Howard identified the different types.

27 **Not all clouds produce rain.** Cumulus humilis clouds are the smallest heap-shaped clouds. In the sky, they look like lumpy, cotton wool sausages! They are too small to produce rain but they can grow into much bigger, rain-carrying cumulus clouds. The biggest cumulus clouds, cumulus congestus, bring heavy showers.

Cumulus clouds bring rain

Cirrus clouds occur at great heights from the ground

Cirrostratus

Contrails are the white streaks created by planes

28
Sometimes the sky is filled with white patches of cloud that look like shimmering fish scales. These are called mackerel skies. It takes lots of gusty wind to break the cloud into these little patches, and so mackerel skies are usually a sign of changeable weather.

29
Not all clouds are made by nature. Contrails are streaky clouds that a plane leaves behind it as it flies. They are made of water vapour that comes from the plane's engines. The second it hits the cold air, the vapour turns into ice crystals, leaving a trail of white snow cloud.

Stratus clouds can bring drizzle or appear as fog

MIX AND MATCH
Can you match the names of these five types of clouds to their meanings?

1. Altostratus	a. heap
2. Cirrus	b. layer
3. Cumulonimbus	c. high + layer
4. Cumulus	d. wisp
5. Stratus	e. heap + rain

Answers:
1.C 2.D 3.E
4.A 5.B

Flood warning

▲ Flooding can cause great damage to buildings and the countryside.

30 **Too much rain brings floods.** There are two different types of floods. Flash floods happen after a short burst of heavy rainfall, usually caused by thunderstorms. Broadscale flooding happens when rain falls steadily over a wide area – for weeks or months – without stopping. When this happens, rivers slowly fill and eventually burst their banks. Tropical storms, such as hurricanes, can also lead to broadscale flooding.

31 **There can be floods in the desert.** When a lot of rain falls very quickly on to land that has been baked dry, it cannot soak in. Instead, it sits on the surface, causing flash floods.

◄ A desert flash flood can create streams of muddy brown water. After the water level falls, vegetation bursts into life.

32 There really was a Great Flood. The Bible tells of a terrible flood, and how a man called Noah was saved. Recently, explorers found the first real evidence of the Flood – a sunken beach 140 metres below the surface of the Black Sea. There are ruins of houses, dating back to 5600BC. Stories of a huge flood in ancient times do not appear only in the Bible – the Babylonians and Greeks told of one, too.

▲ In the Bible story, Noah survived the Great Flood by building a huge wooden boat called an ark.

33 Mud can flood. When rain mixes with earth it makes mud. On bare mountainsides, there are no tree roots to hold the soil together. An avalanche of mud can slide off the mountain. The worst-ever mudslide happened after flooding in Colombia, South America in 1985. It buried 23,000 people from the town of Armero.

▼ Mudslides can devastate whole towns and villages, as the flow of mud covers everything it meets.

I DON'T BELIEVE IT!

The ancient Egyptians had a story to explain the yearly flooding of the Nile. They said the goddess Isis filled the river with tears, as she cried for her lost husband.

Deep freeze

34 Snow is made of tiny ice crystals. When air temperatures are very cold – around 0°C – the water droplets in the clouds freeze to make tiny ice crystals. Sometimes, individual crystals fall, but usually they clump together into snowflakes.

I DON'T BELIEVE IT!

Antarctica is the coldest place on Earth. Temperatures of –89.2°C have been recorded there.

35 No two snowflakes are the same. This is because snowflakes are made up of ice crystals, and every ice crystal is as unique as your fingerprint. Most crystals look like six-pointed stars, but they come in other shapes too.

▲ Falling snow is made worse by strong winds, which can form deep drifts.

▶ Ice crystals seen under a microscope. A snowflake that is several centimetres across will be made up of lots of crystals like these.

► An avalanche gathers speed as it thunders down the mountainside.

38 **Avalanches are like giant snowballs.** They happen after lots of snow falls on a mountain. The slightest movement or sudden noise can jolt the pile of snow and start it moving down the slope. As it crashes down, the avalanche picks up extra snow and can end up large enough to bury whole towns.

39 **Marksmen shoot at snowy mountains.** One way to prevent deadly avalanches is to stop too much snow from building up. In mountain areas, marksmen set off mini avalanches on purpose. They make sure people are out of the danger zone, then fire guns to trigger a snowslide.

36 **Ice can stay frozen for millions of years.** At the North and South Poles, the weather never warms up enough for the ice to thaw. When fresh snow falls, it presses down on the snow already there, forming thick sheets. Some ice may not have melted for a million years or more.

37 **Black ice is not really black.** Drizzle or rain turns to ice when it touches freezing-cold ground. This 'black' ice is see-through, and hard to spot against a road's dark tarmac. It is also terribly slippery – like a deadly ice rink.

▲ Antarctica is a frozen wilderness. The ice piles up to form amazing shapes, like this arch.

When the wind blows

40 Wind is moving air. Winds blow because air is constantly moving from areas of high pressure to areas of low pressure. The bigger the difference in temperature between the two areas, the faster the wind blows.

▶ These trees have been forced into strange shapes by the wind.

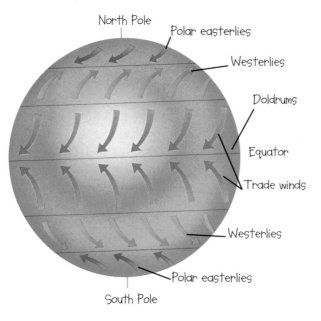

North Pole
Polar easterlies
Westerlies
Doldrums
Equator
Trade winds
Westerlies
Polar easterlies
South Pole

▲ This map shows the pattern of the world's main winds.

42 **Winds have names.** World wind patterns are called global winds. The most famous are the trade winds that blow towards the Equator. There are also well-known local winds, such as the cold, dry mistral that blows down to southern France, or the hot, dry sirroco that blows north of the Sahara.

41 **Trade winds blow one way north of the Equator, and another way in the south.** Trade winds blow in the tropics, where air is moving to an area of low pressure at the Equator. Their name comes from their importance to traders, when goods travelled by sailing ship.

QUIZ
1. At what temperature does water freeze?
2. What does the Beaufort Scale measure?
3. What are the mistral and sirroco?
4. How many sides does an ice crystal usually have?

Answers:
1. 0°C
2. Wind strength
3. Local winds 4. Six

43

You can tell how windy it is by looking at the leaves on a tree. Wind ranges from light breezes to hurricanes. Its strength is measured on the Beaufort Scale, named after the Irish admiral who devised it. The scale ranges from Force 0, meaning total calm, to Force 12, which is a hurricane

▶ The Beaufort Scale.

Force 0: Calm

Force 1: Light air

Force 2: Light breeze

Force 3: Gentle breeze

Force 4: Moderate breeze

Force 5: Fresh breeze

Force 6: Strong breeze

Force 7: Near gale

Force 8: Gale

Force 9: Strong gale

Force 10: Storm

Force 11: Violent storm

Force 12: Hurricane

44

Wind can turn on your TV. People can harness the energy of the wind to make electricity for our homes. Tall turbines are positioned in windy spots. As the wind turns the turbine, the movement powers a generator and produces electrical energy.

45

Wind can make you mad! The Föhn wind, which blows across Switzerland, Austria and Bavaria in southern Germany, brings with it changeable weather. This has been blamed for road accidents and even bouts of madness!

Thunderbolts and lightning

46 **Thunderstorms are most likely in summer.** Hot weather creates warm, moist air that rises and forms towering cumulonimbus clouds. Inside each cloud, water droplets and ice crystals bang about, building up positive and negative electrical charges. Electricity flows between the charges, creating a flash that heats the air around it. Lightning is so hot that it makes the air expand, making a loud noise or thunderclap. Cloud-to-cloud lightning is called sheet lightning, while lightning travelling from the cloud to the ground is called fork lightning.

47 Lightning comes in different colours. If there is rain in the thundercloud, the lightning looks red; if there's hail, it looks blue. Lightning can also be yellow or white.

▼ Lightning conductors absorb the shock and protect tall buildings.

▶ Dramatic lightning flashes light up the sky.

48 Tall buildings are protected from lightning. Church steeples and other tall structures are often struck by bolts of lightning. This could damage the building, or give electric shocks to people inside, so lightning conductors are placed on the roof. These channel the lightning safely away.

HOW CLOSE?

Lightning and thunder happen at the same time, but light travels faster than sound. Count the seconds between the flash and the clap and divide them by three. This is how many kilometres away the storm is.

49 A person can survive a lightning strike. Lightning is very dangerous and can give a big enough shock to kill you. However, an American park ranger called Roy Sullivan survived being struck seven times.

▼ A sudden hail storm can leave the ground littered with small chunks of ice.

50 Hailstones can be as big as melons! These chunks of ice can fall from thunderclouds. The biggest ever fell in Gopaljang, Bangladesh, in 1986 and weighed 1 kilogram each!

Eye of the hurricane

51 Some winds travel at speeds of more than 120 kilometres per hour. Violent tropical storms happen when strong winds blow into an area of low pressure and start spinning very fast. They develop over warm seas and pick up speed until they reach land, where there is no more moist sea air to feed them. Such storms bring torrential rain.

52 The centre of a hurricane is calm and still. This part is called the 'eye'. As the eye of the storm passes over, there is a pause in the terrifying rains and wind.

▼ This satellite photograph of a hurricane shows how the storm whirls around a central, still 'eye'.

I DON'T BELIEVE IT!

Tropical storms are called different names. Hurricanes develop over the Atlantic, typhoons over the Pacific, and cyclones over the Indian Ocean.

▶ A Hurricane Hunter heads into the storm.

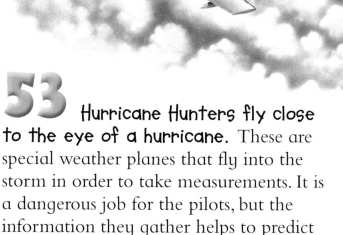

53 Hurricane Hunters fly close to the eye of a hurricane. These are special weather planes that fly into the storm in order to take measurements. It is a dangerous job for the pilots, but the information they gather helps to predict the hurricane's path – and saves lives.

▲ A hurricane brings battering rain and massive waves.

54 **Hurricanes have names.** One of the worst hurricanes was Hurricane Andrew, which battered the coast of Florida in 1992. Perhaps there is a hurricane named after you!

55 **Hurricanes whip up wild waves.** As the storm races over the ocean, the winds create giant waves. These hit the shore as a huge sea surge. In 1961, the sea surge following Hurricane Hattie washed away Belize City in South America.

56 **Typhoons saved the Japanese from Genghis Khan.** The 13th-century Mongol leader made two attempts to invade Japan – and both times, a terrible typhoon battered his fleet and saved the Japanese!

▶ A typhoon prevented Genghis Khan's navy from invading Japan.

Wild whirling winds

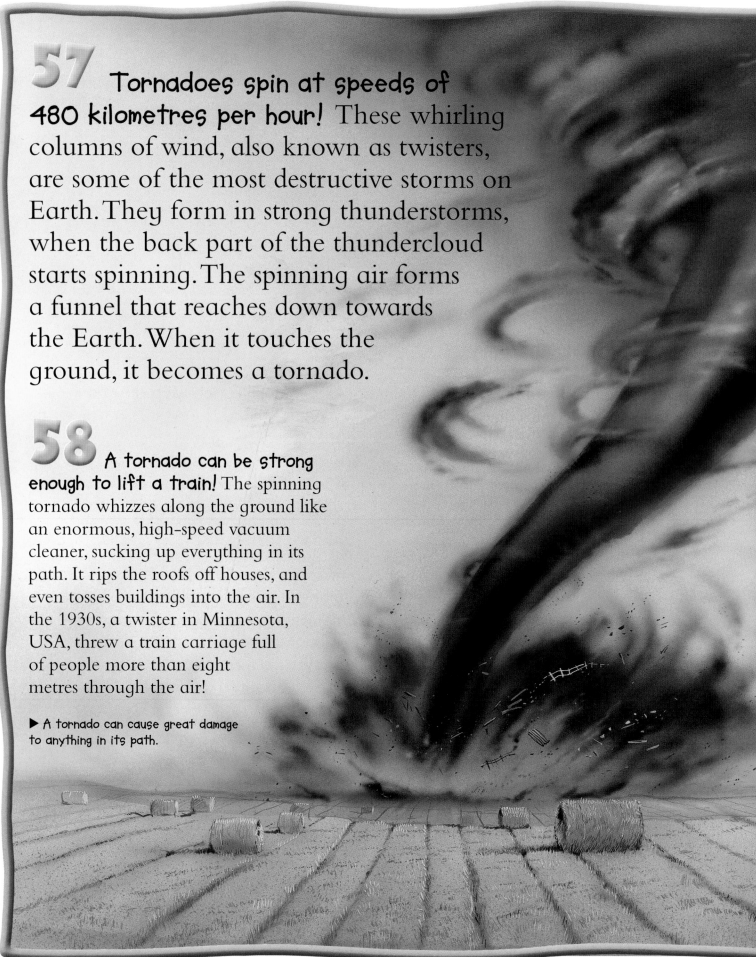

57 **Tornadoes spin at speeds of 480 kilometres per hour!** These whirling columns of wind, also known as twisters, are some of the most destructive storms on Earth. They form in strong thunderstorms, when the back part of the thundercloud starts spinning. The spinning air forms a funnel that reaches down towards the Earth. When it touches the ground, it becomes a tornado.

58 **A tornado can be strong enough to lift a train!** The spinning tornado whizzes along the ground like an enormous, high-speed vacuum cleaner, sucking up everything in its path. It rips the roofs off houses, and even tosses buildings into the air. In the 1930s, a twister in Minnesota, USA, threw a train carriage full of people more than eight metres through the air!

▶ A tornado can cause great damage to anything in its path.

59 Tornado Alley is a twister hotspot in the American Mid-West. This is where hot air travelling north from the Gulf of Mexico meets cold polar winds travelling south, and creates huge thunderclouds. Of course, tornadoes can happen anywhere in the world when the conditions are right.

▲ The shaded area shows Tornado Alley, where there are hundreds of tornadoes each year.

60 A pillar of whirling water can rise out of a lake or the sea. Waterspouts are spiralling columns of water that can be sucked up by a tornado as it forms over a lake or the sea. They tend to spin more slowly than tornadoes, because water is much heavier than air.

▲ Waterspouts can suck up fish living in a lake!

I DON'T BELIEVE IT !

Loch Ness in Scotland is famous for sightings of a monster nicknamed Nessie. Perhaps people who have seen Nessie were really seeing a waterspout.

61 Dust devils are desert tornadoes. They shift tonnes of sand and cause terrible damage – they can strip the paintwork from a car in seconds!

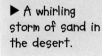

▶ A whirling storm of sand in the desert.

Pretty lights

62 **Rainbows are made up of seven colours.** They are caused by sunlight passing through falling raindrops. The water acts like a glass prism, splitting the light. White light is made up of seven colours – red, orange, yellow, green, blue, indigo and violet – so these are the colours, from top to bottom, that make up the rainbow.

REMEMBER IT!

Richard Of York Gave Battle In Vain

The first letter of every word of this rhyme gives the first letter of each colour of the rainbow – as it appears in the sky:

**Red Orange Yellow
Green Blue
Indigo Violet**

63 Two rainbows can appear at once. The top rainbow is a reflection of the bottom one, so its colours appear the opposite way round, with the violet band at the top and red at the bottom.

64 Some rainbows appear at night. They happen when falling raindrops split moonlight, rather than sunlight. This sort of rainbow is called a moonbow.

▲ Although a fogbow is colourless, its inner edge may appear slightly blue and its outer edge slightly red.

65 **It is not just angels that wear halos!** When you look at the Sun or Moon through a curtain of ice crystals, they seem to be surrounded by a glowing ring of light called a halo.

66 **Three suns can appear in our sky!** 'Mock suns' are two bright spots that appear on either side of the Sun. They often happen at the same time as a halo, and have the same cause – light passing through ice crystals in the air.

▼ An aurora – the most dazzling natural light show on Earth!

▶ Mock suns are also known as parhelia or sundogs.

67 **Some rainbows are just white.** Fogbows happen when sunlight passes through a patch of fog. The water droplets in the fog are too small to work like prisms, so the arching bow is white or colourless.

▲ A halo looks like a circle of light surrounding the Sun or Moon.

68 **Auroras are curtains of lights in the sky.** They happen in the far north or south of the world when light particles from the Sun smash into molecules in the air – at speeds of 1600 kilometres per hour. The lights may be blue, red or yellow.

Made for weather

69 Camels can go for two weeks without a drink. These animals are adapted to life in a hot, dry climate. They do not sweat until their body temperature hits 40°C, which helps them to save water. The humps on their backs are fat stores, which are used for energy when food and drink is scarce.

70 Lizards lose salt through their noses. Most animals get rid of excess salt in their urine, but lizards, such as iguanas and geckos, live in dry parts of the world. They need to lose as little water from their bodies as possible.

71 Even toads can survive in the desert. The spadefoot toad copes with desert conditions by staying underground in a burrow for most of the year. It only comes to the surface after a shower of rain.

Camel

Iguana

Banded gecko

◄ These animals have adapted to life in very dry climates. However, they live in different deserts around the world.

Spadefoot toad

▶ Beneath its gleaming-white fur, the polar bear's skin is black to absorb heat from the Sun.

72 **Polar bears have black skin.** Polar bears have all sorts of special ways to survive the polar climate. Plenty of body fat and thick fur keeps them snug and warm, while their black skin soaks up as much warmth from the Sun as possible.

73 **Acorn woodpeckers store nuts for winter.** Animals in temperate climates have to be prepared if they are to survive the cold winter months. Acorn woodpeckers turn tree trunks into larders. During autumn, when acorns are ripe, the birds collect as many as they can, storing them in holes that they bore into a tree.

▶ Storing acorns helps this woodpecker survive the cold winter months.

Weather myths

74 **People once thought the Sun was a god.** The sun god was often considered to be the most important god of all, because he brought light and warmth and ripened crops. The ancient Egyptians built pyramids that pointed up to their sun god, Re, while the Aztecs believed that their sun god, Huitzilpochtli, had even shown them where to build their capital city.

75 **The Vikings thought a god brought thunder.** Thor was the god of war and thunder, worshipped across what is now Scandinavia. The Vikings pictured Thor as a red-bearded giant. He carried a hammer that produced bolts of lightning. Our day, Thursday, is named in Thor's honour.

◄ In Scandinavian mythology, Thor was the god of thunder.

▲ The Egyptian sun god, Re, was often shown with the head of a falcon.

76 **Hurricanes are named after a god.** The Mayan people lived in Central America, the part of the world that is most affected by hurricanes. Their creator god was called Huracan.

77 Totem poles honoured the Thunderbird.

Certain tribes of Native American Indians built tall, painted totem poles, carved in the image of the Thunderbird. They wanted to keep the spirit happy, because they thought it brought rain to feed the plants.

▶ A Native American Indian totem pole depicting the spirit of the Thunderbird.

78 People once danced for rain.

In hot places such as Africa, people developed dances to bring rain. These were performed by the village shaman (religious woman or man), using wooden instruments such as bullroarers. Sometimes water was sprinkled on the ground. Rain dances are still performed in some countries today.

◀ Shamans wore a special costume for their rain dance.

MAKE A BULLROARER

You will need:

a wooden ruler   some string

Ask an adult to drill a hole in one end of the ruler. Thread through the string, and knot it, to stop it slipping through the hole. In an open space, whirl the instrument above your head to create a wind noise!

Rain or shine?

79 **Seaweed can tell us if rain is on the way.** Long ago, people looked to nature for clues about the weather. One traditional way of forecasting was to hang up strands of seaweed. If the seaweed stayed slimy, the air was damp and rain was likely. If the seaweed shrivelled up, the weather would be dry.

▲ Kelp picks up any moisture in the air, so it is a good way of telling how damp the atmosphere is.

I DON'T BELIEVE IT!

People used to say that cows lay down when rain was coming – but there is no truth in it! They lie down whether rain is on the way or not!

80 **'Red sky at night is the sailor's delight'.** This is one of the most famous pieces of weather lore and means that a glorious sunset is followed by a fine morning. The saying is also known as 'shepherd's delight'. There is no evidence that the saying is true, though.

81 **Groundhogs tell the weather when they wake.** Of course, they don't really, but in parts of the USA, Groundhog Day is a huge celebration. On 2 February, people gather to see the groundhog come out. If you see the creature's shadow, it means there are six more weeks of cold to come.

▼ A blood-red sunset is delightful to look at, but it can't help a sailor to predict the next day's weather.

▲ The Moon is clearly visible in a cloudless night sky. Its light casts a silvery glow over the Earth.

82 "Clear moon, frost soon". This old saying does have some truth in it. If there are few clouds in the sky, the view of the Moon will be clear – and there will also be no blanket of cloud to keep in the Earth's heat. That makes a frost more likely – during the colder months, at least.

83 The earliest weather records are over 3000 years old. They were found on a piece of tortoiseshell and had been written down by Chinese weather watchers. The inscriptions describe when it rained or snowed and how windy it was.

◄ Records of ancient weather were scratched on to this piece of shell.

Instruments and inventors

84 The Tower of Winds was built 2000 years ago. It was an eight-sided building and is the first known weather station. It had a wind vane on the roof and a water clock inside.

▲ The Tower of Winds was built by Andronicus of Cyrrhus in Athens around 75BC. Its eight sides faced the points of the compass: north, northeast, east, southeast, south, southwest, west and northwest.

85 The first barometer was made by one of Galileo's students. Barometers measure air pressure. The first person to describe air pressure – and to make an nstrument for measuring it – was an Italian, Evangelista Torricelli. He had studied under the great scientist Galileo. Torricelli made his barometer in 1643.

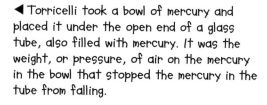

◄ Torricelli took a bowl of mercury and placed it under the open end of a glass tube, also filled with mercury. It was the weight, or pressure, of air on the mercury in the bowl that stopped the mercury in the tube from falling.

86 Weather cocks have a special meaning. They have four pointers that show the directions of north, south, east and west. The cockerel at the top swivels so that its head always shows the direction of the wind.

▶ Weather cocks are often placed on top of church steeples.

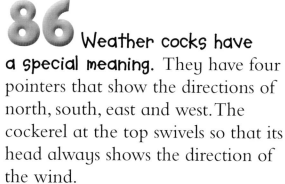

87

A weather house really can predict the weather. It is a type of hygrometer – an instrument that detects how much moisture is in the air. If there is lots, the rainy-day character comes out of the door!

▶ Weather houses have two figures. One comes out when the air is damp and the other when the air is dry.

88

Fahrenheit made the first thermometer in 1714. Thermometers are instruments that measure temperature. Gabriel Daniel Fahrenheit invented the thermometer using a blob of mercury sealed in an airtight tube. The Fahrenheit scale for measuring heat was named after him. The Centigrade scale was introduced in 1742 by the Swedish scientist Anders Celsius.

◀ This early thermometer shows both the Fahrenheit and the Celsius temperature scales.

QUIZ
1. What is another name for the liquid metal, mercury?
2. What does an anemometer measure?
3. What does a wind vane measure?
4. On the Fahrenheit scale, at what temperature does water freeze?

Answers:
1. Quicksilver 2. Wind speed 3. Wind direction 4. 32°F

World of weather

89 Working out what the weather will be like is called forecasting. By looking at changes in the atmosphere, and comparing them to weather patterns of the past, forecasters can make an accurate guess at what the weather will be tomorrow, the next day, or even further ahead than that. But even forecasters get it wrong sometimes!

90 The first national weather offices appeared in the 1800s. This was when people realized that science could explain how weather worked – and save people from disasters. The first network of weather stations was set up in France, in 1855. This was after the scientist Le Verrier showed how a French warship, sunk in a storm, could have been saved. Le Verrier explained how the path of the storm could have been tracked, and the ship sailed to safety.

A cold front is shown by a blue triangle

A warm front is shown by a red semi-circle

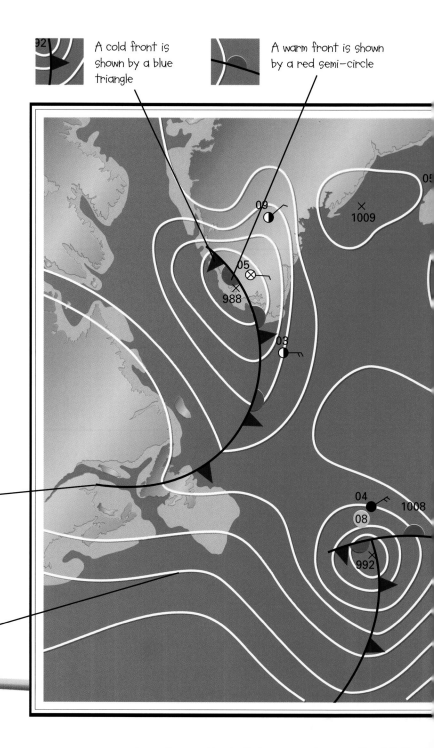

Look for the black lines with red semi-circles and blue triangles – they represent an occluded front, where a cold front meets a warm front

These white lines are isobars – they connect places where air pressure is the same

WEATHER SYMBOLS

Learn how to represent the weather on your own synoptic charts. Here are some of the basic symbols to get you started. You may come across them in newspapers or while watching television. Can you guess what they mean?

91 **Nations need to share weather data.** By 1865, nearly 60 weather stations across Europe were swapping information. These early weather scientists, or meteorologists, realized that they needed to present their information using symbols that they could all understand. To this day, meteorologists plot their findings on maps called synoptic charts. They use lines called isobars to show which areas have the same air pressure. The Internet makes it easier for meteorologists to access information.

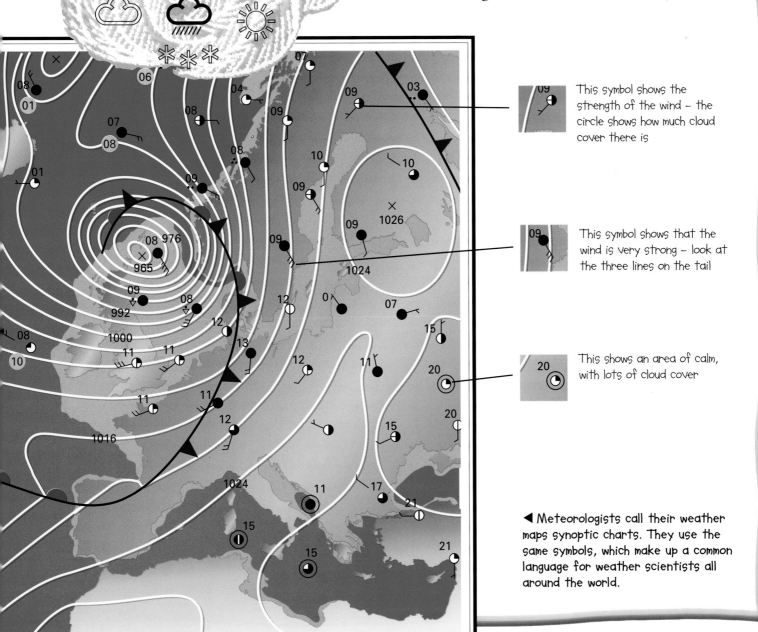

This symbol shows the strength of the wind – the circle shows how much cloud cover there is

This symbol shows that the wind is very strong – look at the three lines on the tail

This shows an area of calm, with lots of cloud cover

◀ Meteorologists call their weather maps synoptic charts. They use the same symbols, which make up a common language for weather scientists all around the world.

Weather watch

92 **Balloons can tell us about the weather.**
Weather balloons are hot-air balloons that are sent
high into the atmosphere. As they rise, onboard
equipment takes readings. These find out air pressure,
and how moist, or humid, the air is, as well as how
warm. The findings are radioed back
to meteorologists on the ground,
using a system called
radiosonde. Hundreds of
balloons are launched
around the world every day.

▶ A weather balloon carries its scientific
instruments high into the atmosphere.

93 **Some planes hound the
weather.** Weather planes provide more
atmospheric measurements than balloons
can. *Snoopy* is the name of one of the British
weather planes. The instruments are carried
on its long, pointy nose, so they can test the
air ahead of the plane.

▼ *Snoopy's* long nose carries all the equipment
needed to monitor the weather.

94 Satellites help save lives. Their birds'-eye view of the Earth allows them to take amazing pictures of our weather systems. They can track hurricanes as they form over the oceans. Satellite-imaging has helped people to leave their homes and get out of a hurricane's path just in time.

I DON'T BELIEVE IT!

Some of the best weather photos have been taken by astronauts in space.

95 Some weather stations are all at sea. Weather buoys float on the surface of the oceans, measuring air pressure, temperature and wind direction. They are fitted with transmitters that beam information to satellites in space – which bounce the readings on to meteorologists. Tracking the buoys is just as important. They are carried along by ocean currents, which have a huge effect on our weather systems.

▲ A weather satellite takes photographs of Earth's weather systems from space.

▶ Currents carry the floating weather buoys around the oceans.

Changing climate

96 Climate change destroyed the dinosaurs – but no one can agree on what caused it. The best explanation is that a huge piece of space rock, called a meteorite, smashed into Earth. It threw up a giant cloud of dust that blocked out the Sun, plunging the world into cold and dark.

▼ Could a meteorite have crashed to Earth and changed the climate? A meteorite crater found in the Gulf of Mexico dates to 65 million years ago – exactly the time that the dinosaurs died out. Perhaps the impact changed the warm climate the dinosaurs were so used to.

▼ Vikings settled on Greenland's coastline. Inland areas were covered in ice.

97 Greenland used to be green! This island lies in the Arctic Ocean and is mostly covered by a huge ice sheet. Even in Viking times, Greenland was cold, but Viking settlers built at least two farming colonies there. These died out around the 1400s, after the climate cooled.

98

A volcano can change the climate! Big volcanic explosions can create dust that blots out the Sun, just as a meteorite impact can. Dust from the 1815 eruption of a volcano called Tambora did this. This made many crops fail around the world and many people starved.

99

Tree-felling is affecting our weather. In areas of Southeast Asia and South America, rainforests are being cleared for farming. When the trees are burned, the fires release carbon dioxide – a greenhouse gas which helps to blanket the Earth and keep in the heat. Unfortunately, high levels of carbon dioxide raise the temperature too much.

◀ Like all plants, rainforest trees take in carbon dioxide and give out oxygen. As rainforests are destroyed, the amount of carbon dioxide in the atmosphere increases.

100

Air temperatures are rising. Scientists think the average world temperature may increase by around 1.5 °C this century. This may not sound like much, but the extra warmth will mean more storms, including hurricanes and tornadoes, and more droughts too.

Carbon dioxide layer traps heat

Heat from the Sun

Trapped heat bounces back to Earth

QUIZ

1. What may have caused the death of the dinosaurs?
2. Which settlers once lived along the coast of Greenland?
3. Which gas do plants take in?

Answers:
1. Meteorite impact 2. Vikings 3. Carbon dioxide

▶ Too much carbon dioxide in the atmosphere creates a 'greenhouse effect'. Just as glass traps heat, so does carbon dioxide. This means more storms and droughts.

Index

A B C
air **14**, **15**, 24
air pressure **15**, 24, 40
Antarctica 22, 23
atmosphere **14–15**
auroras **33**
autumn 9, 34
avalanches **23**
barometer **40**
Beaufort Scale **25**
black ice **23**
bullroarers 37
camels, and the desert 34
carbon dioxide gas 47
Centigrade/Celsius scale 41
climate **6**, 46
clouds 14, **16–17**
    types of **18–19**, 26
coldest place on Earth 22
contrails 19
currents, sea/ocean 13, 45
cyclones 28

D E F G
day 9
deserts 12, 20, 31
    animals 34
    peoples 12
droughts **13**
Dust Bowl, America 13
dust devils 31
Earth, orbit around Sun 8, 9
El Niño 13
electricity 24, 26
Fahrenheit scale 41
fogbows 32
floods 10, **20–21**
forecasting **38–39**, **42–43**
gods and goddesses 21, 36
Great Flood **21**
Greenland **46**
Groundhog Day 38

H I L M
hailstones 27
heat 12, 14
high pressure 15, 24
hottest place on Earth 12
Hurricane Hunters 28
hurricanes **28–29**
    names 29, 36

hygrometer 41
ice crystals **22**
ice sheets 23, 46
lightning **26–27**
    conductors 27
low pressure 15, 24
mackerel skies **19**
meteorologists 43, 44
Midsummer's Eve, Sweden 9
mirages **13**
monsoons **10**
Moon
    and frost 39
    halo **33**
moonbows 32
mountains 15, **16**, 21, 23
mudslides **21**

N O P R
Noah's ark 21
North Pole 6, 8, 9, 23
oxygen 15, 47
polar bear, black skin of 35
polar climate **6**
rain **16–17**
rain dances 37
rainbows **32–33**
rainforests 11, 47
rainy season 10, 11
radiosonde 45
red sky at night 39

S
Sahara, Africa 12
satellite-imaging 45
seasons **8–9**, **10–11**
seawater 16
seaweed, and forecasting 38
snow **22–23**
snowflakes **22**
snowslides 23
South Pole 6, 8, 23
stratosphere 14
summer 8, 9
Sun 8, 9, **12**, 13
    halo **33**
sun gods 36
sunniest place on Earth 12
suns, mock (sundogs) **33**
synoptic charts 43

T

temperate climate **6**
temperature 16, 17
    rising 47
temperature scales 41
thermometers **41**
Thunderbird 37
thunderclouds 30, 31
thunderstorms 20, **26–27**
    calculating distance of 27
Tornado Alley, America 31
tornadoes **30–31**
totem poles 37
Tower of Winds 40
trade winds **24**, 25
tree-felling 47
trees, change of leaf colour 9
tropical climate **6**
tropical storms 20, 28
tropics **10**, **11**, 24
troposphere **14**, 15, 18
twisters 30
typhoons 28, 29

V W
virga **17**
volcanic explosions 47
water cycle **16**
water vapour 15, **16**, 17, 19
waterspouts **31**
waves, giant 29
weather **6–7**, 14
    balloons **44**
    buoys **45**
    cocks 40
    house 40
    maps 43
    planes 28, **44**
    records, earliest (Chinese) 39
    stations 40, **42**, 43
    see also forecasting
wind turbines 24
winds **24–25**
    measurement of 25
    names 25
winter 8
woodpeckers, acorn 35

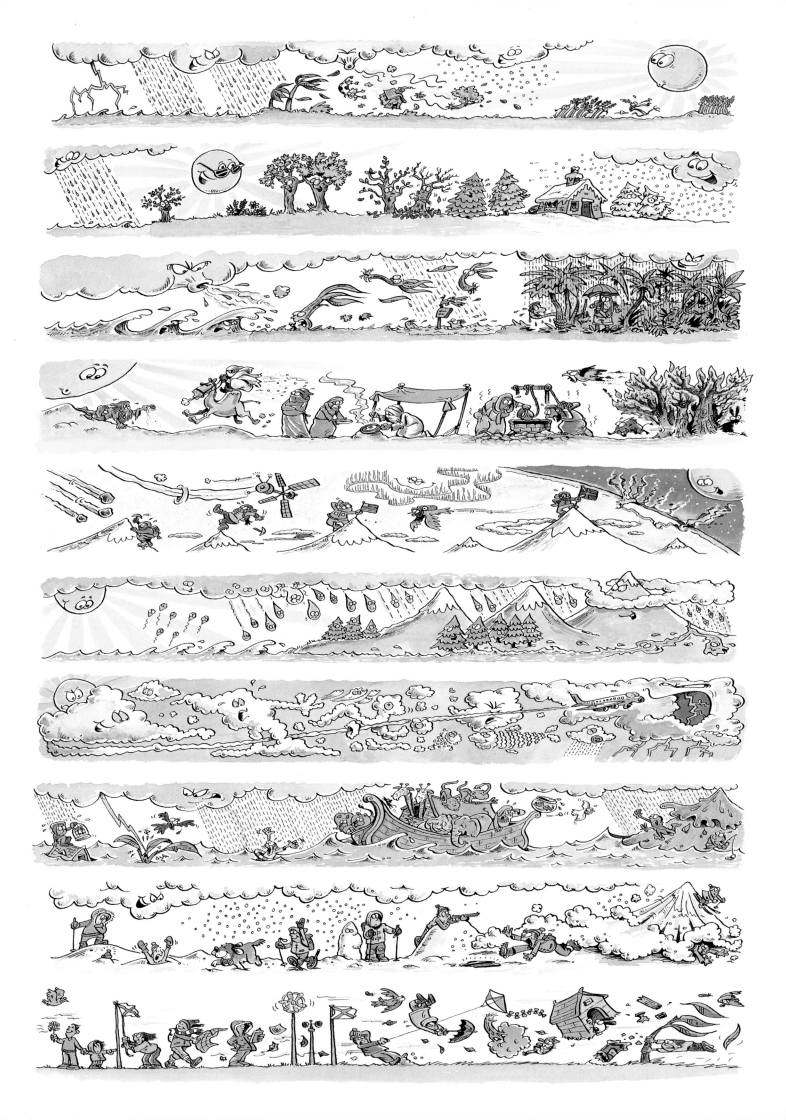